I0557328

Never Too Much

A story of love, life, and consequence.

By Danette Maroney

Envisage Publishing
Queens, New York
Atlanta, Georgia

Envisage Publishing

Copyright © 2004, 2008, 2011 by Danette Maroney

First printing 2008

Typesetting by Danette Maroney

Editing by Monique Maroney & Michael Spence

ISBN: 978-0-9729042-2-3

ATTENTION CORPORATIONS, UNIVERSITIES, COLLEGES, AND PROFESSIONAL ORGANIZATIONS: Quantity discounts are available on bulk purchases of this book. For information, please cotact Envisage Publishing by email at envisagepub1@gmail.com.

Acknowledgements

We did it again! You and I have met again to embark on another journey. Therefore, this time I start by thanking you the fans of Quinton, Imani, Charisse, and Rodney for making this book possible. I promise that if it was not for you constant pursuit for a sequel, the story would have been on line one for years to come. I hope that our journey in literature never ends.

To my son, Rahsaun, because everything I do, I do for you. You are my strength and my heart. I love you always. To my family and friends, those who always believed that I could overcome everything and stuck with me through it all, thank you for you constant support, encouragement, and love.

I have made so many new friends over the years and let go of twice as many fake ones. Therefore, I would like to give a very special thank you to Luz, Marisa, Natasha, Mayra G., Mayra R., Liz and Tomiko C. my good friends and hang out partners. In addition, another special thanks to Samantha, Marie, Ed, LeKeisha, Kareemah, Bernadette and Tamiko B, friends who I have deemed family, thanks for the love and the laughs. A special thanks to my new friends who have become like family here in Georgia. I appreciate you all for being in my corner and being by my side through the good, bad and ugly.

Last but not least, to my bestfriend and soulmate, Mike. You are the motivation I need to strive to succeed. Thanks for all your encouraging words, support and blessings. Your companionship means so much to me. Fate brough us here and faith will bring us through.

It so hard to find good friends and even harder to keep them. I appreciate all of you for your unique personalities and special friendship.

Love You All,
Danette Maroney

"Maturity is a part of life that can bring about many changes. Some will be unexpected, but the experience will always be welcomed."
— *Imani Wright-Banks*

IN THE BEGINNING

QUINTON

Leaving New York was the best thing for my family yet over the first year I had periods of apprehension as to whether I made the right decision. In order for us to survive, we had to leave behind the temptations of the streets and the pressures of our families. There was no doubt that I missed my life as it was but I knew the streets would eventually take me away from the one thing I love more than myself – my family. Although life before was easy, it was also empty. Now love has shown me a new light in life, a light that gets brighter with every waking day. It amazes me how much we are willing to endure for our own happiness but in actuality, it is never too much.

ᴆᴕᴐᴇ·ᴐᴇ·ᴐᴇ·ᴇᴆ

IMANI

At first, I carried anger inside blaming the world for tearing me apart when in actuality it was my mother who destroyed me. No matter how much I wanted her in my life, I finally realized I didn't need her but that wasn't until it was too late. However, the experience helped me to move onto the next level. I have matured as a woman, a mother, and a wife. For that, the heartache was welcomed. When all was said and done, all that I was looking for was set right before me. It wasn't clear until the smoke cleared. Our family, our children looked for me to be the backbone therefore, I had to be complete within myself to satisfy their needs and fulfill their expectations. Time has helped me escape the years of despair and become their superwoman.

CHAPTER 1

QUINTON

The neighborhood brought back memories as Imani and I drove through the nearly empty blocks of Brooklyn. So many stores closed down due to inflation, adding to the numerous abandoned buildings that lined every other street, making room for more overpriced homes and corporate-owned businesses run by people that have no idea of the real value in Brownsville.

Imani checked her make-up in the passenger visor mirror as I circled the block in search of parking. Once we parked, Imani gathered her belongings as I grabbed the pan of vegetable lasagna she prepared and locked the car. Music blared through the hallways from the party that was going on three flights up in my mother's apartment. The party was well in motion by the time we stepped through the door. Our four children were already there since they spent the week with my mother, known to everyone as Mama J, and my stepfather, James.

Every six months my mother gathered our families together for her semi-annual family reunions. At first, we all thought it was odd to reunite twice a year but our families were constantly changing or moving so it never felt like only six months past. It was an intimate gathering, Imani's brothers— John and Jordan—brought their wives, Mia and Tashii, children and Imani's baby-sister, Anissa. Jada came alone as usual. Jada's daughter, Diamond was staying with her father ever since she and her mother had an argument some weeks back. Diamond would arrive later with her father, Craig. My stepbrother, Shea, was accompanied by his latest girlfriend, Jorgette. Everyone knew by the next reunion, she would be old news. My childhood friend, Rodney, his parents and sisters were enjoying the food, folks, and family along with his three children and their mother, Imani's best friend, Charisse. The apartment was crowded from wall to wall with family having a good time while sharing flashbacks, drinking, and dancing.

After all the excitement of the past, our families have grown stronger and tighter. It was a blessing to enjoy these blissful moments without the threat of drama.

Charisse sat in the family room of our home in Pennsylvania breast-feeding her baby girl, Alaire, while her other two children, Christian and Damien, played at Naadira's paint table. Charisse, known to family and friends as Reese, was always there for every family event, no matter how small. I guess that was how she and Imani stayed tight. Rodney, my childhood friend was doing who knows what in Brooklyn. We all thought after three kids he would settle down with Reese. Nevertheless, it seemed they would only get along long enough to make babies and then they are back on the outs. Rodney confided in me on several nights that if Charisse left him, he would not be able to handle it. In his words, "Reese is my air." However, he could not find the strength to commit.

Charisse on the other hand had enough of Rodney and "his empty promises" as she would say. She and Imani have been looking at houses in Allentown for her and the kids. Imani said Charisse had plans to leave Rodney within the upcoming months. Been there, done that and do not care to revisit that period in history. At this point, Imani and I have been married for almost six years and although they have not been the easiest, I could not see us any other way.

"Quinton, did you call your mother back?" Imani hollered.

"Haven't had the time. Did she say it was important?" I replied.

"No." She paused. "Naadira, you have two seconds to find your shoe or you're getting left!" Imani screamed from the top of the staircase.

"Mommy, I can't find it." Naadira cried as she spun around in circles.

"Kai, help her find her shoe, please." I asked our eldest daughter who was obviously too occupied with her hair and appearance to hear me.

"Ok, Daddy." She replied before returning to the standing mirror in the family room.

Kai-Aja much like her mother was a mini-diva, she loved to dress and be noticed. Kai wore her hair long and wavy underneath her favorite black engineer's cap. Kai was also a fan of name-brand, but was so meticulous that every piece she wore had to be by the same designer. Her designer today was GUCCI, so of course, she wore the sneakers, button-down pin-stripped blouse however her jeans were plain old black GAP jeans. She made sure though to borrow her mother's Gucci wristlet to carry her lip-gloss and mirror.

"Kai! Find Naadira's damn shoe!" Raising my voice meant trouble and Kai knew if she did not move soon, I was going to move her myself.

Imani slowly descended the stairs while putting on her earrings. Her full hips and wide bottom filled her jeans perfectly. After Naadira, her breasts grew an extra cup size and no form of exercise could help her lose her thick thighs and plush rear. Personally, I found the extra cushion sexy but still she felt the need to 'tighten up.' The burgundy v-neck cotton shirt she wore complemented her freshly tanned skin and the stretch denim jeans complemented her every curve. Of course, Imani had to accessorize her outfit with her favorite GUCCI sneakers and matching handbag. She loved GUCCI to no end. Kai-Aja reaped the benefits. Every time Imani shopped for herself, Kai's wardrobe got bigger. Whether it was something Imani took out of her own or something new.

Jahlek followed behind her like a shadow, as usual. Jahlek in his usual wear, an Aeropostale logo t-shirt, faded blue jeans and black and white VANS was brushing his hair as he followed Imani down the steps. It seemed as if Imani could not move without Jahlek right behind her. Our family, short of one—Bryan—was complete and almost ready to go.

The Parent-Teacher Committee arranged a charity basketball game at Bryan's school. Bryan and a couple of his team-mates as well as some basketball players from other schools were playing what they considered an All-Star game. These young men were known as their school superstars. Bryan was at the top of his game and began receiving scholarships from major colleges. At fifteen, his six foot two frame caused him to stand above most of his classmen but his skills stood out above all others. As a father, I was naturally proud of my son's accomplishments as an athlete but as an ex-high school all-star, I had my concerns.

"Daddy, Mommy's going to leave me." Naadira cried as Imani walked to the kitchen to pack a snack bag for the kids.

"Mommy's not going to leave you." I said trying to calm Naadira.

"Don't baby her, Q. Make her find that shoe!" Imani hollered from the kitchen.

"Why can't she wear her sneakers?" Kai asked holding Naadira's black K-Swiss.

"Give me the sneakers, Kai." I said reaching out my hand.

"The point was to get her to find her shoe. Y'all give in to her." Imani said obviously frustrated.

"Baby, we'll look for it when we get back." I spoke to Imani while tying Naadira's sneakers.

"Whatever, we got to go. It's almost four o'clock. Let's go. I'm getting in the car."

Charisse gathered her children and loaded them into Rodney's Lincoln Navigator.

"Christian, pass mommy the diaper bag." She called to her oldest son who was named by his godfather, me.

The young replica of Rodney passed the diaper bag before hopping into his booster seat and buckling his seatbelt.

Charisse placed Alaire in her car seat before lifting two-year old, Damien, and putting him in his seat. Meanwhile, my kids— as hardheaded as they want to be—were still inside the house.

"Ma, can I get a movie to watch in the van," Jahlek asked.

"Don't pick nothing corny, Jay." Kai-Aja teased.

"Shut up, Kai." Jahlek countered.

"Make me." Kai-Aja replied.

"If you two start fighting, I'm going to kick both of y'all asses. Go get in the car." I said before turning off the lights and locking the door.

There have been light arguments over the years between Imani and me. Considering all we had to do to get here, the arguments are a part of the good times. Our move to Pennsylvania was the best move for Imani and the kids. As for me, whenever I became bored with the quiet lifestyle, I find my way back to Brooklyn. My mother and Rodney were still in Brooklyn. Brooklyn was my drug.

Imani's brother John, his wife Mia, and the girls Amber and Anissa moved to Connecticut with his job. Their son, Matthew kept their house in Brooklyn while their other son, Steve lived near us in Allentown. Jada, Imani's sister was still in Queens and her daughter, Diamond was living between homes. Craig, Jada's ex-husband was done with rehab but he and Jada never got back together.

ഔഔഔഇഇഇ

CHARISSE

Stevie Wonder's *'My Cherie Amour'* played quietly as we started on the road. Rodney dedicated this song to me while we were on vacation six years ago and it became my favorite. It brought back the sweetest memories of him. He would sing it to me while I was pregnant with Christian substituting Cherie with Charisse. That was when the times were fun and we were in love.

'Enough of that.' I thought before changing to the next song on the I-Pod. Christian was trying his hardest to rhyme along with MASE as *Welcome Back* blared through the speakers. Damien and Alaire had fallen asleep as soon as I started the car. I lowered the window and turned down the air conditioning noticing how Christian began to fidget in his seat trying to dodge the cool air from the vents, instead of closing them. Sometimes I wondered about him. When you think he has that much common sense, he does something to make you take it all back.

"Mommy, am I staying with Uncle Q today?" Christian asked.

"No. We are going home after the game. Your dad is going to be waiting for us." I said half-heartedly.

Rodney and I were definitely no Quinton and Imani. No lovey-dovey shit was in our picture. Rodney had not made up his mind whether his first priority was our family or the streets. Frankly, I did not care anymore. My babies were fine with or without him. However, I *knew* I would be torn if he left. Although, we argued with every passing wind, I loved him. After Christian was born, Rodney fussed and bitched that he was not ready to get married and I never asked him about it again. All I wanted for him to do is to act as if he had a family, give us the respect we deserved. Christian was at that age where he was starting to figure things out. Even he understood what Rodney was and was not doing. It was wrong and above all selfish.

I ran my free hand over Christian's freshly braided hair and thought about what tomorrow would have in store. Ten more hang-ups, five more excuses, two more arguments, and then one night of heavy make-up sex. That was pretty much our new life. A life that I had grown tired. Rodney's deadline was rapidly approaching and the outcome was not looking promising on his behalf.

"Christian, do you like Uncle Quinton's house better than our house?" I asked out of concern.

It seemed as if lately Christian always wanted to stay with Quinton and Imani.

"I don't know." He replied.

"What do you mean you don't know? It's a yes or no question." I replied.

"Sometimes." He replied. "I like playing with Naadira."

"You know I want you to be able to tell me anything, right?" I asked. He nodded his head.

"If there's anything you want to tell or ask me, just say it. We are going to talk about everything, okay? Who's your best friend?" I asked. It was like our secret club motto.

"You, Mommy." Christian answered with a smile. "Who is your best friend, Mommy?"

"Well you know me and Auntie Imani go way back...." I teased.

"Mommy!" He broke into laughter.

"You are my best, best friend, Christian." I finally answered with the widest smile.

I have not smiled in so long; I almost didn't recognize myself as I looked in the rear-view mirror.

"Mommy, can I tell you a secret." He said with a serious expression. And there she was again, no smile, no joy.

"Yes, Christian." I said as I prepared myself for what he might say.

"Sometimes, I get mad at Daddy. He's always screaming. It's better when he's not home."

Christian folded his arms and stared out the window. His face was full of attitude and anger.

With that, I realized that Rodney's deadline was past due. I could not continue to put my kids through that, even if it was their father. They deserved better. Rodney was going to drive his kids away from him next.

"Christian, next time daddy comes home, I'll talk to him. And if he starts screaming again, we are going to move to a house closer to Naadira."

Christian looked over to me and a small smile began to creep across his face.

I tickled his sides so I could hear his innocent laugh. It always seemed to cheer me up.

"I love you, Christian." I said as I held his hand.

"I know." He replied, like his father.

Seconds later, my cell phone began to ring. The Caller ID displayed Rodney's phone number and a picture of the kids I took with my camera phone. I put the phone on speaker, passed it to Christian, and let him answer. My tolerance level was low so Rodney and his bullshit would have to take a backseat.

"Hi, Daddy." Christian said. His smile began to fade.

"Where's your mother?" Rodney asked.

"She's driving." Christian replied.

"Tell her I'm at the school. I'm waiting for y'all outside." Rodney said.

"Hold on." Christian put the phone in his lap then relayed Rodney's message as if I hadn't heard him already.

"Alright." I said and continued watching the road.

Christian picked up the phone and waited for Rodney to finish talking to who ever was in the background.

"Daddy, Mommy said 'alright'." Christian said.

"Let me speak to your mom."

Christian passed the phone. After I turned off the speaker phone, I let Rodney speak and listened unenthusiastically. Christian was watching me and I did not want to say anything that he would repeat.

"Alright, uh-huh. Ookay. Yeah." Were my simple replies to avoid being nasty.

"Reese, are you even listening to me?" He asked.

"Rodney, I heard everything you said. You are sitting in front of the school. You got a tune-up. You bought Alaire some earrings. And, you wanted to pick up the boy's sneakers. I heard you." I replied.

"What's up, Mama? Why you sound so angry?" Rodney asked.

"I'm tired, not angry." *'Tired of you.'* I thought. "We are in the parking lot now. Meet me at the car. Umm ... Aisle 6, by the flag pole."

"Alright, I'll be there in a minute." He said before disconnecting.

I parked in the lot directly in front of Imani. She was still fussing with her kids. Quinton was taking Naadira out of her booster seat. Kai-Aja was stretching her long limbs and Jahlek was right behind Imani, like always. Quinton and Imani started towards our vehicle as I unbuckled Christian's seat belt. Damien had sat up as soon as we parked. Imani opened the back car door and reached for Alaire's car seat.

"Imani, grab this bag please." I said as I passed her the kids diaper bag. "Rodney's here. He can get the car seat."

"What's up?" Quinton said to Rodney as he approached the jeep.

They greeted each other with their traditional handshake. Rodney then came to the driver's side and opened the door.

"You alright, Ma." He said then placed a soft kiss on my forehead.

Then I was right back were I started. In love all over again. His soft brown eyes melted my insides as he took my pocket book and offered his hand to help me from the SUV. Christian climbed over me and stretched for his father. Rodney eyes lit up as he picked Christian up and kissed his cheeks. Quinton and Imani went back to their family as Rodney and I gathered ours.

Rodney pushed the stroller to the gymnasium while I carried Damien and held Christian's hand. I admired Rodney from behind imagining him undressed in our bed at home. The way I missed him.

14

He gained some weight over the years but it only made him more desirable. His locks, traveled down the length of his back, were pulled into a ponytail. Rodney talked of putting locks in Christian's hair but I was against it. I liked him better in cornrows. Damien short curly hair refused to grow so we never discussed locking his hair. Rodney wore a black Sean John velour sweat suit with a white Sean John monogram T-shirt and a pair of all black Sean John sneakers. The autumn wind caused his locks to sway from side to side as his jacket blew open. Rodney stopped to zip his jacket then tucked Alaire's blanket shielding her from the wind. He turned around to wait for the boys and me.

"Christian, close your jacket." He said when we got closer to where he stood.

Damien reached for Rodney. Rodney took him and mentioned for me to push the stroller. Before I could grab the stroller, Christian had already begun to push it along the sidewalk. Rodney reached for my hand and I first looked at him awkwardly then figured, *'what the hell'* and went with the flow.

ೞೞೞೲೲೲ

<u>IMANI</u>

Quinton and Jahlek went to the men's room while I took the girls to find seats. Bryan walked with us as we search the gymnasium for enough seats for the eleven of us. Kai was all smiles while she walked with Bryan. She liked to be under him especially now with him being a popular basketball star. The fact that the boy's on his team were cute and that she was at the age were she was learning to flirt were bonuses. Bryan threatened his teammates to stay away from his sister who, by the way had blossomed breasts for Christmas. *What a gift?*

Charisse and Rodney were entering the gym as we found seats close to the floor. I thought something was wrong with my eyes but when I looked again, Rodney was holding her hand. I waved to them so they could claim the seats we had saved for them. Quinton and Jahlek walked in behind them and walked in our direction.

Years have matured Quinton features but that only made him sexier. At a young thirty-seven he had began to sprout some gray hairs in his goatee and head but I didn't want him to change a thing. His body was wider and more defined. Last year he added a gym to our garage and put together a workout regimen for him and Bryan. Quinton decided to let his hair grow about four inches. His full curly hair kept him looking young and handsome. Quinton turned me on without trying and there was no doubt that I loved him but I couldn't help but feel as if something was always brewing in the mist. Something that kept us at odds. We talked everyday, keeping our bond strong but if we did not argue once a day our day was not complete. Still, no matter how much we fussed and fought, Quinton let it be known there was nothing he would not do to keep his home happy and safe.

"Mani, did you want something from the concession stand? They got one set up outside." Quinton asked without even making eye contact with me.

He was too busy watching Kai-Aja as she sat with Bryan's team.

"Q, Bryan's not going to let none of his boys touch her." Rodney said as he took Alalre from her stroller.

Charisse sat beside me with Damien on her lap and Christian on the opposite side. She did not seem enthused with Rodney's interpretation of the *perfect daddy*. In fact, she looked like she wanted to fight him. Her top lip curled to one side as she muttered words underneath her breath.

"Reese, stop looking at him like that." I said trying not to bust out in laughter.

"He makes me sick. He is so fucking phony." She whispered.

Rodney and Quinton stood in the aisle talking. Naadira held tight to Quinton as he tried to usher her in our direction. I looked around to see the number of people in attendance only to stop on some woman three rows up who continued to stare in Quinton and Rodney's direction. Quinton did not notice but Rodney did. He tried to make eye contact with her but he must have felt my eyes on him and looked towards Reese and me.

"And he's busted." Reese said.

Obviously, she noticed the little exchange as well. She used her index finger to signal for Rodney to come to her. I knew this was going to turn into something ugly so I did my best to defuse the situation.

"Reese, please wait until we get back to the house to curse him out. It's not worth making a scene over." I said.

"He can't keep disrespecting me, Imani. This is getting out of hand." Charisse said as she stood from her seat and placed Damien beside me.

I put my head in my hands and began to rub my temples. Last time she approached him on the same subject, we were escorted out of a restaurant, on my anniversary.

Rodney met Charisse half way. The look in his eyes said he did not want to argue. Before Reese was able to say a word, he kissed her. Nice save. Then he put Alaire in her arms and walked with them back to our seats. Quinton noticed the exchange then looked at me quizzically. Bryan brought Kai to our seats with Quinton, Jahlek, and Naadira in tow.

"Dad, after the game me and my boys are going downtown." Bryan said before kissing my cheek.

"So you're telling me or asking me? I must have missed something." Quinton replied in his same no-nonsense tone he always used with the kids.

"I'm asking you. Can I go with my boys downtown?" He replied with slight attitude.

Quinton jaws tightened before he responded. It seems that lately he has been extra hard on Bryan. At the same time, Bryan did any and every thing that he knew would get Quinton started. I tried to talk to Quinton about his temper but I was told to mind my business every time.

Quinton and Bryan stood face to face. Q folded his arms and displayed the imprint of his muscle under his white button down shirt. I watched the standoff for as long as I could before interfering.

"What time are you trying to come in the house?" I asked Bryan.

Quinton shot a look that could have knocked me back into my seat. I stood my ground. Bryan was our son not one of his employees under his supervision.

"I'll be in before eleven. I know we got Karate class tomorrow." Bryan replied while staring Quinton in his eyes.

"Quinton, do you need him for anything important tonight?" I asked as I sat in my seat.

"The game is about to start." Quinton said then sat beside me.

His vibe made me feel uncomfortable so I switched seats with Kai, who was three seats from Quinton.

ಐಐಐೞೞೞ

RODNEY

It must have been something in the air because it seemed as if everyone was walking on eggshells. Reese and I were always at each other throats, so it was nothing new but Quinton and Imani have been quarreling more than normal. Charisse did not tell me what she knew anymore so I could only assume that Quinton and Imani are in need of some serious alone time away from their kids and responsibilities. Despite the circumstances, I thought they have been handling the whole family and marriage situation really well. However, their bridge was beginning to look a little shaky.

"Rodney, pass a bottle out of the bag." Charisse said as she made cooing sounds to our newborn daughter.

"Do you want me to feed her?" I asked before giving her the bottle and burp cloth.

"No, I got it. Check Damien's pull-up. He hasn't been to the bathroom since we left Imani's." She replied without looking in my direction.

"Reese, why are you acting like this? Giving me the cold shoulder and shit. Why can't you drop the fucking attitude?" I asked, in a demanding whisper.

Damien was in earshot and I did not want him or Christian to think we were arguing.

"Rodney, please watch your mouth. Now is not the time or place. Look..." She paused. "Bryan shot a three!"

Annoyed with her abrupt change of conversation, I sat back and watched the game. The players scrambled back and forth across the court. Q sat at the edge of his seat watching intently as Bryan played defense and all I could think of was why I was still with Charisse. Over the past six years, things have only gotten progressively worse. I think her biggest problem is the fact that I do not want to get married. When we first got together, Charisse and I agreed that we were comfortable with the way things were between us. Nevertheless, by the time Damien was born, our relationship seemed to have gotten very deep, too deep. I gave her everything she wanted but she still was not satisfied. She wanted me to stop hustling. I stopped doing it around her. Move out of my apartment in Brownsville, not a problem. We bought a house in Canarsie. She did not have to work, she had my truck, while I paid the bills and took care of the kids, but no, she wanted to draw blood. She was a fucking bourgeois spoiled brat that could not accept that not everything always goes her way.

Charisse tapped my leg and it seemed to flare something inside me. There was a time when she could look at me and I would get rock hard. Now it was like a mental obstacle course to keep from cursing her out. I tried to ignore her hoping she would leave me alone but she tapped me again.

"What?" I answered angrily.

"I don't want to fight with you." She replied.

Her sweet tone and irresistible lips replaced the anger with forgiveness instantly. I loved Reese and no matter how much we fought, it was not going to change. She entwined her fingers with mine and motioned for me to move closer to her on the bleacher style seats. Putting Damien on my lap closed the gap between us. She leaned in and placed a soft kiss on my neck.

"Don't do that, Ma." I said trying to fight the erection that was building.

I admired Reese as she sat beside me still holding Alaire. She wore her long black hair tied back in a ponytail. Her mahogany skin seemed to glow brighter than before. Her facial features were still the same. Most women change after kids, weight gain, wide nose, acne, but Reese bounced right back to her perfect size six and flawless beauty every time. She considered going back into modeling but I did not think she could handle being away from the kids for more than a couple of hours, let alone days.

"Rodney, are you sure you want to drive back to Brooklyn tonight?" She asked. Her eyes were full of desire and longing.

"You got other ideas." I played into her game.

"Maybe." She replied.

"Come here, Ma." I said before taking her lips in mine.

"Get a room." Imani shouted.

Charisse put her face into my chest and laughed. For that moment, the tension was gone and we were back to normal, but we both knew it was only temporary.

One of the boys from the opposing team knocked Bryan down and Quinton damn near jumped on the court. Kai-Aja grabbed his shirt.

"He's okay, Daddy. Chill." Kai said as she pulled him back into his seat.

Imani shook her head in disgust in regards to Quinton's behavior. Q returned to the edge of his chair and continued watching the game. I do not know what was opening the gap between Quinton and Imani but I hoped for their kids' sake they would figure it out soon.

CHAPTER 2

CHARISSE

Rodney and I sat in the living room playing with the kids while another shouting match between Quinton and Imani echoed in the background.

"Rodney, don't you think you should step in and calm Quinton down." I suggested while looking over the saddened expression on Naadira's face.

"Ma, it's really not my place to be getting in their fights." Rodney replied.

"I know, Baby. And you know any other time I wouldn't suggest this but look at the kids."

Rodney looked at Jahlek who was sitting on the window ledge looking out the window, trying to be anywhere but home. Then he looked over to Kai who played the part of 'Mother' as she tried to soothe a very upset Naadira.

The sound of a shattered glass rang through out the house and it was at that moment Rodney rose from his seat to check on Quinton and Imani. I set Alaire in her playpen and followed. When we entered the dining room, Quinton was rubbing his fist, a shattered lamped lie on the floor and Imani sat in a chair staring off into space.

"Quinton, please calm down. The kids are in the next room." I said as I placed a comforting hand on Imani's shoulder.

"Reese, mind your business." Rodney whispered which, through the silence, was loud and clear.

"Rodney, this is my business." I said as I motioned toward Imani who was clearly on the brink of losing it.

Her eyes were blood shot from crying and she nervously tapped a foot against the hardwood floor.

Rodney followed Quinton as he left the dining room and started for the front door. I continued to sit with Imani while they exchanged words. It was well after eleven and Bryan hadn't called or showed. Quinton must have cursed for what seemed like forever before Rodney managed to get him out the house. Imani was so upset she began to shake. As Quinton gathered his keys and jacket, Rodney returned to the dining room to give me a quick peck then dashed out the house to catch up with his comrade. Quinton and Rodney went to get beers while Imani and I talked. When Imani looked as though she was calm, we prepared the kids for bed. Red nose and eyes full of tears, Imani continue to be strong. She refused to let another tear fall. Not with Naadira and Kai-Aja watching. Jahlek was in the living room watching television while Christian lay next to him half sleep.

"Jah, get in the shower." Imani said while she put Kai's scarf on her head.

"Mommy, did you call Bryan's cell phone?" Jahlek said as his eyes began to well with water.

He was the most sensitive when it came to Imani. He didn't like to see her upset and went out his way to help her.

"Yeah, he has it turned off." She answered absently.

"Dag, why Bryan got to be such a butt munch?" Kai questioned.

It seemed that all the kids suffered when Q was upset. Normally on Friday and Saturday nights, they could stay up all night, but not this Friday night. Quinton demanded that all the kids be in bed by the time he returned.

"Kai, watch your mouth." I said. "Naadira and Christian are quick to repeat."

"Sorry, Auntie." She apologized. "Good night." She placed a kiss on my forehead and then one on her mother's followed by a tight hug. "Mom, don't stress yourself please. Naadi, let's go upstairs."

"Good Night, Mommy." Naadira said then gave Imani a huge hug.

"Night, Night. I love you." Imani said as the girls walked up the stairs.

"Love you, too." They replied in unison.

Alaire began to cry. As I was about to check on her, Damien began to cry. This was one of those moments I wish I had earplugs. Imani went to pick up Alaire as I started for Damien.

"Mani, what's going on between you and Quinton?"

"Quinton thinks I am one of the kids and not his wife. He doesn't listen to me when I try talking to him about our kids. We aren't the team we used to be."

As Imani put the period on her sentence, Bryan walked through the door. I took Alaire from her arms and went into the living room with Damien and Christian.

"Mom, I'm sorry. I lost track of time." He offered as an excuse.

"Are you out of your mind? Do you know what I had to endure because you lost track of time? Your father is beyond angry." Imani hollered as she stood in front of Bryan who towered over her.

"Bryan, you need to be more responsible. Besides the fact that you are supposed to be an example for your brother and sisters, your mother put her neck on the chopping block for you?" I said as I paced in and out of the dining room.

"I said I'm sorry. What do you want me to do?" Bryan said as he tried to walk around Imani.

"What were you doing that you had to turn off your cell phone? And why are you trying to dodge me? Look at me!" She hollered.

"Mom, chill. Can I take a shower?" Bryan brushed passed Imani.

That was all she wrote. Imani grabbed the hood of his jacket and tried to choke him.

"I said look at me." She grabbed his face and pressed her fingers into his cheeks. She sniffed his breath and then landed a blinding smack across his face. "Since when did you start drinking? And I know that's not a hickie on your neck."

Bryan stumbled to the ground and Imani pounced on top of him.

"Get off of me. Mom, you're bugging out." He pleaded.

I put Alaire in her car seat and ran over to try to break them up. I managed to pull Imani off him but it was hard as hell holding her back. Bryan sat there looking stupid.

Imani looked at me with tears streaming down her face. "Reese, you don't know how hard it is trying to keep this house together. Quinton has become someone I don't even know. Bryan is changing too. I cannot loose *my kids* and *my husband*."

I knew Imani's anger stemmed from more than Bryan staying out past his curfew. The tension between Quinton and Imani had become so thick; it was uncomfortable being around them.

Quinton and Rodney walked in the house with their hands full of bags. Quinton took one look at Imani in tears again and immediately started on his rampage.

"What the ... Bryan what the hell happened in here?" Quinton shouted.

"Mom tried to kill me." He responded while rubbing his neck.

"Why did you come in the house so late? You're grown now?" Quinton asked as he faced off with Bryan.

"I lost track of the time." Bryan answered with attitude.

Imani went to the kitchen to get some water. "He was out drinking with a girl. Lord knows what else they were doing. Check his neck." She hollered from inside.

"I can smell he was drinking. I'm trying to figure out why he came here if he's so grown. Why didn't you stay where you were at?" Quinton said, as he got closer to Bryan.

"Because I wanted to come home." Bryan answered meekly.

Imani took Alaire and went into the living room with the kids. Rodney and I stood in the dining room with Quinton and Bryan to make sure things didn't get out of hand. Rodney placed his arm around my shoulder and I laid my head back, easing into the comfort.

"You think you're grown because you're fucking?" Quinton questioned.

Bryan didn't answer.

"You're grounded. The only time you leave this house is with your mother or me. Don't touch the damn phone and don't think about company!" Quinton said with finality.

Bryan went to walk off and go to his room but mumbled something before getting out of Quinton's earshot.

"What did you say?" Quinton asked.

"Nothing." He responded then sucked his teeth.

Within a blink, Quinton had punched Bryan right in the mouth.

Bryan must have drunk some courage with his vodka because he turned and landed a blow to Quinton's chest. Before you knew it, the two were fighting like men in the street. Rodney and I tried to break it up but they continued swinging at each other. Imani ran back into the dining room and placed herself between Quinton and Bryan while Rodney pulled Bryan into the living room.

"What the hell is wrong with you, Man?" Rodney said as he backed Bryan into a corner.

Imani stood in front of Q crying for him to calm down.

"Quinton, that's our son." Imani cried.

"He thinks he's a man. I'm going to teach him what it's like in a man's world." Quinton replied.

"Fighting him isn't going to solve anything!" She shouted.

"Imani, back off! This is between Bryan and me." Quinton stated before walking towards the living room.

By now, Kai and Jahlek were on their way down the stairs.

"Go back to your rooms!" I hollered from the living room.

"You can't fight your father." Rodney yelled in Bryan's face.

"He hit me first." Bryan hollered as if he wanted the neighbors to come save him.

"He's your father, B." Rodney tried to reason.

"No, he's not!" Bryan replied.

Time stood still for two seconds as the last syllable rolled from his tongue.

"Bryan, go to your room!" Imani screamed.

Quinton stormed out the house slamming the screen door. Rodney ran behind him. I threw my head back and tried not to let the tears fall. My heart went out to Imani. She turned to me and said, "Let's get your kids in bed." with tears steadily streaming from her eyes. I wrapped my arm around her shoulder as we headed into the family room.

ಭಿಭಿಭಿ೮ಽ೮ಽ೮ಽ

<u>QUINTON</u>

Rodney sat beside me as we drove down the street towards the makeshift pool hall. Bryan's words haunted me as I tried to focus on the road. Somehow, I knew that the sudden rift between Bryan and me was more than Imani and I not being his biological parents. I refused to believe that he would act out without reason. Up until a couple of months ago, Bryan and I were like best friends. He would roll with me when I went to hangout with Rodney in Brooklyn. Even if I was stepping out the house for a couple minutes, he wanted to be with me. It's not as if he's lashing out at his brother, sisters or Imani — just me.

"I haven't done anything but raise Bryan like my own for him to treat me like shit." I said as I pounded the steering wheel.

"He's at that age, Q. Everything and everybody is against him, in his warped mind. Plus, he was drinking. Don't take what he said to heart." Rodney stated.

"You know a drunk speaks a sober mind. Remember my mother was the worst alcoholic but nothing she said was ever a lie. And the truth is I'm not his father." Quinton replied.

"Then who is? Even when they were alive, they weren't there for him. Bryan was only concerned with his money and hos; he didn't give a fuck about Trina or those kids." Rodney said with conviction.

"But they were still his parents." I parked in the lot and waited a few seconds before exiting the car.

Rodney was talking on his phone by the car when I opened the door to the bar. I was going to wait but by the way he was whispering into the phone he was talking with Reese and I knew it would be a while.

"Yo, Q. What's up? Haven't seen you around here in a while?" The bartender shouted as he prepared my drink.

"Hey, Silk. I've been trying to lay low. You know what I mean." I responded.

"I hear ya', Man." He replied.

I sat at my regular seat on the far end of the bar where I would be invisible to anyone coming in the bar. Rodney walked through the door and greeted a couple of people before walking over to my corner.

"Sorry about that. Reese wanted to know if you were all right. I told her you'll call home in a few." Rodney said as he took the seat next to mine.

"How's Imani? Did she say?" I asked.

"She said Imani and Bryan were in your room talking. Every few seconds she heard Imani screaming but they weren't fighting." He replied.

Rodney put up his hand to signal the bartender. Silk walked over to our corner and took his order. When he returned with the drink, I ordered another.

"You're driving, so don't over do it." Rodney offered while watching the big screen.

My mind was sifting through the years trying to find a moment when I didn't treat Bryan as if he were my own. Never. As far as he or anyone else was concerned, Bryan didn't have to be my biological son for me to love him anymore. The only way you would think different was that he looked like his father. Tall with coffee-colored skin and deep brown wide eyes. His features were nowhere similar to Jahlek. Outside of their hair color, which was damn near black, like Trina's there wasn't anything else. Bryan had his father's wide nose, full lips, and thick eyebrows. Unlike his father who resembled a big ole' ugly gorilla, he was good-looking and well kept. Until tonight, he had manners and was respectful.

"Q, what's on your mind? Talk about it and let it go." Rodney said.

"That little motherfucker is lucky I didn't kill his punk ass." I stated, releasing some of the anger that was bottled inside.

"Man, you couldn't really hurt that boy. He's feeling himself right now, Q. I'm sure he'll be apologizing in the morning."

"I doubt it. If I learned anything over the years, Bryan is hardheaded like his mother. Even if he's wrong, he will try to make you believe why he feels he wasn't." I replied then downed my second glass of Jack Daniels.

"Do you want to talk about what's going on between you and Imani?" Rodney offered.

"There's nothing to talk about." I replied.

Honestly, I didn't know what was going on with Imani and me. It seemed as if we couldn't get it right. The harder I tried; the more she pulled away. Rodney and I sat in the bar for a little over an hour and talked about what needed to be done with Bryan. If we didn't find a way to calm him down, his attitude will wind up getting him in more trouble than he could handle.

We walked through the front door a little after three in the morning. Christian and Damien were on the pullout sofa bed. The sounds of the television in the guest room were the only noise in the house.

"Let me go talk to Reese, Man. I know she's still up. She can't sleep with the set on." Rodney said as he began towards the bedroom on the first level.

I started up the stairs to my bedroom when I saw a light coming from the boys' room. I slightly opened the door to peek inside. Bryan was sitting at his computer table with his feet kicked up and an ice pack on his jaw. He was talking on the phone. Not wanting to startle him, I tapped lightly on the door.

"Yeah." He answered.

"You want to talk?" I asked.

"Yeah, Dad. Come in." He replied.

I entered his room and sat on the end of Jahlek's bed. He was knocked out. I kissed his cheek and pulled the blanket up.

"I'm going to call you tomorrow. Yeah, I'm alright. My father's here I gotta go. Bye." He said to the caller.

"What's up, Bryan?" I asked to start conversation between us.

"Nothing." He replied.

"That was your girl." I questioned.

"Something like that." He answered.

"When were you going to talk to me about it?" I asked as I looked around their room.

"I didn't think it was anything to talk about."

"Well when she starts causing you to break rules, it is something to talk about. Did you tell your mom you're seeing somebody?"

"She asked me was I having sex. She didn't ask if I had a girl." Bryan stated.

"Are you?" I asked.

"Am I what?" Bryan tried to avoid answering the question.

"Are you stupid? You know what I'm asking you. Are you having sex?" I became frustrated with his act of ignorance.

"Yeah." He answered.

"How long have you been having sex?" I continued to question.

"For a while." He replied.

"What's a while? Stop playing stupid. Open your damn mouth and talk." My irritation was getting the better part of me.

"I've been seeing her for a couple of months. We started ... like three weeks ago. And yes, she is the only girl I've been with and we used protection every time" He responded.

I put my head in my hands and waited before I said anything irrational.

"Does she go to school with you?" I asked.

"No, she's in college." He answered with a slight smirk and chuckle.

"So I take it that you're proud of yourself. Got you a college shorty."

I waited for his response. He nodded.

"Still doesn't give you the right to disrespect me or your mother. You could have called."

"I know, Dad. I'm sorry. I told Mom I'm sorry too. I really didn't want to make you mad. But you keep treating me like I'm a little kid."

"You are! Just because you get your dick wet doesn't mean you're grown. And when the hell did you start drinking?" I asked.

"Today was the first time. I only had two drinks. Dad, why can't you and mom cut me some slack? I'm fifteen now about to turn sixteen soon. I've never been in any trouble and I'm doing well in school but y'all are always so hard on me." Tears began to form in his eyes.

It was tearing me up on the inside but I had to make sure he understood that his actions wouldn't be tolerated and find his reason for acting out.

"Doing what you did today will not get you the extra freedom you want. Your mom and I will cut you some slack once we feel comfortable that you will make the right choices. I don't want to see you end up in the same situation I was in when I was your age." I said on the verge of tears, memories burning through my heart.

"Dad, give me the chance to make some mistakes." He argued.

"Some mistakes can kill you." I countered.

We were quiet for several short seconds.

"Bryan, you are the oldest and you are supposed to set an example for you brother and sisters. Imagine if it were Kai out past curfew drinking and doing whatever. How would you feel?" I asked.

He sat up in his seat and looked me directly in my eyes.

"I would hurt her." He replied.

"Exactly." I said. "Look, Bryan. Your mom and I are trying to look out for you. There are many influences out there to get you caught up. There are women who look for men with a promising future so they can live the high life, on your dime and care nothing about you. You know you can play ball. Don't let anybody mess that up for you."

"Mom said the same thing. Dad, Sierra doesn't want to have kids or mess up my game. She wants to be with me. And I'm cool with that." He said.

I stood from my seat and walked toward Bryan. He stood to his feet as well.

"I want to meet her."

"Mom does too."

"Alright." I said before gently grabbing his chin. "I am really sorry about hitting you. Let me see your face."

I turned his head from side to side inspecting. He had a little lump but otherwise he was fine.

"I'm sorry about what I said, Dad. I didn't mean it." He said.

"I know." I said then grabbed him and hugged him tighter than ever before. "Next time try talking to me or your mom if you feel we're being unfair."

"So, am I still grounded?" He asked as I started for the door.

"Oh, for sure. You still have to suffer the consequences for your actions." I replied.

"Can we talk about this?" He asked.

"Tomorrow." I answered then closed the door behind me.

I entered my bedroom to find Imani tucked under the covers. I grabbed my robe from the chair and headed for the shower. The warmth of the water eased my body into a state of relaxation. My headache began to dissipate as the beads of water rolled over my head and shoulders. I allowed the shower to comfort me as I tried to purge the day's events. After I was completely at peace, I brushed my teeth and headed to the bed. My first thought was to put on a pair of pajama pants but I enjoyed sleeping in the buff so I threw my robe on the chair and slid in the bed. Imani stirred in her sleep. I kissed her nose then her lips. She didn't wake so I put my arms around her and closed my eyes.

CHAPTER 3

<u>RODNEY</u>

Charisse always slept hard. I couldn't see how she could sleep through the baby crying though. I went to the kitchen to warm her bottle while I carried her in my arms. When I held her something always stirred inside me. It was like that with all the kids. It was like a burst of emotion. I remember when Quinton said the same thing to me when he first held Kai-Aja and now I understand what he meant.

It was only six in the morning so I tried to be very quiet not to wake anyone else. I went back to the bedroom and searched for her burp cloth while I held the bottle in her mouth with my chin.

"Where the hell is the rag?" I said to myself.

"Over here." Reese said from the bed.

"I didn't know you were awake." I said.

"I felt you get out the bed." She replied.

"So, why didn't you get the baby?" I asked.

"I knew you would." She answered. "Bring her here. I'll take her."

"I got it now." I said as I returned to the bed.

Charisse sat up and reached her arms out for Alaire but I continued doing what I was doing.

"Go back to sleep. I told you I got it." I said.

Charisse got out of bed and started for the door.

"Where are you going?" I asked.

"Can I go to the bathroom or do I need permission?" She replied.

"Your smart ass mouth is getting out of hand." I said as she close the door.

When Charisse returned Alaire was in her bassinet fed and changed. She fell asleep after I put her down.

I watched Charisse as she walked around the bed. Her full breasts almost spilled out of her small tank top. As she climbed back in the bed,

I turned towards her and motioned for her to come closer. At first, she was hesitant because it was in her nature to be defiant but she gave in and rested on my chest. I kissed the top of her head and wrapped my arms around her. Charisse draped her long leg over mine and placed butterfly kisses on my chest. I tried to concentrate on the ceiling fan to avoid getting an erection but it didn't work.

"You see what you're doing to me." I said as I placed her hand on my throbbing penis.

"Nice to see I still have the touch." She replied as she massaged.

"Do you really?" I teased.

"You want to find out." She replied.

Before I could reply, she had already taken off her shorts and climbed on top. I held onto her hips as she rode as if she was on a mission. The way her body accepted mine was a feeling too hard to describe. I couldn't allow Reese to have total control so I flipped her onto the bed and took charge of the situation.

"Oh, Daddy. You sure you can handle this." She said between nibbling on my nipples. Something she knew would drive me to the brink.

"Ma, you know I got this." I said as I doubled each thrust.

The sound of the bedsprings and Charisse's moans filled the room. I tried to muffle the sounds with kisses but she was still loud.

"Reese, you are going to wake up the house." I said as I motioned for her to turn over.

She buried her face in the pillow as I began to hit it from the back. She loved doggie-style. She loved almost any position.

"Rodney, stop. Wait. Wait." She panted between thrusts.

I eased back and lay on top of her as she lay flat on the bed. My locks fell freely over my shoulders covering her face as I used my tongue to play with her ears.

"Baby, hold up. Get up." She said.

"What's up?" I asked as I lay besides her running a finger up and down her spine.

She sat up and took off her top. Her breasts bounced.

"I was getting milk all on my shirt. I don't like the way it feels when the shirt is wet and rubbing against me." She said before pulling me closer to her.

I placed one of her breasts in my mouth and sampled the baby's milk. Ever since Christian was born, I've grown to like the taste of breast milk. She moaned in pleasure as I took my time pleasing her. I traced her torso with my tongue until I reached her bare vagina. Reese threw her head back as I nestled my face between her legs. Her body began to shudder as my tongue tamed her.

"Rodney, I want you inside of me. I want you to come with me." She said as she pulled on my locks.

Without hesitation, I slid back inside her. My thrusts became faster as we neared our climax. Charisse dug her nails in my back as we began to release.

"Ma, you can't be doing me like this. I'm getting old." I teased although I was really out of breath.

She didn't answer. She continued to lay on my chest playing with my locks.

"What's up, baby? You alright." I asked.

"Yeah, I'm fine." She replied.

"So, why are you quiet?"

"I don't have anything to say." She replied.

"Is that it? Is there something you want to talk about?" I asked dreading what her answer would be. I honestly did not want to start on the marriage topic right now.

"No, Rodney. I'm resting." She replied.

I wasn't totally convinced but I didn't want to start an argument so I didn't press her any more.

"I love you." She said.

"I know." I replied.

ଊଊଊଔଔଔ

IMANI

Quinton jumped out of bed early in the morning. It was routine for him and Bryan to get up and run before the sun-up. Quinton tried to get Bryan in the habit of exercise ever since he made the team. I looked over to the clock to see that it was after eight. I had to get the kids up and ready for their classes. Kai-Aja was in dance and Jahlek and Bryan were still in Karate. Naadira would stay home with Q. Quinton didn't want her in dance yet. He felt she was too young. Kai started dance at the same age and she loved it.

I sat on the edge of my bed and searched for my slippers. Quinton came upstairs as I was walking over to the bathroom. Still in his sweated T-shirt and shorts, he wrapped his arms around me.

"Q, get off of me. That is nasty." I hollered as I struggled to move away.

"When I'm sweating on top of you, you don't care." He replied as he started towards the bathroom.

"That's different." I responded.

He quickly undressed and jumped in the shower. Although I was still angry with him for our argument the night before, temptation caused me to join him. Quinton was covered with lather when I stepped into the porcelain tub. Playfully, he threw water over his shoulder into my face.

"Q, don't start this again." I said.

"Why? You're not in the mood?" He said before tossing another hand full of water.

I playfully slapped his back and he turned around and grabbed me.

"Who's the man?" He said as he slapped my bottom.

His comment caused me to think about the argument. *That's part of our problem now.'* I thought. I fought against myself to pick a fight with Quinton.

We began to playfully fight in the shower. If it wasn't for the non-skid pads in the tub, we would have killed our selves. Quinton held me under the stream of warm water until I gave up.

"All I see in here is a little boy." I said then turned my back to him and continued to lather my body sponge.

"Oh, really? Then I guess this won't interest you." Quinton pressed his rock hard penis against my behind and began to grind.

I tried to act unfazed by his manhood rubbing against my wet flesh but I was passed aroused, I was down right horny.

"If you want it, you got to take it." I replied as I tried to ignore the throbbing between my legs.

"You ain't saying nothing but a word." Quinton turned me to face him then lifted my legs around his waist as he pressed my back against the wall.

"You sure you know what you doing, little boy." I teased as I titled my pelvis towards him.

"I've had my practice." He replied.

Quinton gently inserted himself while nibbling along my neck to my breasts. He took his time as he caressed my body. Allowing myself to be swept away by his kisses, I ran my hands down his smooth chocolate skin, over his muscular arms, tracing his sculpted abdomen and across his strong back.

"So, Mrs. Banks, do you think your husband would be mad that you have a young man in the shower with you?" He joked.

"I hope not. I plan to have you over more often." I teased.

"Imani, tell me how you like it." He demanded as his loving became more passionate.

"Just the way you're doing it, Q. Keep... doing it...oh, Quinton." I sang as I neared my climax.

"Sing it for me, baby. Tell me." He said as his force intensified.

I could barely breathe let alone talk. The look on my face alone should have told him all he needed to know. I was heading home and he was joining me. Quinton roared as he released all his love. He held me tightly as he rested against my chest.

Tap, tap, tap

"Daddy, Mommy, Jahlek is burning down the house." Naadira cried as she entered the bathroom.

"Naadira, sweetie. Wait for Mommy on the bed. I'll be out in one minute." I said as I picked up the sponge and peppermint body wash.

"Is Daddy in there?" She asked.

"Maybe. Go do what I told you to do." I said trying to stifle my laughter.

"But I need to tell Daddy something." She continued.

"What is it, Naadira? Tell me and I'll make sure to tell him."

"Can you tell him that I already pulled out the paintbrushes and the paper?" She said.

"Yes, I will tell him." I replied.

"Okay, don't forget Mommy." She said before exiting the bathroom.

Quinton kissed my shoulder before washing again and stepping out of the shower.

"Quinton, don't walk out yet. Give me two seconds and I'll take her out the room." I said as I turned off the water and hung my sponge on the showerhead.

"I have to shave anyway. Go ahead take your time." He replied.

After I quickly dried my skin I slipped into my plush bathrobe before exiting the bathroom.

When I entered the bedroom, I saw Naadira sitting on the edge of the bed flipping through the channels still in her footed pajamas.

"Kai didn't dress you, sweetie?"

"Nope, she won't get out the bathroom either. She ran out the room and locked herself in the bathroom. Bryan was banging on the door but she told him to go away." Naadira said as she put her arms across her chest.

"Come on, Baby. Let's go see what's wrong with your sister." I said only imagining what it could be.

As I reached the kids bathroom, the smell of burning food flooded the hallway. Bryan sat outside the bathroom door trying to talk to Kai-Aja but she wouldn't answer. I knocked on the door but she still didn't answer.

"Kai, open the door. It's Mommy." I said trying to stay calm.

"Mommy," She cried. The door slowly opened.

"Take Naadira downstairs and fix her some cereal and tell Jahlek to get away from the stove." I said to Bryan as I entered the bathroom.

Kai-Aja sat on the toilet. Her face flushed and eyes full of tears.

"Mommy, I woke up and there was blood all over the sheets. It scared me. I ran in the bathroom and tried to wash my pajama pants and the sheets." She cried.

I almost passed out. No matter how much I talked to her about puberty and sex, I would never be ready to accept her going through those changes. I looked in the tub and saw the sheet, her pajama bottoms, and panties all soaking in water.

"Well, I know you know what this means. You got your period, Baby." I said as I squatted in front of her and wiped the tears from her eyes. "Don't cry. You'll be okay."

"Do we have to tell everybody?" She asked as she blew her nose.

"We have to tell Daddy and Auntie Reese. But you don't have to tell anybody else." I replied.

There was a knock at the door and then the doorknob began to wiggle.

"Who is it?" I called out.

"It's Daddy. Are you okay, Kai?" Quinton answered.

"Do you want me to let Daddy in?" I asked as I grabbed her housecoat off the floor.

She waited before responding.

"No, I don't want to talk to him in here. Wait 'til I go in my room." She replied.

"She's okay, Q. I'll be right out." I hollered towards the closed door.

"Are you sure, Imani?" He asked.

"I'll talk to you when I get out, Q." I replied.

"Alright, I'm going downstairs then." He said.

"No, wait for me in the girls' room. We need to talk." I replied.

Kai-Aja walked towards the bathtub to finish cleaning the stained cloths. As I walked towards her, I noticed some red spots on the back of her pajama shirt. Not wanting to embarrass her any further, I waited until she wrung out the sheet and put them in the laundry basket before I suggested she take a shower and meet me in her room. She took off the shirt, placed it with the other laundry, and entered the shower. I picked up the basket and carried it out of the bathroom.

"What happened to Kai?" Quinton asked as I walked past the girls' room.

"Are you sure you want to know?" I returned.

"Not really but give it to me anyway." He replied.

"Our baby girl is growing up. She got her first visit from her friend." I said as we walked to our bedroom.

I needed to change out of my robe and get dressed for the day before I could bring the clothes to the laundry room.

"Are you serious?" He yelled.

"What the hell are you yelling for? You can't scare it away." I replied.

"How is she feeling?" He asked in the concerned parent tone.

"A little scared and embarrassed but she'll be fine." I replied.

"What do you need me to do then?" He asked.

"Can you take the boys to class? I want to stay home with Kai today." I answered.

Quinton sat on the wooden chest at the foot of the bed. I walked towards our walk-in closet and searched for one of my favorite weekend warm-up suits. After Naadira was born, my behind never completely returned to its pre-baby shape. All I have been able to fit were my sweat pants and select stretch jeans, which I hated. Quinton liked my new assets; it was like his new toy.

As I applied baby oil to my skin, Quinton applied his cologne and selected his jewelry. He had dressed in a pair of blue jeans and a black pullover Nautica shirt. He never buttoned the top two buttons. He pulled his chain over his neck and centered it so he could show off the diamond-filled pendant that read, *Mr. Banks* under a king's crown. Rodney bought it as a birthday gift for him last year and he hasn't stopped wearing it since. Charisse almost killed Rodney after she found the receipt for it.

Quinton carried the basket to the laundry room as I went to check on Kai.

"Baby, send Naadira upstairs so I can get her dressed please?" I said as he walked down the stairs.

"Alright." He replied.

Kai was in her room preparing her underwear with the sanitary napkin I put on her bed before I pulled out Naadira's clothes. She had the towel tied tightly around her as her wet hair stuck to her bare shoulders.

"Do you want me to press your hair today?" I said as I ran my hand over her curls.

"No, I'm going to wear it curly." She replied without looking my way.

"Kai, are you okay? Do you want me to leave while you finish?" I asked not wanting to make her feel anymore uncomfortable.

"I'm okay ... well, my stomach hurts a little, but you can stay here." She replied.

Kai-Aja now towered above me at a height of five-nine. All my kids were tall; I was the shorty in the house. Naadira and me, anyway. Kai-Aja no longer favored Quinton. If she were compared to anyone in the family, everyone would say she resembled John. Outside of her having Quinton's curly hair texture and chinky eyes, she had John's pointy chin, light brown eyes, slim face, and our rusty hair color and tanned skin. Jahlek and Naadira favored Quinton all the way, chocolate brown skin, curly dark brown hair, chinky brown eyes and full lips. Jahlek wore his hair in braids like Bryan. Naadira was very tender-headed and dreaded anyone messing in her curls. Normally I put her hair in ponytails and call it done. Kai-Aja had hair like Kelis. She could were it loose for a while before it got too wild. However, when pressed, the sunset color complemented her tan skin as it flowed down her back.

Naadira walked in the room with her hands held out in front of her.

"What's on your hands, Baby?" I said as she walked towards me.

"Syrup." She replied.

"Go wash your hands then come get dressed and get your hair done." I said as I went into their closet and pulled out a pink top with *Diva* in silver rhinestones across the front to pair with pink jeans.

"Are you hungry, Kai?"

"Yeah, I'm going to go downstairs and make some toast and tea. After my stomach stops hurting I'll eat a sandwich or something." She replied.

Sometimes it was hard to believe she was only twelve then there are the days when I am hollering, *'Damn, she's twelve already.'*

"After you eat, I'll take you down to the pharmacy to pick up some sanitary napkins and something for the cramps." I said as I kissed her cheek.

"So, I'm not going to dance today?" She asked.

"I didn't think you would feel up to it. You can go if you want." I replied.

She buckled her belt then pull on her DKNY logo t-shirt. Her body was deceiving. Her face and voice were still young but her body was like that of a seventeen or eighteen year-old. Quinton had a hell of a job on his hands.

"I think I rather sleep." She said.

"I figured you would." I agreed.

With that, she walked out the room and left me to dress Naadira.

CHAPTER 4

QUINTON

Charisse was in the kitchen making pancakes while Rodney was outside smoking a cigarette. I offered to help but Charisse said she could handle it. This was a treat for the kids because Imani never cooked a big breakfast on Saturdays, dinner either for that matter. However, she made breakfast and dinner any other day. Bryan and Jahlek were in the dining room finishing breakfast while Christian and Damien sat in the kitchen with their mother.

"Q, you want me to make a plate for you and Imani." Charisse asked.

"No, I'll grab something after I drop off the boys. And Imani doesn't eat pancakes." I replied.

"Since when, *'Imani doesn't eat pancakes?'*" She questioned.

"Ever since she felt she needed to lose weight." I replied as I poured a glass of apple juice and leaned against the counter.

"She's a mess. Imani has a nice body. Shit, most women would love to have her body after two kids." She said.

"I tried to tell her she looks good but she's not trying to hear me. Now if some next dude told her, she'd believe him." I joked.

"Yeah, right. Once that girl gets something in her mind no one can make her believe different." Reese countered.

We shared a brief laugh before Rodney came inside kissing all over Charisse.

"Get off of me please. You stink like cigarettes." She complained.

"Come on, Reese. Stop acting like you don't like it." I said while I gave Rodney a hand dap.

"Where's Imani? Why are you taking the boys?" She asked ignoring my last comment trying not to blush.

"Kai is not feeling well so she's going to stay home with the girls.

Oh yeah, let me make her some tea." I said as I thought that the tea might alleviate some of the nausea.

Bryan walked into the kitchen and placed two sets of dishes in the sink.

"Dad, Is Mom ready? Me and Jah are going to be late." He said.

"I'm taking y'all. You ready?" I asked.

"Yeah, we left our bags in Mom's car though." He replied.

I reached into my pocket and removed my keys.

"Here, this is her key. Get the stuff and then start my car." I said as I passed Bryan the keys.

"Can I drive?" He asked excitedly.

"Later on tonight. I'll let you drive me to the supermarket." I replied.

"Imani is going to have a fit if she finds out your letting Bryan drive." Charisse added.

"She'll be alright." I finished the juice in my glass then continued. "He's going to be sixteen soon. He got to learn somehow."

"Damn, we are getting old, dawg. Bryan's going to be sixteen, Kai recently turned twelve, and how old is Jahlek now?" Rodney asked.

"Eleven. Naadira and Christian are six already. Where the hell have you been?" I laughed.

Charisse made a low huffing sound.

I took that as my cue to leave. Imani was on her way down the stairs as I was leaving the kitchen and heading towards the front door. I waited for her to come down the stairs so I could ask her about Kai.

"She's fine." Imani responded then reach for a kiss. Naadira stood besides her waiting for a kiss as well with her lips poked out.

I bent over to kiss her then said, "I put on the tea kettle. The water should be hot now. After I drop the boy's off, I'm going to the car wash. You need anything while I'm out?"

"No thank you, Baby. The girls and I are going out after Kai and I eat." She replied as she stepped off the last step.

"Reese and Rodney are in the kitchen. Be careful. They were cool when I left but you know how long that could last." I said before walking toward the door.

"When aren't they arguing?" She responded.

Bryan and Jah were in my Benz blasting Planet Patrol's 'Play at your own risk.' I must have left my CD in last night. As I opened the door, Bryan turned down the volume.

"Dad, what was up with Kai? I tried to get to the bathroom and she had the door locked. Me and Jahlek had to use the guest bathroom in the basement." Bryan said as we backed out the driveway.

"She wasn't feeling good. She'll be all right. Your mom is going to take care of her." I replied.

"Is she pregnant?" Jahlek asked from the back seat.

Bryan nor I could respond fast enough, "NO!"

"What made you say that, Jah?" I questioned.

"Because, when I spent the night at cousin Matt's house, Santita ran to the bathroom like that and when I asked him what was wrong with her, he said she was pregnant and she gets sick like that every morning. Morning sickness" He replied.

"I didn't know they were having another baby." I said.

"Well, maybe nobody was supposed to know." Bryan said as he looked back at Jahlek.

"Don't matter. Kai is not pregnant. She is only twelve." I said trying to dismiss the thought.

"Dad, you know girls can have babies at twelve? Remember Tiffany from up the block..." Bryan offered his input.

"Yes, I do. Nobody asked for your two cents either. Now drop the conversation. Kai is not having a baby anytime soon. Point, blank and period." I said with frustration.

"You sound like Mom. She always says that, *point, blank and period.*" Jah said with a slight laugh.

"You are such a Mama's boy, Jah." Bryan said as he turned the volume on the radio up.

My cell phone rang as I was about to chastise Bryan about teasing Jahlek.

"Answer it, Bryan." I said as I passed him the phone.

"Hello," He said as he greeted the caller. "Yeah, he's here. Hold on." He covered the mouthpiece, "Some lady named Sandra."

The named made my heart beat double time. Sandra was Trina's friend. She called my office recently about something to do with money left to Bryan's kids. I told her to keep everything and spilt it between her two. After that, there should have been nothing left to talk about. How did she get my cell phone number?

"Give me the phone. Yeah, hello."

"Q, you have to bring Bryan to New York. Justice and Renee won't let me have the money unless you and Bryan show up and tell them that you don't want any parts of the money." She said in one breath.

Justice and Renee were Bryan's uncle and aunt – his father brother and sister. They had money and other valuables that were rescued from the house and divided between their family. Bryan's portion however was still unclaimed.

"I have to talk to Imani first. Let me see what I can do from here. Is this your number?" I asked.

"Yeah. Why you can't come to New York? It will be much quicker." Sandra added.

"Because, I don't want to make an unnecessary trip." I replied.

"Or, you don't want Bryan to meet his real family." She replied.

"Sandra, stay out of my business. Worry about your own family." I said before disconnecting.

Immediately, I dialed the house. Kai-Aja picked up.

"Where's your mother?" I asked. "Put her on the phone please."

Kai called for her mother to answer the phone. Imani picked up another extension. Kai hung up.

"Are you going out right now?" I asked.

"No, where are you?" She questioned

"A block from the boys' school. Look, I'm coming straight back home so don't leave." I stated.

"Is everything okay, Q?" She asked.

"We need to talk. Give me fifteen minutes to get back." I said before hanging up.

I pulled in front of the boys' school and gave Bryan a twenty-dollar bill.

"Buy something to eat after class. Call me and let me know where you are so I can pick you up from there." I said.

"Is everything okay, Dad?" He asked.

"It will be." I replied. "Don't worry about it. Your mom and I will take care of everything. Keep your phone on."

৪০৪০৪০৫৫৫৫

<u>CHARISSE</u>

Rodney bathed Christian and Damien while I ironed their clothes. I always kept a spare change of clothes at Imani's house for the kids and me. There had been many times when I would come here to get away from Rodney so it only made sense to keep an extra set of everything. Imani and Naadira were in the living room with Alaire. Kai-Aja had been in her bed all morning.

Rodney returned to the bedroom with the boys wrapped in towels.

"Where are the lotion and underwear?" He asked.

"Look in the baby's diaper bag for their lotion, powder, and Damien's pull-ups. Here's Christian's underwear." I said as I passed the red and white Superman underwear to Rodney.

"Are you going to be ready to leave after the kids are dressed?" He asked.

It seemed as if anything he said would annoy the hell out of me. It wasn't what he said; it's how he said it. No doubt he wanted to rush back to New York to drop me and the kids to the house so he could hit the streets. I tried to remain calm though.

"Are you in a rush? I don't have anything to do today." I replied.

"I wanted us to take the kids over to my mother's. Today is Shemeka's birthday and their having a small party for her." He said.

I felt foolish for assuming he was trying to shuck his family responsibilities but history proves Rodney was infamous for just that.

Shemeka was one of his four younger sisters. He was the only boy. His sisters, all a year behind the other – Shemeka, Kareemah, Keisha, and Stephanie were like my younger sisters. My actual sisters were somewhere in New Jersey enjoying their married lives. I hardly ever

46

heard from them after they found husbands. That's how Rodney's sisters and I became so close. Especially after Imani moved out of New York and left me with no one else to talk to, Rodney sisters and I have been inseparable.

"Did you pick up a gift then?" I asked.

"Not yet, why?" Rodney replied as he began to dress Damien.

"Because Shemeka had mentioned that she wanted this necklace she saw in Howard's. As a matter of fact I think she put it on lay-a-way." I said.

Shemeka had actually taken me to the store to see the necklace but we both knew she couldn't afford it. I put a deposit on it because I had planned to get it as a Christmas gift but I figured Rodney could pick it up now. It would be a nice surprise for Shemeka.

I waited for Rodney to finish dressing the boys before I went into the bathroom. I turned on the shower then wrapped my hair to put on the shower cap. As I began to step into the shower, I heard a light tap on the door. Without question, I knew it was Rodney so I unlocked the door and opened it slightly. He stepped in as I wrapped myself with a towel.

"What happened?" I asked as he sat on the toilet lid.

"Nothing really. I was thinking about us and wanted to talk." He said as he rested an arm on the sink.

"Well, if you don't mind talking while I'm in the shower..." I paused as I motioned towards the shower.

"I don't mind." He replied.

I stepped inside of the tub and placed my towel on the ring on the wall outside of the shower.

"What's on your mind, Rodney?" I said as I prepared myself for another meaningless conversation that will leave us right back where we started, nowhere.

Every now and again Rodney would bore me with the obvious problems in our relationship then after approximately twenty minutes he would conclude the conversation as if something had been fixed. Meanwhile the only thing he did was make me realize how much bullshit I was actually tolerating. He would feel as if his conscious was clear while I had a building tension headache.

"Reese, I know you're not happy. I really don't know what else to do to make you happy. I gave you a house and the truck. You don't have to work. The kids are always taken care of. What am I doing wrong? Most women would be satisfied with that but you want more. What more can I give you?" Rodney said.

Whoa! I wasn't expecting for anything that stupid to fly out of his mouth. Obviously, Rodney really didn't have a clue.

"I guess most of the *superficial women* you know would be happy with a drug dealing baby daddy that never spends time at home with them or the kids but have their hair and nails done with that same tax-free, drug money. Most *materialistic women* would be satisfied with a big house, a nice car, and a bank account but that's not why I stood with you. Contrary to popular belief, there is a small percent of women that actually want a real man. No, excuse me a husband. I need attention and affection, Rodney. And that's more than money and a big dick can fix!" I said trying to suppress the anger that began to build in my chest.

"I give you and the kids plenty of my time. You want me to stay in the house all fucking day and lay up beside you but that's not me, Reese. When we met you knew I was always out in the street..."

"That was before we had three fucking kids!" I said as I cut him off. "You know what, Rodney. Personally, I don't give a rat's ass if you are in the house or not. However, you have two boys that need their father. And if you can't handle that, then I'm sure there is someone that can." I said, thoroughly frustrated with where this conversation was going.

"So, you are seeing someone else now? That's why you're always in Pennsylvania. You got a man out here. That's what you're trying to tell me, Charisse?" Rodney said as he pulled the shower curtain back and looked me in the face.

"Rodney, I wish it were that easy. I only wish I was seeing someone else, instead wasting all my time loving a man that will never love me back." I said, as I stood naked under the running water.

"Now you're telling me how I feel. If I didn't love you, Reese, I wouldn't be trying to work things out between us." He said as he backed away from the shower.

I closed the curtains again. I wanted to hide the tears that mixed in with the water and ran down my face.

"Rodney, if staying out six days of the week, almost never calling home to check in on the kids or me for that matter is how you show someone you love them then you are doing a fantastic job. Maybe there's something wrong with me for wanting more. I need more than that, Rodney. I need to feel the love." I said as I washed the lather off my skin and turned off the water.

Rodney passed a towel through the curtains. I made sure my face was free of any tears before opening the curtains and facing him.

"Reese, baby. If you want me home more, I'm there. But I really don't see how that will change everything between us." He said as he ran a finger down the side of my face.

"Why don't we try it out first and see? We have to do this one-step at a time. We've been together over six years; we can't let it go to waste."

Rodney pulled me close to him and held me tightly. I wrapped my arms around his neck as we kissed. For the first time, in a long time, I felt something move inside me.

"Come on, baby. Let's go get this gift for Meka and drop the kids by my mother's so we can spend sometime alone." He took off my shower cap and hung it on the back of the door.

"I think I'll like that." I responded as I grabbed my lotion and began to massage it onto my skin.

A loud slamming sound interrupted our quiet moment as Rodney rushed out of the bathroom to make sure it wasn't one of the kids. I tried to finish pulling myself together as quick as possible to find out what was going on.

When I walked into the living room, Quinton was talking to Rodney in a hushed tone as Imani took the kids into the playroom. I stood beside Rodney as I combed my hair and listened to Quinton going on about some woman named Sandra.

"If it's only to sign papers, what's the problem?" I asked as Imani returned.

"Not sign papers, divide paper – money. I don't believe it's only for the money. Sandra wants Bryan for something else. She seems more concerned with us going to New York." Quinton responded then put an arm around Imani.

"Bryan can't go back to New York, Q. He saw the niggas that killed his father. It's not safe for him to go back." Rodney said as he paced back and forth.

"After all these years you think they are still looking for him?" Imani asked. "That doesn't sound like it makes sense."

"Q, we need to handle this shit, Man." Rodney said.

"No you don't. What are you going to do? Go out there looking for trouble, Rodney. You and Quinton have families now. It's really time for you to leave the streets before you get locked up again or get killed." I said as I thought back to when I went to visit Rodney on Riker's Island.

"Reese, this is not the time for us to be arguing. Q and I can't sit back and do nothing." Rodney shouted.

"Look, there's no need for any of us to argue. Bryan is not going back to New York. Point, blank and period. We will get Sandra the money some how or find some other way to help her that will not put Bryan in the middle." Imani said as she looked up to Quinton who had yet to say a word.

"Sandra was right about one thing." Quinton said. "Bryan will eventually have to meet his family. After I pick up the boys, we'll talk to him about it and see how he feels. Bryan knows he has family in New York. We never gave him the opportunity to decide what *he* wanted to do."

"What family? Where were they all these years then, Q? They are coming around now because they exhausted all the money Bryan's father left them. Now they want Bryan's share. Bryan ain't going to New York and that's final!" Imani turned and walked out of the family room.

"Rodney, uhmm, we need to get to your mother's house." I said suggestively.

"Yeah. Q, I'll give you a holler later and see what's going on. Reese, you get the kids together and I'll get their stuff." Rodney said as he headed towards the guest room.

Quinton headed up the stairs to follow Imani as Rodney and I got the kids ready to ride back to New York. Rodney seemed distracted as he took Damien car seat from the Navigator and put it in my car.

"Christian is going to ride with you, Rodney?" I asked.

"Don't matter." He responded without looking in my direction.

"Are you okay, Rodney?" I said hoping he wasn't going to change his mind about tonight.

He walked over to me and kissed the tip of my nose with his full lips.

"Yeah, Mama. I'm okay. Let's get home." He ran his hand through my hair. "Your hair looks cute in that style. Don't cut it anymore." He said as he touched my bangs then ran his fingers down my face – his way of saying, 'I love you.'

I carried Alaire to the truck as Christian struggled with our overnight bag. Damien and Rodney were in the car and just about ready to leave while I was still buckling in Christian and Alaire. There was a faint ringing sound coming from somewhere inside the truck. I looked around until I found Rodney's cell phone inside the baby's bag. I started to give him his phone but the woman in me wanted to know who was calling.

I hid behind the seats as I flipped open the phone and said, "Hello." The caller hung up.

I search the phone for the last received call but the number was blocked. As I turned around, I was face to face with Rodney.

"So, you're snooping through my phone now?" He said.

"It was ringing, so I answered it. Is there a problem with that?" I responded.

"Can I have my phone, Charisse?" He asked.

Using formal names meant he was upset.

"Of course, *Rodney*. And when your girlfriend calls back, tell her I was trying to say hi." I added before I closed both of the passenger side doors.

He didn't respond.

CHAPTER 5

IMANI

Bryan sat on the edge of our bed as I sought the right words to say. Quinton wanted to tell Bryan about his relatives back in New York that have started asking for him and the money his biological father left for him. Personally, I didn't think he needed to know and there I was trying to find the best way to tell him.

"Bryan, I...I...I can't do this. Q, you want him to know, you tell him." I said.

"Mom, if this is about last night, Dad and I already talked. I apologized. Everything is good." Bryan said as he looked from me to Quinton who stood bold-faced as if he were angry with us.

Nevertheless, I knew that was his serious, in-deep-thought expression.

"Bryan, remember the call I got this morning from a woman named Sandra." Quinton waited for Bryan to respond. "Sandra is your sisters', Sharay and Jasmine's, mother. I don't know if you remember or even if you want to but we need to talk about this."

"Dad, I don't think I want to talk about this. I've been getting calls from Sharay for like the past two weeks. I *really* don't want to talk about it." Bryan said as he looked about the room, avoiding eye contact with Quinton and me.

"Why didn't you tell me? How did they get your number?" Quinton said as he walked towards Bryan.

"She said she got it from Diamond. She said her and Diamond went to school together and was best friends for a long time." Bryan replied. "Anyhow, she's been stressing me about coming to visit her in New York. I told her to come here."

"What did she say?" I asked as I sat beside him on the bed.

"She said she can't because her mother doesn't like you or Dad and doesn't want her anywhere near y'all." Bryan said as he looked into my eyes. "What happened between you and Sandra?"

"This has nothing to do with your mom." Quinton spoke in a low voice. "Sandra thinks that I am trying to keep you away from your father's family. A small part of me did, but the larger part wants you to be safe. Until I feel that this is legit, that all she wants is your money, then we should stay out of New York." Quinton stated before reaching for his cell phone.

"But what if I do want to meet them? They are my family. Shouldn't I have a choice? I don't have a choice with the money and I understand that but I should be able to meet my family." Bryan asked.

"Do you?" I asked. "Are you thinking about going back to New York? Going to see the family that didn't give a damn about you?"

Before Bryan could answer, my mind had filled with thoughts of Bryan following in the footsteps of Quinton and Bryan senior.

"I want to meet them. Find out what they're all about. Find out a little about my background. Mom, I'm not trying to leave you and Dad. I want to know who they are. Who am I?" Bryan answered innocently.

With that, I left the room. My heart felt like it was being pulled from my chest. Kai-Aja was standing right outside the door. She stood there for a moment before speaking.

"Bryan you are the most popular boy in your school, my big brother and idol. You don't need to go to New York to know this." Kai answered Bryan's insecurities with innocence then turned to me. "Are you alright?" She asked.

"Yes. Do you want to ride with me? I'm going to the Pharmacy now." I responded.

"If you need me to ride with you, I'll go." She replied.

"Get your jacket. We'll leave Naadira with Jahlek. Your father and Bryan need to talk alone." I said as I started down the stairs.

"Mom, is this still about last night?" Kai asked referring to the fight.

"I hope not." I replied.

Kai took one last look at Bryan then her father before closing the door and start down the stairs.

Naadira and Jahlek were in the family room watching a movie. She was lying on his back as he lay on his stomach using his arms as a pillow. I started to sneak out with out telling them I was leaving but when I looked again I realized they were sleeping. As Kai came down the stairs, I pressed a finger against my lips, signaling for her to be quiet. She looked inside the family room and began to laugh. I went into the office to get my camera. I had all kinds of candid shots of the kids around the house and always found room for more. This was one for the photo album.

After taking several pictures, I asked Kai to help me as I lifted Naadira off Jahlek and laid her on the floor beside him. Kai put Nana's quilt on the floor then covered Jahlek with a WWF sheet that Jahlek kept on the single seat. Gently, I woke Jahlek for him to lie on the quilt and then I laid Naadira beside him and used the same wrestling sheet to cover her. Kai turned off the television and we left.

As we drove down the street, Kai-Aja flipped through the station looking for some Rap music. No matter how much we argued about it, she insisted on torturing me. I was never a fan of Rap. Hip-Hop, R&B, and maybe some of the old school Rap, but not too much of the new Rap. After several minutes of being unsuccessful, she decided to play one of my mix CD's.

"Mom, can you put anything from the last five years in your car? This stuff is so old." She complained as Donnell Jones poured through the speakers.

"Well, I like it. You used to love this song. Now all you want to hear is that hardcore music. And as a matter of fact I do have some rap in here." I said as I pressed the button to change the CD. "You want to hear some Jay-Z."

Kai got excited. "Yes! Please something other than this slow, 'I'm in love' music."

I laughed at her expression.

The CD began to play and cuts from Jay-Z's *Reasonable Doubt* album accompanied us to the Pharmacy. I'm sure she was expecting something more current but she knew not to complain. Next would have been Jazz.

My mind wondered over reasons Quinton might have for not telling me about the money or Sandra. There was no reason for Quinton to wait until it was beyond his control for me to find out. That was one of the things that upset me about Quinton. He would always take family issues and try to handle them without consulting the *family*.

"Mom, not to be in the business or nothing but why is Daddy always so hard on Bryan?" Kai-Aja asked.

"That's your dad's way of being a strict parent. Your dad wants all of you to be the best you can. Somewhere in his mind, he thinks if he's hard on you, you will learn to make the right decision. Strange but it's true." I replied thinking about the many arguments Quinton and I had about the same thing.

"Sometimes, it seems like he's being *really* hard on Bryan." Kai-Aja said while bopping her head to the music.

"When I scream at you, do you think I hate you? When your dad scolds you and Jahlek, you think he hates you too?" I asked.

"You want me to tell you the truth?" Kai asked.

"What do you mean? Lying is not an option." I became angry but tried to maintain an even tone.

"I never thought you or dad hated us. But there are a lot of times that you hurt my feelings and it's really hard to forgive you." Kai-Aja explained.

"Well, your father and I always tell you and your brothers to speak your mind. Why don't you say any of this when we're talking? When I scold or punish you, it is never because I want to hurt you. It's only to make you think about what you have done. You need to know that all of your actions have consequences." I tried to explain but I remember a time when no matter what Mia said I swore John hated me.

"Kai, no matter what you, your brothers, or your sister does, your father and I will always love you. Do you understand me?" I assured Kai-Aja.

"Yes, Mommy." She replied and displayed that same sweet smile that always warms my heart. That same sweet smile also won her some leniency on many occasions when her punishment could have been a lot worse.

We decided to go to the Supermarket instead of the Pharmacy. It was Quinton job to do the food shopping on Saturday's but since we were already out, I figured Kai and I could handle it. As we walked through the Supermarket, we began sharing girl talk. Once Kai started, she was an open book. Any gossip she knew, you knew. I mentioned to Kai that her mouth would eventually get her in trouble but she continued to volunteer information.

I decided to pick up tacos for dinner then went to the meat section for some ground turkey while I tried to drown out Kai's continuous yapping. As I looked over the packages of meat, someone tapped my shoulder.

"Kai-Aja, I thought I told you about tapping me." I replied without looking towards her.

"Hello, your name is Imani, right?" The voice responded.

"Excuse me." I said as I turned to face the voice beside me.

"I didn't mean to bother you. I thought you were someone...never mind." The woman replied then turned to walk away.

"Miss, hold on. How do you know my name?" I asked as I followed the woman who began to head down the frozen foods aisle.

She turned abruptly and stared at me quizzically. Then she took an awkward stance and twisted her lips to the side.

"You are Imani." The woman stated.

"Who are you?" I replied.

Kai-Aja stood beside me in her own stance as if she was ready for whatever.

"I don't remember where we met but your face is unforgettable." The woman said while posing a fake smile.

"Are you from New York?" I asked knowing that if this woman did indeed know me it would have had to be from New York.

"I work in New York but I've lived here all my life." She replied.

"Maybe we've worked for the same firm. I used to work for P. G. Johnson." I stated hoping this would help.

"Ahh, now I know where I know you from. We did a conference in Atlantic City together. Wow, it must have been like six, maybe seven years ago."

"Atlantic City?" I questioned as I thought to the last conference I attended.

Six or seven years ago, Atlantic City, Conference. Why can't I remember any of this?

"I'm sorry. I can't recall. Anyway, how are you? What's your name again?"

"Shandi. I was one of Omar's co-workers. You remember him don't you? Wasn't you good friends with him?" She asked.

"Nope. We weren't friends at all. Anyway, it was nice seeing you." I said trying quickly to get away from this woman. I didn't need any visits from the past.

The reason I could not remember was because I did not want to. My mind had this habit of purging bad memories. Omar and all the drama of that year hit the recycle bin a long time ago.

"Mommy, is everything okay? You don't look okay." Kai-Aja said as we headed towards the register.

"There are some things from the past that should stay right there, in the past." I said as I began to unload the items in the shopping cart onto to the counter.

 జుజుజుళుళుళు

RODNEY

Charisse sat in my mother's bedroom watching television while everyone else participated in the celebration that took place in the living room. She said she wanted to watch Alaire while she slept but Alaire had been awake for sometime and Reese has yet to join the rest of the family. I wasn't in the mood to play apart in her pity party so I left her alone. Besides, the longer she stayed in the room, the more opportunity I gained to flirt with Shemeka's friend, Natalie. Natalie was one of those 'don't-give-a-damn' kind of girls. She knew about Reese and me – hell, her baby father was sitting right beside her – nevertheless, every chance she got; she subtly hinted that she was interested in sampling a taste.

"Hey, Reese. What's going on?" Natalie hollered over the music.

When I turned around Charisse was standing right behind me. She placed her hand on my shoulder and stared at Natalie. Charisse never paid Natalie any attention. She dismissed Natalie's childish antics and deemed her harmless and foolish teenager. But, Natalie was of age and definitely willing to prove Reese wrong.

"Baby, I'm going to go home and get the kids stuff together for school. Do you want me to take the boys?" Charisse said as she ran her soft slender hand down the length of my arm.

"Are you feeling alright? You stayed in the room the whole time we were here." I asked as I took Alaire from her arms.

"Rodney, I'm fine just ready to go home. Did Meka like her gift?" Charisse asked.

"She hasn't taken it off since she opened the damned box. I still think it's a little too flashy for her to be wearing around the hood." I said as we watched Shemeka dance with her man-for-the week.

"Rodney she's a grown woman now. She's not going to be wearing it to go to the grocery store, I'm sure." Charisse said with a slight laugh. "She is too classy for that."

When she smiled the room lit up.

Kareemah came over to where we were standing. She extended her arms to receive Alaire.

"I hope you two know that undercover love shit you're doing is annoying. Keisha and I were over there watching you. It's okay to be affectionate. Y'all damn near married." Kareemah added her two cents before stepping away into the crowd with our baby girl.

"Looks like we can't front for the public anymore. Damn!" I said playfully.

I pulled Charisse into my arms and began to dance.

Jordin Sparks and Chris Brown poured through the speakers with 'No Air'. Charisse loved that song. She ran her hands through my locks as she began to sing along.

"Oh, so I'm your air now." I whispered in her ear.

"Yeah, something like that." She replied.

For the first time in a long time, Charisse and I were enjoying each other's company as if all our problems never existed and we had a perfect home. We danced for at least another four songs before reality took us away from our special moment. Christian stood beside me as I trailed kisses down his mother's neck. Her body was accepting my invitation for some intimacy.

"Daddy, my stomach hurts." Christian cried.

Charisse broke away from embrace and immediately sprung into Mommy mode. "You must have eaten too much. Let's go see if Grandma has something for your stomach in the cabinet. Rodney, are you ready to go home?" Charisse looked at me as if she wanted to finish what had begun on the dance floor.

"Yeah, let me get Damien and Alaire ready. Do you want Ma to pack a plate for you? You haven't eaten anything since we got here." I replied.

"Oh, no sweetie. Stephanie brought me some food before she left. Get the kids." She responded.

I went to get Damien who had fallen asleep on my mother's lap while Alaire was being spoiled by Keisha and Kareemah. Shemeka and Natalie were standing against the wall behind me. As I bent over to collect Alaire and her things, Natalie took it upon herself to cop a feel. She and Shemeka stood there giggling as I continued to gather my daughter's things as if nothing happened. After I passed the plotting duo, I looked over towards Charisse who was so immersed in taking care of the Christian that she missed Natalie's play. I turned towards Natalie and cut my eyes. Her games made her immaturity shine through.

"Meka, enjoy the rest of your party." I said as I kissed her cheek.

"Rodney, call me." Natalie added.

"Yeah. Okay. Keep your phone on." I answered sarcastically.

"Oh, it's like that now?" Natalie asked.

I answered with silence.

By the time I reached Charisse and Christian, she was holding him over the garbage pail. Ma stood beside Charisse holding a wet cloth around his neck.

"Rodney, he's running a fever. I want to take him to the emergency room." Charisse said with worry covering her face.

"Okay, baby. I'll meet you down stairs in the jeep." I replied.

"Give my keys to Keisha and ask her to bring your car home." Charisse replied while rubbing Christian's back.

Christian cried out for me as I turned to leave the kitchen. Reese and I switched duties. She took the keys to Keisha and held Alaire while I carried Christian down the stairs. By the time Charisse reached the jeep, Keisha and Kareemah were in tow.

"We are going to take Damien and Alaire to your house and stay with them until you get back." Keisha said as she hit the alarm on my car.

"Thank you. Reese, let's go!" I yelled as Christian began to vomit again in the bag I gave him.

Charisse hopped in the backseat and before she could close the door, I had peeled off the block.

The hospital's emergency room was full. Christian had begun to shiver as if he had chills but his skin was burning hot. The more I demanded immediate attention for my son, the more my demands went unheard. A nurse finally came to take Christian's temperature and when she read the results, she rushed him to a bed. A doctor rushed over and began to shout all kinds of instructions as he checked Christian's pulse. One of the nurse's was asking Reese questions regarding his age and all these other questions that seemed to have faded out. My thoughts were so far away I did not even notice when the doctor's began to roll him away to a room. Charisse tugged on my jeans and mentioned for me to follow the doctors as she stood behind to fill out paperwork. A nurse prepped Christian's arm to draw blood while another tried to hold him still. Christian began to shake more and an indescribable anger rose inside me. I knew they were trying to help him but I wanted to snatch him away from them. Charisse then walked beside me.

"Baby, he's going to be fine. Calm down." She said as she held my hand.

We sat, waited, and watched over Christian while he slept. An hour earlier, he was given some antibiotics and Tylenol through the I.V. that was inserted in Christian's little hand. The doctor managed to break the fever and stop the vomiting but wanted to keep him over night to observe him. Charisse wanted to call home and check on the kids but it was two o'clock in the morning and we knew everyone was sleep. I tried to get her to go home but she was determined to be there in case he woke early.

"Charisse, tomorrow I want you to take some time for yourself. You have been running yourself tired with the kids and your own projects. When was the last time you went to Cornerstone?" I asked.

Cornerstone Healing was where Charisse would go to get a bi-weekly body massage and acupuncture.

"Now is not the time, Rodney. I can't be thinking about massages and shit." Charisse responded.

"Reese, I'm offering a suggestion. Lately you've been real moody. I was thinking that maybe if you had some rest we wouldn't be arguing all the time. Let me handle the house and kids for a while." I said as I placed a hand on the side of Christian's small face.

"If I left you with the kids, I would be nothing but a nervous wreck. Can't you see this is not about the kids or my *projects*? I'm tired of you and your bullshit. Rodney, there was a time when I could honestly say that we wanted the same thing but I've grown over the years and you haven't. All day all I could think about was where are we going? Where will we be in one or two years? I kept coming up with the same answer. Nowhere! Rodney, I really wanted us to work but...I don't think us being together is a good idea anymore." Charisse looked directly in my eyes and shook her head. "I think its best that we move on."

"Charisse, we got three kids. You can't make that kind of decision without discussing the options with me." Charisse caught me completely off-guard.

"What are the options? I continue to play into your games and be miserable for the rest of my life or I do what is right for me. I choose option number two and that includes me learning how to be by myself."

"What about the kids? How do you think they're going to react to having two homes? They need both of their parents." I tried to find reason but my mind was spinning too fast from Charisse's verbal attack.

"And you should have thought about that a long time ago. You are never there for us anyway so what will be the big difference. It's over, Rodney. I'm not going to put up with another seven years of the same bad luck." Charisse walked across the room without once meeting my gaze. I watched as she collected her things and prepared to leave.

"You going to put me out like that. Like this! While our baby is sick and need us most. I'm sorry, Reese. I can't do that." I stood to meet Charisse who was standing by the door.

"Rodney, it's not about what you can or can't do. It's about what you're going to do. You don't have to leave right away but you got to go." Charisse said before walking out the door.

Although I knew Charisse was serious, I couldn't stop my mind from contemplating ways to make her change her mind. Ultimately, the results will all be the same. I wasted seven years taking advantage of Charisse's devotion to our relationship and her commitment to our family. As I looked over Christian innocent face, a single tear fell from my eye. I couldn't leave my kids. Not after all the shit I've been through. Charisse and the kids were my balance. If they left ... I would be nothing.

CHAPTER 6

QUINTON

"Slow down, Bryan. Watch your speed." I said as he drove towards his school.

"Dad, I got this." Bryan replied as he turned the corner treating my Expedition like a Versa.

"Did you know that SUV's have the tendency to tip over when you make turns like that?" I asked as my patience began to wear thin.

"You're killing me, Dad. I'm not going to kill us. I'm telling you I got this." He tried to reassure me as we sat at a stoplight.

After dropping off Kai and Jahlek, I allowed Bryan to drive. Bryan decided that since he had some extra time he would pick up his girlfriend, Sierra. He told Imani and me how she worked part-time as a secretary aide in his school to pay for her evening college classes. When we reached Sierra's house, Bryan pulled out his cell and called to let her know he was waiting outside.

While we waited, I began to ask questions about Sierra.

"So, she lives alone?" I asked as I watched the building door waiting to see what caused Bryan to drive like a madman.

"She lives with her parents but she is trying to get her own spot." Bryan said as he unbuckled his seat belt.

The front door opened and a young woman with a baby carrier exited the building. Bryan opened his door and started towards the woman who I had been praying was another tenant in the building but by the way her eyes lit up when he approached her, I knew it was Sierra.

"Imani is going to have a heart attack." I said to myself as Bryan helped Sierra carry her things to the car.

I thought of the multiple possibilities. Maybe she was baby-sitting one of her siblings or maybe she had nieces or nephews. The fair-skinned girl looked as if she was all of sixteen years old. Her long ponytail swung from side to side as she walked around the front of the car. I doubt she weighed over a hundred and five pounds. Her small thin frame did not fit the picture of a mother to an infant. Sierra opened the back door and greeted me with a huge smile.

"Hello, Mr. Banks." She said as she placed the diaper bag on the back seat and helped Bryan secure the baby seat.

"Good morning." was the only response I could offer.

When Bryan returned to the driver's seat I gave him a questionable stare he returned my look with a look that said, 'We'll talk later.'

First, we stopped at a day care center that was along the way to his school then we switched seats and I dropped him and Sierra in front of the school. Before he walked away from the car, he put his hand through the window and put his palm out. I almost lost control by this point but I managed to stay calm long enough to give him a twenty, roll up my window and drive away.

"I thought I seen it all but that was some new shit. He wants to be a man but still ask me for money. I should have only given him five dollars and see how he gets by with that." I said aloud to myself as I started towards work.

As I sat at the light, I realized there really wasn't any reason to be angry with him and dismissed the thought of bringing it to Imani's attention. It wasn't his kid. Time would reveal all we should know.

As I pulled my car into its designated parking spot, my cell phone began to vibrate. The Caller ID read, *HOME*.

"Yeah, what's up?" I said as I collected my brief case and suit jacket from the passenger seat.

"Hi, Daddy." Naadira's innocent voice sang through the line.

"Hey, baby. How are you doing?"

"I'm okay." She replied.

"That's it. You're okay?" I asked playfully as I hit the locks and alarm.

"No, I'm really, really good." She said then broke into a fit of giggles.

"I'm about to get in the elevator. I just got to work. Can I call you back from my desk?" I said as I checked my watch.

"Okay, how long are you going to take?" She asked.

"A little while. It will be quicker than you think."

"I'm going to be waiting for you. I'm not even going to leave the phone." She said in her most serious tone.

"I love you. I'm going to call you right back. Now hang up." I waited for the line to go dead before I stepped on the elevator.

My secretary, Eva greeted me as I stepped off the elevator on the eleventh floor. She gave me a basic run down of the day's agenda. Her arms were full of folders as she walked with me to my office. It seemed as if it was going to be another long day.

"A young woman named Sandra called and asked that you call her back at your earliest convenience. She also said it was urgent." Eva said as she passed me a few messages.

Without hesitation, I tossed Sandra's message into a waste basket and headed into my office. Sandra had been calling ever since that Saturday. For a whole week, she had tried everything from begging to threats and back to begging. Her persistence was annoying. I was beginning to believe she was also calling our house and hanging up when Imani answered. It was time to end Sandra's nonsense before it was completely out of hand.

"Eva, I have to call home. I'll probably be on the phone for a while so could you take messages. I'll notify you when I am free."

"That's fine, Mr. Banks. Oh, by the way, your brother is in your office." She said then returned to her desk.

When I turned on the lights, Rodney was there, knocked out on the sofa. I chose not to bother him until after I called Naadira. Whatever drama brought him out could wait a couple more minutes.

Naadira and I talked for over twenty minutes. She was excited because she had learned how to use the speakerphone. Imani was in her office beating away at her keyboard. She created her own nine to five at home. Imani started every morning with a thought and by the end of the day her thought was a new topic for her advice column in the local newspaper. She had become so obsessed with writing that she was even considering writing a novel but she wanted to use her own experiences. I said autobiography, she said novel, and I said whatever.

"Listen, Naadira. Daddy has some work to do. Can I call you back later?" I asked as I turned on my laptop. "I'll call you at lunchtime."

"I probably will be busy later helping Mommy write. When we finish we will call you, okay." Naadira replied.

Her response brought a huge smile to my face as I tried not to laugh. "I guess that's okay." I answered.

"I love you, Daddy." Then Naadira sent one of the juiciest kisses through the phone.

"Love you, too." I sent a juicy kiss back before ending the call.

I pressed the intercom to let Eva know that I was off my call and she could start sending calls through. Rodney began to wake up as the first call came through.

"Hold one minute." I said to my client as I put them on hold and turned my attention to the wide-eyed Rodney who had the look of a beat down dog.

"Charisse left me. She packed the kids, all their stuff and moved back to Harlem. I didn't even know she still had her spot out there. I thought she rented it out a long time ago. She had to have been planning this." Rodney babbled on and on as I sat there trying to find the right time to say, *I told you so.*

"Rodney, let me take this last call and then we'll go grab something to eat and talk about you and Reese." I said as I held the handset in my hand.

"I'm sorry about that Ms. Reed. Yes, the paperwork for your license is complete. You can come by the office any time after one to pick it up." I concluded my conversation then hit the intercom.

"Yes, Mr. Banks." Eva answered.

"I'm sorry. Can you hold my calls again? I am going to step outside for a minute. Would you like anything from downstairs?" I asked as I gathered my jacket and keys.

"No, I'm fine. Thank you." She replied.

Rodney grabbed his jacket, which moments earlier doubled as a blanket, shook it vigorously in an effort to remove the wrinkles and then followed me out the door.

Rodney and I decided to go to the diner down the street from the office. No sooner than the waiter showed us a booth, Rodney began running his mouth.

"At first I thought I had bought some time by staying in the house but she packed up and left without looking back. I knew refusing to let her have the house wasn't going to make her take me back but I figured it would at least give us sometime to let things cool down like usual. It's like she never even gave us a second thought." Rodney stopped talking long enough for me to get a word or two in before he started rambling again.

"The worst part is that she had been feeling this way for some time and never even mentioned to me that she was thinking about leaving. It's like we had been living a lie." Rodney took a sip of his water then stared absently out of the window.

"How long did you think you would be able to string Reese along before she got tired of chasing after you? How many "second thoughts" do you think she needed to realize she needed to move on?" I asked.

Rodney didn't respond.

"Rodney, stop kidding yourself. You knew for some time now that Reese was unhappy. You figured that the mother of your kids, your *girl friend* for seven long years would never leave you. Shit, she stuck it through longer than any other woman I know excluding Imani. You know I'm on your side even when you are wrong but you fucked up this time."

Rodney dropped his head after my comment.

"She wasn't supposed to leave. I gave her everything she wanted but it never seemed to be enough." Rodney said as he stirred his coffee.

"Do you hear yourself? Better yet, do you even believe what you are saying? You were the one who told me years ago that sometimes change is a good thing. You need to change your standards of what a relationship consists of because if what you were giving was your best, then Rodney you need to seriously consider counseling. This is definitely one of those times when your best isn't good enough." I looked at Rodney and wondered what he was actually thinking.

"Q, don't say another word. You know we are tighter than family but if you dig any deeper I might react."

Rodney looked at me as if I was a stranger for a brief moment before he sipped his coffee.

"So, what are you going to do to get your woman back?" I asked as I chewed a piece of bacon.

"I'm not even sure I want to try. I don't play the revolving door. Once it's closed, that's it. Charisse walked out the door. I have to accept the fact that it's over." Rodney replied as he looked at the time.

"Rodney, are you actually willing to let your family go because you are too stubborn to accept that you were wrong?" I questioned.

"Q, who's to say I was wrong and she was right? We have different ideals on family and marriage. You and I know there's somebody for every body. Maybe Reese and I weren't meant to be together." Rodney said.

It was obvious he had lost his mind somewhere between New York and Pennsylvania. The Rodney I knew considered family much too important to let go. The Rodney I knew helped me save my relationship. Years ago he told me, *'Imani is your wife; your lifeline and that means more than any amount of money.'* Yet, he was about to throw it all away at any cost.

"What about the kids, Rodney? Reese loves you Rodney. Together you two are a team. Shit, Reese had your back under any circumstance. You will never find another woman like that. If you think that your family and your woman ain't worth fighting for, then what is?"

My blood began to boil. My brother was trying to take the easy road out and that was not our style.

"Reese and I will figure something out. We need this time apart, to figure out what means the most to us." Rodney replied with confidence as if this break up was his decision all of a sudden.

৪০৪০৪০৪৩৪৩৪৩

CHARISSE

"It's only been two days, Reese. Give him a chance to really absorb the fact that the life he knew is no longer the same." Myra said as

68

she helped unpack the kids' clothes and place them on the bed.

Myra had rented my place after Rodney and I moved in together. I definitely missed the comforts of the house and the memories it contained but my sanity was far more important. Myra hadn't really changed anything in the apartment after all those years. The only real change was to change the extra room back into a bedroom for the kids. All my clothes, handbags, and shoes from the years I had been modeling were going into storage. Well, not exactly *all* of it, the real extravagant things. I always had a large wardrobe and since Rodney and I have been together, I didn't have much use for the old things. If he didn't do anything else, he definitely provided clothes, jewelry, and money for the kids and me.

"Maybe I can donate some of these things or sell them." I said as I looked over some of the shoes. "Half of it hasn't been touched or only worn once."

"Designer made one of a kind definitely can bring in a nice profit. People are always looking to buy discounted one of a kind items. Try Craigslist or EBay." Myra replied.

"Myra, I really appreciate you helping me out. I mean after what we been through I really feel bad for having to ask for your help." I said as I thought of the way I broke off our engagement.

When we came back from Puerto Rico, Rodney and I didn't really think we were going to be together. However, fate has its way of throwing a major wrench in your plans. We continued to see each other but it was awkward for me. I was living with my fiancée, Myra, and having sex with a man, Rodney, whom years ago I could barely stomach. Nevertheless, when Rodney and I found out I was pregnant we knew Myra was going to have to go. Therefore, without any explanations I packed a weekend bag and moved into Rodney's place. Myra called for about the first week, trying to figure out where I went and what happened but I couldn't bring myself to tell her the truth. Not right away. Her calls withered to about three a week to once a month. During my sixth month, we passed each other on the street. She turned her head the other way as Rodney and I strolled down Fifth Avenue hand in hand shopping for baby things.

"Reese, it's alright. We were always friends if nothing else. Keep in mind that I have my own life now. We are going to figure out some kind of schedule so your kids won't be exposed to *my* lifestyle." Myra said before taking a stack of Alaire's clothes and putting them into a clear plastic storage container.

Her words stung, rocked my core.

"Look, I'm not even trying to be here too long. Give us six months and then we are out of your hair. I already started setting up some connections to get back on the road. Me and my kids. We need some time to get our money together and we are gone!" I replied curtly.

"I didn't mean it like that, Reese. Really!" Myra said apologetically.

"Don't stress. I'm a little edgy."

Bullshit. She said exactly what she meant and so did I.

Christian and Damien were watching cartoons while Alaire was sleeping in her swing. It's funny how I didn't feel any hurt or lost over the fact that Rodney and I weren't together. For some strange reason I felt like I only lost my house. Nothing more.

I picked up my cell phone and headset to call Imani. Her phone rang twice before Naadira answered.

"Hello, Angel. Is your mom busy?" I asked.

"Hold on, Auntie." Naadira set the phone down then next you heard the faint sound of bare feet slapping across the wood floor.

'Mommy, Auntie Cherries is on the phone.' She hollered in the background.

Imani picked up the extension that was in her room.

"*'Naadira, hang up your phone.'* Reese, hold on one minute. Q called my office line. Let me finish with him real quick." Imani stated.

"*'Q, Baby. Yeah, I heard you. No. No. Q, I got Reese on the other phone. Yeah, I call you later.'* Yeah, what's up, Momma." Imani said as she returned to the line.

"I'm alive and barely doing that right." I sighed as I walked into the kitchen.

"Rodney was at Q's job early this morning. It seems both of you are not doing so well. According to Q, if Rodney was capable of manufacturing tears he would have cried." Imani said.

"Then why won't he call?" I said before a small tear trickled down my cheek.

"Reese, it's not easy for Rodney to admit that he has been an asshole. He does love you and the kids. He'll come around." Imani tried to sound convincing but even she knew that Rodney had no intentions on calling.

"Imani, I am so drained. I can't believe I let him get me like this. The worst part is that the kids are asking for him. If it were any other day they wouldn't mention *'Daddy'*."

"Reese, kids can definitely feel when something is wrong. As a matter of fact, how is Christian doing?"

"He's doing alright. He started coughing this morning but no fever or anything. He's almost done taking that nasty ass Augmentin. Remember that pink shit they said it taste like bubble gum. They don't have that anymore. "

Imani and I shared a brief laugh before Damien entered the kitchen. He stretched his arms up and began to whine.

"This little boy here whines for everything. He is so spoiled. His Nana did this." I said as I held him in my arms and began looking for his training cup.

"Reese, you know if you ever need a break, you can bring the kids up here with me for a couple of days." Imani offered.

"Thanks, Sis. I'm fine. We'll probably come by this weekend though. You know so Myra can have some space." I responded.

"How is ole' girl doing anyway? How does it feel? You know, *sleeping* together but not really *sleeping* together." Imani was as nosey as ever.

"It doesn't really bother me. I think it's a problem for her though. When we're finish cleaning out the extra bedroom, I'm going to put a little bed in there for myself or sleep with the boys. Right now, Christian and Damien are sleeping on the convertible. I thought about sleeping with them but they sleep too wild." I replied as I poured juice in Damien's cup and sent him back into the living room.

"Why hasn't Myra offered to take the couch and allow you to share the room with the kids until you get the extra room together?"

"She did but I felt uncomfortable putting her out of her room."

"Your room!" Imani countered.

"I left her the apartment. It's her room. I can't shit on the girl twice in one lifetime. First I kick her to the curb for Rodney then kick her out of her home because he and I didn't work out. I'm sure this is uncomfortable enough."

"Bullshit. She loves every bit of it. Especially since she can have you in her bed at night."

"I know, Sis. I know. I really hate the way this feels."

"Charisse, it's temporary. Our doors are always open if you want to come home. Listen, Reese it's about time for me to drop Naadira to school. These backwards ass half days are killing me. They want the kids to come in from twelve to four this week so they could have their meetings in the morning." Imani exhaled in a sigh of annoyance.

"Alright, let me bathe the kids then and get to the supermarket. Myra wants to cook a big dinner tonight."

"Awhh, the happy family going to have dinner together." Imani teased.

"Fuck you, Imani." I replied.

"You know how I like it, Reese. If it isn't stiff, it's not for me." She replied.

We laughed some before we disconnected.

Myra walked into the kitchen with a bright-eyed Alaire in her arms.

"Say hi, Mommy." Myra said a she carried Alaire over to the cabinets that had her baby cereal.

"I can handle it, Myra." I said as I held out my hands for Alaire.

"Why don't you go tend to the boys? That's your problem. You don't know how to say thank you and move on. I can handle this. Go on. The boys are getting tired of those cartoons anyway." She replied as she reached for the baby's bowl and spoon. I passed her the container of milk and exited the kitchen.

Christian ran freely down the aisles while Myra pushed the shopping cart with Damien sitting in front of her sucking on his fingers. I carried Alaire in her Snugli carrier as we walked behind Myra. It felt somewhat weird being with my ex-girlfriend and my kids going grocery shopping but time has a strange way of bringing people together.

While walking down the cereal aisle, a tall, sweet smelling brother with the most handsome green eyes strolled beside me and I couldn't help but stare. His broad chest filled his beige dress shirt perfectly and his brown slacks left me wanting to discover what was hiding inside. I never thought that I would be fawning over a yellow brother but I had to admit he was gorgeous. I was tempted to reach out and grab his ass as he passed but I maintained my composure however I continued to gawk.

Christian was trying to decide which cereal he liked better, Apple Jacks or Froot Loops as Alaire began to whimper. I tried to place her pacifier into her mouth but it fumbled out of my hands, to the floor, in front of the feet of Mr. Sexy-Sexy. I called to Christian to pick up the pacifier as Mr. Sexy-Sexy bent over, giving me the opportunity to check out his ass, and picked it up. With a box of Golden Grahams in one hand and the pacifier in the other, he walked towards me as he licked his succulent lips. *Lawd,* this man was too damn sexy.

'*With my luck, he is gay or married.*' I thought.

"Excuse me; I believe this belongs to you." He said with a hint of spearmint on his breath.

"Thank you. That was really nice of you." I said, passing one of my most sexy smiles.

"It was nothing. Actually, I was trying to find a way to speak to you. I guess I kinda willed the pacifier to fall." He said and then unleashed the his own sexy smile.

"Come on now. You mean to tell me as hard as I was checking you out, you was scared to approach me." I playfully sucked my teeth.

"Oh, don't get it twisted. I wasn't scared, maybe a little apprehensive." He replied.

"Oh, really. *Apprehensive*?" I questioned.

"Yeah. You see I have this feeling I've seen you before. By the way you were staring at me..."

"I wasn't staring." I interrupted.

"Okay. By the way you were *looking* at me I thought we had some kind of beef." He concluded.

"No, I don't think we have ever met. Maybe, you've seen me in an ad or something. I used to get that a lot when I was modeling."

I figured that would be the only way he could have seen me before.

"Unless you posed for KING magazine, I don't think so." He replied.

"That has been a fantasy of mine for some time now." I said jokingly.

"I can help you get there." His response tempted me in more ways then one.

When I finally built up the nerve to ask for his name, his pager began to vibrate.

"Excuse me, I have to go. Umm, here's my card. If you are ever looking into going back into modeling, give me a call." He said as he passed an ivory business card.

"Thanks. I will." I said without once looking down to the card.

He began to walk away but paused and said, "I'm sorry. I didn't get your name."

"Charisse." I replied. "Charisse Nettles."

"Alright, Ms. Nettles. I'll be looking forward to your call." He added before walking out of the aisle.

When I turned around to see what Christian had finally selected, a very angry Myra stood with a hand on her hip and despise in her eyes.

Back at the apartment, Myra had somewhat cooled down but made it her business not to utter a peep. We both knew that in order to keep the peace, we needed to keep our distance. Therefore, while she cooked dinner, I played with the boys on the living room floor.

"Charisse, your cell phone is going off." She said.

Myra tossed the cell phone my way. *Imani Home* flashed across the screen.

"What's up, Chica?" I answered.

"Nothing, Baby. How was your day?" Imani asked.

"Well, let's say I can't complain." I replied half-heartedly.

"Can't talk right now, huh?" She responded.

"Hold on." I said as I walked into another room. "Myra is acting out."

"Oh lawd, what the hell happened now?" Imani asked.

"I was checking out this fine-ass brother in the supermarket and she got this big ass attitude. Stomping around the supermarket with her lip poked out. Girl, I almost laughed in her face." I sat on the window ledge and let out an exasperated sigh.

"It's an emotion. She'll get over it. I want to hear about the guy at the supermarket." Imani's curiosity always took the better part of her.

"Well, I never thought that I would have been interested in a light skinned man, hell I never thought I'd be interested in another man, but he definitely did something for me. He wasn't as light as you but not too much darker. You know what I mean, like a toffee complexion. Something like Terrence Howard's fine ass. Oh Sis, he had the sexiest eyes." I said as I replayed the image of Mr. Sexy repeatedly in my mind.

"What kind of eyes? Was it the color or the shape that make it sexy?" Imani continued to question.

"Both. He had small, yet not beady eyes. When he looked at you, it was if he could read your thoughts. They were kind of like green, gray, or something in between."

"And his name was?" Imani asked.

"Girl, I don't even know. I was so busy running all kind of kinky scenarios through my head I didn't remember to ask. However, he did give me a card. Hold on; let me get it out of my bag." I said before reaching for my pocketbook "Where the hell did I put that card?"

"Oh, don't tell me you lost your only contact to Mr. Sexy because I am going to fall out." Imani joked.

"No, I got it somewhere. I could have sworn I put it right here." I said as I looked through the smaller section of my tan Coach Hobo bag.

"What the fu..?" I caught myself before I let one slip in front of Damien who was staring in my face.

"Listen, Reese. Take your time. You know how junky your bags are. I'm going to call you later on tonight. You know I have to start dinner before Q gets home or else he'll complain all night." Imani said.

"Alright. If I find the number before then, you know I'm going to call you." I responded.

"Later, Sis." Imani replied before hanging up.

Myra walked through the living room, headed straight to the bedroom, and slammed the door. Alaire jumped from the thunderous sound and began to cry. Now my nerves were jumping and if Myra didn't check her attitude soon there was going to be some smoke in the fucking city.

Christian and Damien sat beside me as I tried to put Alaire back to sleep. Damien kept planting drool filled kisses on her forehead as Christian tried to take her pacifier out her mouth. Something he must have saw his father do. No one hated pacifiers more than Rodney. The boys weren't allowed to have one. The thought actually caused a small smile to cross my face. With that I decided it was finally time to give him a call. The kids shouldn't have to suffer because of our misery. I will be the bigger person.

The phone rang once then switched to voicemail. My normal response would have been to leave a hate message but I am not going down that road again. Again, I will be the bigger person.

"Rodney, this is Reese. When you get a minute, give us a call. We miss you."

CHAPTER 7

IMANI

Naadira played with the celery stalks as I cut tomatoes, cucumbers, and lettuce for our dinner salad. Quinton came in about fifteen minutes early. Kai-Aja and Jahlek were running behind Bryan and would be home before seven. In between cooking and entertaining Naadira, I checked emails, edited some of my story, and started laundry. Normally I wouldn't complain but today it seemed as if I were more tired than usual. My body and mind yearned for a break in the worst way. Charisse and I talked about taking a short trip, a little girlfriend get-a-way but I didn't think that idea would fly with Quinton. Seeing that Rodney was no longer in the picture, I knew it was harder than ever for Charisse to get help with her babies. Therefore, I never brought it up to anyone.

Naadira began to snack on her makeshift drumsticks as Quinton grabbed a bag of baby carrots and snacked on them while he relaxed in the living room. Dinner was done but we were still waiting for the other three to come home.

"Mommy, I'm really hungry. My stomach is growling." Naadira said with bits of celery falling through the gaps of missing teeth.

As I began to respond, the front door opened and the rest of our troop walked in still in their school uniforms. Kai-Aja walked towards the kitchen with a shopping bag in each hand while Jahlek and Bryan shot straight to their room.

"You two hurry up and get ready for dinner. Your father and sister are starving." I hollered up the stairs at the fleeting duo.

"Ma, look at this shirt Sierra picked out for me." Kai said as she held up the shirt against her chest.

It was a lilac sleeveless cotton button-down shirt-dress with a small K on the top left decorated with iridescent rhinestones. It was a form fitting dress which would show off the curves of her blossoming body. Something she was going to have a hard time wearing without her father commenting. Kai-Aja brought the shirt closer to show the numbers 15, which was Bryan's numbers, stitched on the collar.

"We had this lady that has a stitching shop put this on. That's what took us so long. We had to wait like forever for her to finish." Kai explained as she pushed the shirt in my face to inspect the stitching.

"This is really cute. How much did it cost? I only gave you twenty dollars this morning." I asked while I went through her other bag, which was from Bath and Body.

"Sierra gave me the money for the stitching. The shirt was on sale for twelve-fifty at Old Navy. Then I used the gift card Aunt Reese gave me for my birthday for the perfumes and lotions and stuff. You know the card had two hundred dollars on it. I only used seventy-five." Kai rambled on and on as Naadira tried to spray the Cucumber Melon mist on her tiny wrists.

"Who's Sierra?" Naadira asked.

"Bryan's girlfriend. She is mad nice." Kai-Aja replied.

"Oh really. Why didn't she come back to the house with you? I told Bryan I wanted to meet her." I looked towards Bryan and Jahlek who were coming down the stairs.

I started to ask why they had taken flight without greeting me but after a couple of seconds, it became clear.

"Who in the hell told you to get your ear pierced?" I yelled as I snatched Jahlek by his ear, examining the cubic zirconia under the kitchen ceiling light.

Quinton made it from the living room to the kitchen within two seconds.

"Bryan, Jahlek, come here now!" Quinton said as he stood in the doorframe of the kitchen.

The boys followed Quinton as he went back into the living room. Kai took that as her cue to get ready for dinner and Naadira followed Kai to their room. I walked to the living room and watched as Quinton chastised the boys.

"You must have lost your minds!" Quinton hollered after slapping both Bryan and Jahlek in the back of their heads.

"It's only one ear." Bryan argued.

"I don't give a damn! Since when are you old enough to make these kind of decisions without talking to me or your father." I interjected.

"Dad, it's really not that bad. We can take it out if you want." Jahlek tried not to let the situation escalate as he nervously tried to remove the earring.

"That's not the point, Jah. You and Bryan have no right to do what you want to do and try to make me and your mom accept it." Quinton explained in a calmer tone.

"But would you have let us get it if we would have asked?" Bryan questioned.

"You know we would have at least given it a thought. Maybe we would have taken you and bought real earrings instead of these bullshit studs you got. But you took it upon your self to not only pierce your ear but your little brother's too." Quinton yelled as he became frustrated with Bryan's constant disrespect.

"Mom, I'm sorry. I'll take it out." Jahlek cried as he began to tug at the gold stud.

"Leave it, Jah." Quinton said as he stared at Bryan who had yet to utter an apology. "You two get ready for dinner while I talk to your mom."

"Bryan." I called as they started to the kitchen. "Even though you were grounded, we let you go out with your girlfriend and hang out with your team and then you go and blow it. So, how am I supposed to respond this time? Do you get some kind of thrill by being defiant?" I asked as his eyes began to well with tears.

He waited for a few seconds before responding. "I'm not trying to be disrespectful."

"Well you're not doing a good job at following rules. Then you bring Jah into it. How fair is that?" I asked before walking towards Quinton who was sitting on the couch.

"I'm sorry." He mumbled before joining Jahlek in the kitchen.

Quinton sat for a few moments longer trying to massage the tension out of his neck. Words formed in my mind of all the things to make him relax and let it go but the delivery was impossible. From the kitchen, I could hear the faint whispers between Kai-Aja and Bryan.

"What are we going to do about that boy, Imani? He is so damn hardheaded. He's going to wind up getting himself into a lot of trouble if he doesn't change his attitude quick." Quinton said as he looked towards the kitchen door.

"Q, we have to give him some room to make mistakes. We can't continue acting as if he is perfect. They're kids and they are bound to do things we don't like but we can't jump down their throats every time. Your temper and harsh tones are only going to push them away. One day at a time, baby." Quinton looked up at me as if I were a traitor.

"Bryan was wrong. I am not arguing that but the approach we have taken to reach him hasn't worked so far. Think about it. When we were teenagers no one could tell us anything. We knew everything." I offered hoping my innocent words and relaxed tone would somehow help him move pass this; If only for the night.

"Were we really that defiant?" Quinton asked with a slight smirk on his face.

"Now that was a dumb question." I responded. "I ran away from home to be with a thug."

"You were kicked out. Plus, I wasn't a thug, I was a young entrepreneur." Quinton replied.

Quinton grabbed my waist and pulled himself from the couch. I laughed at his silliness and began walking towards the kitchen. Quinton and I took turns stealing kisses until we entered the kitchen. That was what made all the arguments and disagreements disappear. Stolen moments when actions spoke louder than words and love echoed through the air.

"Mommy, I am starving. Can we please eat?" Naadira begged as we entered the kitchen.

"Naadira, you are such a drama queen." Quinton said as he ran his hand over her loose curls.

"Bryan, can you please bring the salad to the table? Kai, why didn't you get the glasses when you set the table? Jah, take the Kool-Aid out of the fridge." I began running off orders while serving the lasagna.

Quinton was helping Naadira with some of her reading homework while Kai and I went over her math homework when the doorbell rang. Quinton and I looked at each other with surprise as the bell rang again. We didn't associate with many people in the area and since we left our families in New York it was odd that someone would visit us unannounced. As I approached the door, I peeked at the time. The wall clock read nine twenty-three and I knew that was much too late for any postal carriers so I was curious to find out what someone found so important that they couldn't call or wait until morning. When I looked out the peek hole I had to take a double take to make sure I was seeing right.

"Diamond, what are you doing here so late?" I asked.

Before Diamond could respond, she broke down in tears. Quinton came to the foyer with Kai and Naadira following right behind.

"What happened, Diamond? Talk to me. Did you and your mother have another fight? Come on, stop crying, and talk to me?" I pulled Diamond into my arms as I tried to find out what brought her to our home.

Quinton took the overnight bag she was carrying and took the girls back into the living room.

"My mother has gone too far, Auntie. Your sister has a serious drinking problem and needs help. First, she slaps me in front of the house. Mind you, Ryan lives right across the street so he probably saw it. Then she calls my father out of all people and starts calling me all kinds of hos and bitches. Excuse me, Auntie. She told my dad I'm sleeping around with all the boys on my block. When I tried to defend myself, she said I was calling her a liar and since I am so f—ing grown get out her house. Then she started swinging again."

"Calm down, Diamond. Do you want me to call her?" I asked as I continued to stroke her back.

Diamond knew if I got involved, it would get ugly. Jada and I never agreed on how she treated Diamond. Mainly because Jada did not like being wrong and she always was.

"I don't even care. She makes me sick. I'm tired of taking care of her for her only to turn around and abuse me. I'm nineteen now. Way too old for her to keep hitting me and thinking its okay." Diamond declared as she looked into my face.

"You know I am nosey, right? I talk to you like a little sister. Are you having sex with this Ryan boy? Not saying that this gives your mother the right to embarrass and insult you."

Before I called Jada, I needed to figure out what kind of thoughts were flying through her mind.

"Auntie, I have been dating Ryan for about a year now. You met him. Remember, he was with me at Amber's birthday party. That's my boo." Diamond never really answered my question so I asked again.

"D, are you having sex?" I asked in a firmer tone.

She looked at me for a while and then looked away.

"It's nothing to be ashamed of. As long as you don't plan to make babies, sex is not a terrible thing. Be safe." I exhaled an exasperated breath before I continued.

"When did your mother find out?"

"Yesterday, after she read my journal." She replied.

"Listen, you know the deal. You can stay here until stuff cools down but eventually you have to go home and work things out. I will call Jada later after the kids go to bed and hear what she has to say. In the meantime go fix yourself up."

Diamond and I shared a long, tight hug before entering the living room.

"Hey, D. What's going on?" Bryan said as he greeted Diamond.

"Nothing, trying to get some peace and quiet for the night." She replied.

"And you came *here*?" He snickered and returned to the basement with a bottle of water and a bowl of pretzels.

Quinton looked as if he wanted to respond but then returned to helping Naadira sound out her short vowel words. Kai-Aja finished her homework and decided to follow Diamond upstairs. Diamond was Kai's best friend and whenever they got together there was a lot of cackling to follow. It was time for everyone to get ready for bed anyway. Quinton called the boys upstairs and told everyone to be showered and in bed before ten. Before I was able to put the last lock on the door, Diamond came dashing down the steps and heading to the front door.

"I left my cell in my car." She shouted as she ran towards her tan Acura that was parked behind our cars in the driveway.

After Diamond came inside, I continued to lock the door and turned off the lights.

ಬಬಬಐಐಐ

<u>RODNEY</u>

Christian and Damien were playing with their remote control cars as I sat on the couch watching television. Reese had called the day before and told me where she had moved. She asked if I wanted to spend sometime with the boys while she went to the hairdresser in other words she needed a babysitter and didn't know whom to call. It was all good though.

Patrice brought in some sandwiches and Capri juice pouches for the boys. Christian pushed the food to the side but Damien was too greedy to refuse. She had been trying to get on Christian's good side all morning but he wasn't trying to acknowledge her. If she wasn't family or Mommy, she didn't exist. I tried to tell her to be patient but she was determined to get him to speak to her.

Charisse called and said that she would pick up the boys by four so that gave me a little over two hours to take them over to my mother's house. She had been complaining about not being able to spend time with her babies. I let Charisse know that we would meet at my mother's place and Patrice nearly hit the ceiling.

"You know your mother don't like me. How are you going to leave me here like that?" She whined as I packed the boys toys away.

"Listen, you already know the deal. Don't start this bullshit crying. You played the understudy for some time now don't start trying to be the star. Reese is not someone new. My mother *not* liking you is not *new*. So, what's your problem?" I hollered.

"My problem, *Rodney*, is that you are not doing anything to make

83

the situation better. Instead of addressing your family and your baby mama, you continue to ignore the fact that there is a problem." Patrice responded with attitude.

"You want me to address Charisse and my mother telling them what? Honestly, I don't feel there is a problem." I paused and stepped closer to Patrice.

With a gentle hand, I traced the side of her face

"Oh I see. You want me to acknowledge you as my woman, let Charisse know I have moved on and that you expect some newfound respect or authority now. Newsflash, 'Not Going to Happen'."

"I don't understand why you always have to be an asshole." She hollered before storming away.

"Oh, I'm a big asshole. Wait and see how much of an asshole I can be. As a matter of fact..." I followed behind Patrice into the bathroom.

She tried to close the door in my face but I stopped it with my foot.

"As a matter of fact, why don't you pack up all the little things you've been leaving around my house and forget you ever met me?"

We stared at each other for a few quiet seconds before she began to put on her desperate whine and cry routine.

"Rodney, it's not that serious. All I was trying to say was..." Patrice tried to explain her way out of this one but I had interrupted her routine apology.

"I heard enough and really don't care what you were trying to say. Get your shit and go." Then without looking back, I walked into the living room and began to help the boys put on their jackets.

Charisse had turned my heart cold and the worst part was she was the only one with the cure. I could not imagine myself in love with anyone else but Charisse.

Kareemah and Keisha were looking at music videos when I arrived with Christian and Damien. My mother and her girlfriends were playing their regular game of POKENO. The house was full with people and food. That's the way my mother liked it. Christian ran over to his grandmother and jumped onto her lap. He loved to collect her money whenever she won. He knew he would get a portion of the winnings at the end of the night. Damien went to sit between Kareemah and Keisha and left me standing alone in the hall. I checked the time and then joined the crowd.

I sat at one of the other tables where the older men were indulging in a game of Spades. They didn't play the way we played with all the new rules and wild cards. They played the old-fashioned straight, raw Spades. I wanted to join in but they were much too serious about their game and my partner wasn't there. Charisse was the best damn partner I had in years and if we couldn't do shit else right, we played Spades and made beautiful children. Suddenly, I realized that Reese and I do have some memories worth cherishing. The more I thought about it, the urge to see her became stronger.

People were moving about making plates or changing tables, trying their luck in a little bit of Poker or even some Pity Pat. Quinton's mother and stepfather came through the door with bags full of beers and sodas. The house was too crowded for me so I decided to step off for a minute. I stood outside the building enjoying the breeze and my cigarette when Sandra came strolling up to me.

"What's up, Rodney?" She slurred. The stench of liquor permeated the air.

"Ain't shit. What's up?" I replied.

"I've been trying to catch up with your boy. I think he's trying to duck me. Have you spoken to Quinton about the money?" She asked.

Sandra stood so close to me I could feel her hot breath on my neck. It was bad enough she looked a mess and I had to be seen talking to her but now she was making it seem like we were intimate. She wore a pair of super tight black jeans with a too small matching jean jacket; an outfit that clearly belong to her sixteen-year-old daughter. Her weaved ponytail needed a serious touch-up and her nails were long over due for a filling but she thought she was sexy. I remember when there was a time when Sandra was one of the baddest women on this block. She was never undone – she was a lady, complete with sex appeal and street knowledge. Sandra knew how to play the game. Using what she had to get everything she wanted and never needed a thing. However, the pressures of drugs and alcohol had taken over. Sandra's two daughters suffer due to negligence. Her oldest daughter, Sharay takes responsibility of her younger one, Jasmine until Sandra is sober enough to handle being a mother.

"Nah, I told you I'm not getting in the middle of that. Whatever you got to do with Quinton and Bryan is none of my business!" I said adamantly.

I wanted to assure Sandra that this would be the last time I had to repeat myself.

"Look, I helped your punk-ass out when Bryan's business was hurting your pockets now I think it's time you returned the favor. I don't want anything to do with Quinton or Bryan. All I want is the money Bryan's father left for his ass. Shit, he doesn't need it. Now, tell Q to have Bryan sign the motherfucking bank papers or I am going to have to tell Q what really went down the night of the fire."

She pressed her finger into my chest before backing away.

Her threat didn't faze me. I sat back for a few seconds letting the urge to slap her subside before I continued.

"As far as I am concerned, we both benefited from that accident. If I am correct, weren't you the one upset about Trina taking your man? If anything, I helped your trifling ass. You got what you wanted now disappear. Leave Quinton and his family alone or it'll be like de-ja-vous on this block. Six years later another house mysteriously burns down." I whispered as passer-bys looked in our direction.

"Rodney, I am going to get that motherfucking money or else your ass is going down." She said as she began to walk away.

"Don't mess with me, Sandra. This is a game you're not ready to play." I hollered.

"Try me, Bitch!" She returned.

It never dawned on me how much the truth would affect Quinton until that night we went to the bar. He laid out all the problems he was having with Bryan and how he felt guilty for Trina's death. Up until that night, I had honestly thought I had done everyone a favor but I was beginning to see that I only caused more problems.

Charisse pulled up in front of the building with Alaire in her child seat crying at the top of her lungs. As soon as the car stopped, she jumped out and opened the back door to get the baby. I began to walk to the car as she took Alaire from her car seat.

"What happened to her, Reese? Why is screaming like that?" I asked as I reached for my angel.

"She started screaming at the top of her lungs about a half-block ago. She was sleeping up until then." Reese was obviously shaken by Alaire's sudden fit.

"Maybe, Daddy's girl had a bad dream." I said as I kissed Alaire's tiny, red nose. "Come upstairs and calm down. My mother is having one of her card parties. It's a little crowded but it's cool."

Reese stood looking puzzled. I admired the way she maintained herself. She always displayed femininity. Her freshly pressed hair hung long and the fresh smell of flowers filled my nostrils as she walked by. Reese wore low-rise jeans that seemed to sit right on her hips revealing a tight midriff and a small tattoo below her navel. No stretch marks or scars, only smooth, silk chocolate skin. Unconsciously, I placed my free hand in the small of her back, leading her toward the building. She first looked at me quizzically but never said a word.

As we ascended the stairs to the apartment, I tried to make small talk.

"So, what's new?" I asked.

"Nothing really. Same old stuff. My agent is looking for some gigs for me but I think he's more interested in the kids, particularly Christian. My agent says he has a lot of personality."

She held the door open as I passed with Alaire.

"I know how you feel about putting the kids in the industry but it doesn't sound like a bad idea. Christian is talented. Look how smart he is, Reese." I said.

"I hear you Rodney but I don't think now is a good time. By the way, next week the kids are going to have to stay with you. I have to fly out to Los Angeles for a photo shoot for some urban clothes designer out there. He's starting a new women's line and heard about me through a friend."

Charisse took Alaire from my arms long enough for me to take off my jacket and then went on to greet everyone. She never waited for my reply.   Charisse knew I was not comfortable with her traveling and leaving the kids for more than a day or two at a time. Neither was she.

I followed Reese into the living room and pulled her aside to a quiet area.

"Reese, you think it's a good idea to start taking assignments so soon after . . . you know. I mean, the kids need you here more so now that we are not living together. You know what I mean, right?" I asked.

Damien came between Reese and me and asked for some water. Reese and I looked at each other before anyone moved. Finally, Keisha came and took Damien into the kitchen as if she knew what was going on.

"Rodney, I can't put my career on hold to please you. I did that already and now I think it's time to please me. The kids are going to be fine. If you can't handle the kids, I'll ask your mother or Imani to take them for me. In fact, forget I asked. My mom and dad are supposed to be coming down; I will leave the kids with them."

Reese began to walk away until I pulled her back.

Quinton's stepfather came over to where we were standing and decided to intervene.

"Rodney, listen. This is not the place for y'all to be talking personal business. Why don't you take it to another room?"

My mother looked over at me with an evil look on her face. A look not to be reckoned with.

"Reese, can we talk in my mother's room?"

Without a response, I began to escort her towards my mother's bedroom. Kareemah took Alaire from Charisse arms as she left the bedroom. Once we were behind closed doors, I struggled to keep my composure. Misplace emotions turned to rage and then passion as I pulled her into my arms. She tried to pull away but I continued to hold her tighter.

"Rodney, please let's not do this to ourselves. It's not right, not now." She begged as she pulled away.

"Reese, I want you. We can work out a babysitting situation later but I need you, right now." I ran my hands through her thick mane as she stood before me.

"No, I can't do this. Are you going to keep the kids or not? That is all I need to know. I really got to go." She started for the door.

"Don't walk out that door, Baby. Stay with me. Only for a few. Let's talk."

Finally, I had been reduced to begging.

Charisse looked at me and the look in her eyes said I was in but treading on thin ice. She stepped away from the door and sat on the edge of the bed.

"Talk to me, Rodney. I've been waiting a long time for this." She said.

"Too long." I replied.

I started the conversation with apologies and explanations for my actions. Charisse didn't look interested. She gathered her hair around her finger, pulled it over her shoulder and stared off into space.

"Is there anything you have to say? Anything you want to ask me?" I asked as she sat silent.

"No, I thought I would let you have the floor. You talk, I listen. Maybe you can hear some of the things I've had to deal with. Think, Rodney! If the tables were turned, how long you would have put up with me?" She replied.

"Why do you always have to make things so difficult? I'm trying to work things out." I said as I stood before her.

"Why do you always try to make things seem so simple? I've been trying to work things out for years." She responded while standing from her seat and meeting me eye to eye.

"So, what's stopping us from trying again?" I placed a hand on the small of her back and pulled her close.

"You tell me." She replied. "What's holding you back?"

Her warm hands caressed my face and I felt my insides tingling. My body and heart agreed that Reese was the missing link to my happiness but my mind had its own agenda. Our conversation was thrown to the wind as desire took over our mind and bodies. Charisse leaned in for a kiss then pushed me against the wall and began to place kisses on my ears and neck. I palmed her backside and held her close, wanting her to feel the erection building. I ran my tongue down the side of her neck until I reached that spot above her collarbone that made her weak. Her body reacted with a spasm as I continued to taste her sweet skin. Reese had her hand in my pants, rubbing my throbbing penis as she bit my neck, leaving marks of passion.

Charisse kept her eyes closed as my hands ran over her breasts then down to her waist. I placed one hand on her back to keep her close as I used the other to unbuckle her jeans. I reached inside, pushing aside the lace material of her underwear, which covered a hot and hairless vagina. Charisse moaned as my fingers parted her lips and played with her pierced clit. She wrapped one leg around mine and pulled me in for a passionate kiss, one that said, "I need you, now."

"Can I have you? Can I taste you?" She asked as she lowered her leg and began to unbuckle my belt.

"Can you handle it?" I asked.

Her sly smirk said enough. Reese pushed my pants down to my ankles and began to handle it. When her mouth encased me, I let my head lay against the wall while fighting the urge to hold her head. She knew what I liked as she massaged my balls occasionally licking and sucking them.

Reese stopped then said, "I like it when you hold my head."

I looked at her and she winked her eye then went back into it.

'How can I let this go?' I wondered.

Reese jerked and sucked until my juices filled her mouth. After she swallowed she said, "You still taste like candy."

She kissed me and turned to leave the room. I grabbed her by the arm and said, "It's not over, Reese."

Before she could respond, I carried her to my mother's bed, took of her sneakers and jeans, and admired her lying there in her t-shirt and thongs. I instructed her to turn around. Above her left cheek she had a tattoo that read, *Rodney*.

"When did you have that done?" I asked as I traced the lettering.

"A while ago. Shows how much you pay attention." Charisse said before attempting to back off the bed.

I pushed down on her back as she kneeled on the edge of the bed, kissed the tattoo, and then apologized. "I'm sorry, Reese. I promise to start paying more attention." Then I kissed her other cheek.

"Well then you can start right now." Reese stated as she opened her legs and invited me in.

I tore the lace material off her body and immediately began handling business.

Reese cried, "Harder. Harder, baby."

"I got this, Ma." I replied as I placed one knee on the bed, held onto her waist and delivered.

Reese played with her pierced clit and continued to give instructions. We moved from the bed, to the floor and then to my mother's rocking chair. Reese rode until neither of us could take anymore. Her back arched as my body tensed, together we climaxed.

CHAPTER 8

CHARISSE

It was our sixth game of Spades and still I could not get my mind off our conversation. After Rodney and I satisfied each other, we tried to talk out our problems. Rodney had a way of always sugar coating his shit. Even while he apologized for all the bullshit he put me through, he had a reason why it was acceptable or appropriate. He even had an excuse for not having any time for his kids. The more he talked, the more I realized that I wasn't in love with Rodney anymore and probably would never be again. I loved him and that was forever but our connection was long gone. That phase has finally come to pass. Our time together was a fantasy built on the love I had for being in love; the love that family shares and a husband shares with his wife. Now, it's time to be in love with me for me. My kids were all I needed to keep me balanced and focused.

Alaire's piercing cry cut through the crowd and pulled me from my thoughts. Rodney sat across from me staring in his hand as if her wailing did not faze him. Obviously he too was immersed in his own thoughts. Without notice, I laid my cards on the table and headed for my baby. It was evident that we had stayed too long. Damien was tucked in the single seat fast asleep sucking his thumb while Christian slept on his grandmother's chest.

"Rodney, I think it's time for us to go. The kids need to get home." I said as I paced back and forth rocking Alaire.

"Okay." He replied and continued to sit back in his seat, staring at me.

I exhaled an exasperated breath before I began to gather the kids' belongings. Keisha offered an extra hand by helping with the boys' jackets. After I collected my jacket and clutch, I returned to rocking Alaire. I searched her diaper bag for a prepared bottle but they were all empty and she was balling by this point. As we started for the door, I looked around to make sure I could not be seen then used my freehand to undo my jacket, lift my shirt, and breast-feed her. Kareemah came from behind with one of Alaire's receiving blankets and draped it over my shoulder while Rodney's rotten ass sat there.

This time Rodney's selfishness didn't cause me to get upset like all the other times but instead only reminded me of the asshole that wasted my time.

"Nothing changes, Imani. Well, I know nothing changes with Rodney's ass anyway." I said to Imani as I prepared a pitcher of formula for Alaire.

"Something ain't right with him. He got me feeling some kind of way right now. Let's change the subject before I say something I can't take back." Imani responded.

"Sis, don't worry about hurting me. Rodney took care of that. I don't think anyone can top him." I laughed cynically.

"Reese, did you ever call that guy from the Supermarket? The one that said he could help you out with the modeling." Imani said changing the subject.

"Nah, I found the card though. I put it in my organizer and forgot all about it." I replied with little interest. "However, I did get a modeling job for next weekend. Who knows? He could have arranged it. I have no idea who these people are but I can definitely use the money."

"Reese, I know as old as you are that you don't actually think he gave you that card solely for business."

"Yeah, yeah, yeah. I'm not in the mood to interview men yet. Better yet, I don't have the time or patience for getting to know someone new. I know eventually I will want a companion but I don't think I'm ready. I feel like I need to be by myself for a while." I explained.

"Sis, what's the harm in one little dinner date? You deserve to be spoiled a little. Speaking of spoiled, how do you feel about taking that sisters' getaway?" Imani asked.

"I wish I could but who's gonna watch my babies. Rodney already showed his ass for one lifetime. It's funny because Taniqua asked me that yesterday. I told her that you and I had talked of planning a trip but I got some issues to deal with."

"You didn't tell her you left Rodney! Why?" Imani questioned with surprise.

"She never liked him. So, she really wouldn't care." I replied.

"But you know that your family always got your back. They would be down here in a heartbeat to help you with the kids. Come on, Reese." Imani sighed.

"Well my parents know that I moved back to Harlem. I thought it would be better to wait a while before telling them that Rodney and I didn't make the move together."

"In case you and Rodney worked it out, huh?" Imani implied.

She was right so I stood quiet while the thought of telling my family that Rodney was gone rolled through my mind. To my parents, I always succeeded at whatever I put my mind to. Finally, I had set my goals too high. The ideal relationship I had once imagined was destroyed and with no way to repair it. The thought of telling my father that I was a single mother and hearing his disappointment broke my heart. My parents weren't happy with the fact that I had three kids out of wedlock. Mainly since both of my *younger* sisters were married. However, Rodney promised my father that the commitment was there and that we would be married. That was five years—and two—kids ago.

"Reese, are you alright? You know I don't want to hurt your feelings, not at a time like this but don't fool yourself and play blind to Rodney's games. He's not worth the stress." Imani paused. "I know I should be the last one to talk when I waited years for Quinton but I rather not see you go through all the same pain I did. Even though Quinton and I are doing well now, I still have the memories. I forgave him but it's hard to forget."

"I hear you, Imani. Still, I have three kids with Rodney. Even if I decide never to see him again, his face will still haunt me. Rodney and I need time apart to grow and heal. If I find that through my healing I can never forgive, then time will mend the wounds. I can't force him out, not when I want him to stay. All I want him to do is understand where I am coming from and find some kind of compromise within him you know, so he can be the family man I need while still feeding his thirst for the streets."

"Do you hear what you are saying? In the end, you will be making the ultimate sacrifice. No matter what you may think about him spending more time at home, the street will ultimately be your demise. If his temptation is not the flocks of women, then his need for more money will eventually kill him. You need to think if this is what you really want to subject your kids to because obviously Rodney doesn't give a flying fuck."

The more Imani talked the more she made sense. The picture became clearer while the hole in my heart tore wider. Rodney and I will never be. Not at the sake of losing my kids or our sanity.

"This shit is making my head hurt. I almost wish I never met his ass. My kids could have had a better father."

I felt myself breaking down and I couldn't allow anyone including Imani see nor hear me fall apart.

"Look, Imani. I need to get some sleep. Get rid of this headache and foul attitude. I am going to snuggle up with Alaire and watch a good movie." I said while cleaning the last of the dishes.

"Alright, but if you need to talk you know you can call me. No matter how late it may be, I'm here for you." Imani replied.

"Okay, goodnight." I said before hanging up.

After putting the phone on its cradle, I fixed Alaire's bottle then checked in on the boys. The bunk bed set Myra bought fit perfectly in my old wardrobe room. Myra had someone come in and paint the boys' faces on the walls with different cartoon characters around them. The room looked better than I had expected. All my clothes were packed in boxes and sent to storage. I really wanted to sell or donate most of it but Myra took it upon herself to take care of everything. At times, I felt she was overstepping her boundaries but on the other hand, I really appreciated her help.

Tonight was Myra's night out so I kept Alaire in the bed with me. I watched *The Sweetest Thing* while I braided Alaire's hair. Alaire fussed a little but not as much as any other night. While I put the elastics on the end of her braids there was a silent knock at the door. I waited for the person to knock again to make sure I wasn't hearing things. I put Alaire in her playpen as I tiptoed to the front door and looked through the peephole. Although it was five after nine, it was still too late for anyone to stop by. As I looked out the peephole, I thought I was hallucinating. I slowly opened the door to find Rodney standing there with his overnight bag.

"Can I help you?" I asked.

"I was hoping you could." He said before stepping inside.

Rodney laid his bag on the floor and stared at me for a few seconds before moving further inside the house. This was unacceptable. I didn't know what kind of woman he mistook me for but a fool I was not.

"Rodney, what are you doing here?" I asked, annoyed with his presence. Yet, a small part of me wanted him to be there.

"Look, I need you. I thought I made it pretty clear earlier but it doesn't seem like you heard me so I'm here to tell you again. I want you to come back home. And, if you don't want to come back, I'll come to you every night until you see that I'm serious."

"I'm not coming back, Rodney. I can't. It wouldn't be fair to the kids or me. Therefore, you can keep showing up but I won't keep letting you in. As a matter of fact, I think its best you go home."

"You think it's best for who? For you? For Myra? Not for my kids because they need me."

"Then you should have been there!" I hollered.

I inhaled deeply in attempt to regain my composure then continued, "Like I said, I think it's best for you to go home. We don't need you anymore. I told you before me and my kids are going to be alright with or without you. What happened earlier was a mistake. Rodney we are no good together."

Rodney stepped in front of me as I tried to move towards the front door. "And we're are no good apart. I'm not going anywhere until you see we need each other to be complete."

The look in his eyes told the truth. Rodney intended on making me fall for his acts of desperation as acts of love. I knew that if I didn't think quickly it would be the longest night of my life.

"Well, since you are determined to make this harder than necessary..." I said then reached for the telephone. "I'll call over some company and we can make this a party."

"Who are you about to call?" Rodney asked with skepticism in his tone.

"Detective Josef. You remember him don't you? Well, he told me that if I ever needed anything to give him a call. I figure why the hell not. Let's have a reunion." I replied.

"So, you're going to stoop to that level now? You gonna call the police on your man? Come on, Reese."

"Your choice. You leave voluntarily or forcefully. I don't think you would want Christian or Damien to wake up and find the police taking their Daddy in handcuffs. So, what's your answer?"

Without response, Rodney picked up his bag and headed out the front door. I watched as he climbed in his car and sped down the street. No last words, no final glances, no feelings.

Alaire began to whine, preparing to let loose her boisterous cry. After putting on all the locks and chain, I returned to my room. My mind was far from the movie or finishing Alaire's hair. I battled the urge to pick up my cell and call Imani. I discovered it was time for me to figure out this situation alone. I took Alaire out of her playpen and finished her hair then went to the kitchen to fix a cup of tea to help me calm down. Alaire sat in her swing while I made my way around the kitchen. When I returned to the living room, I settled into the comfort of the plush sofa only for the phone to ring and take away my serenity. My first instinct was to turn off the ringer and let the voicemail pick it up. Instead, I rushed to the kitchen to grab the cordless as it went into its fourth ring.

"Yes." I answered without checking the caller ID.

"Did I catch you at a bad time?" Imani asked.

"Nope, I was thinking about calling you." I replied.

"What's up? Everything okay?" She questioned with concern.

"Yeah, I wanted to talk. It's kind of lonely." I lied.

"Are you still coming up this weekend?"

"Me and my troop will be there Friday before eight. So, what's up?

What do I owe the honor of this call?" I playfully questioned.

"Oh, I forgot to tell you earlier that I received an invitation to an album release party and wanted to know if you would join me?"

"Who invited lame ass Imani to an album release party?"

"Kiss my ass, Reese. Rahsaun is some kind of promoter/manager/agent kind of thing out there in New York and he has been sending me invites for sometime now but I never took him up on the others."

"And why this one?"

"I figured it would do you some good to mingle, maybe you will meet someone that might take your mind away from your situation. Plus, I heard there are all kinds of people at these affairs maybe I could meet someone that could help me out with getting my book in the right hands." She replied.

"When and where is this event? Hold on. Q doesn't have a problem with you hanging out?"

"He's my husband not my father. Quinton understands that in order for me to be recognized as an author I need to network. Anyway, it's in December around Christmas at someplace called Tangerines in The Village. Rahsaun said the place is very nice. I think it's Thai. You like Thai food, right?"

"Girl, you know I love Thai food. Shit, I craved for Thai with all my pregnancies. Damn, I have to find somebody to watch the kids."

"Quinton said he'd watch them. I already asked him. He's planning to drive the kids and me up there after they get out of school. Christmas vacation our kids always stay with his mother. So while you and I go out, they'll watch your babies too. Everything is set."

"Well, I guess I'm down then. I haven't been out in so long; I have to find something to wear. Damn, I almost forgot I am supposed to be leaving for L.A next week and haven't found anyone to watch the kids. I guess I'll have to cancel once again."

"Reese, bring the kids to our house. I have no problem taking care of your beautiful babies. Plus, I have big kids. They can help if necessary." Imani offered.

"Maybe it is too soon for me to go back to work. Thanks, Sis. I'll keep that invitation in mind if another opportunity comes up in the near future."

Alaire began to gum her hand and whine. I took a Beechnut cookie from the box and gave it to her. She had been trying to grow teeth for sometime and was growing cranky.

"I hear little momma in the back. Is it time for bed?" Imani asked.

"No, she slept almost all day. She is teething." I replied. "So, Rahsaun is big time now, huh. Damn it's been so long since I heard his name. I didn't know you two still kept in contact. Now that was one sexy brother."

"He was okay, if yellow brothers are your thing now." She joked then continued. "We call each other for the holidays and birthdays but we don't really talk about much. He used to stop by Quinton's mother house for her card games and such but that stopped about a year or two ago. Last time I spoke to him, he and his wife were going through a divorce. He was ecstatic though. However, Q was around and we couldn't really talk because Q was acting immature. Quinton would pick up the other line; call me for little things and so on. He kills me."

Imani and I shared a good laugh then continued talking, mostly reminiscing. I took Alaire out of her walker and into the bedroom to wipe her face and hands. After Imani and I ended our conversation, I was ready for bed. Alaire began to rub her eyes, a sure sign that she was ready for bed also, so I gave her a warm bottle, and we were sleep within seconds.

As I turned over in the bed, the house phone began to ring again. I thought to ignore it and let the caller leave a message. Then I thought if it was important enough for them to call this time of night, I should answer.

"Hello."

"Hey, Sweetheart, how are you holding up?" My father voice filled the line.

"Daddy." I said before bursting into tears.

My father offered words of encouragement and support. He continued to calm me with his soothing tone. My father was always my best friend and confidant.

"Listen, Baby. You know you can always come home. Your mother and I don't mind helping you with those babies, Reese. You don't have to do this alone."

"I know, Daddy. It's …it's ." I searched for the right words.

My father was always able read my mind.

"It's that you don't want to be too far in case Rodney changes his ways."

As he finished my sentence, I cried some more.

"It's all right, sweetheart. If you want when your mother and I come down, we could stay there for a while. We love you. It's breaking my heart thinking that you are alone and hurting." He stated.

"I don't want to feel like this, Daddy. I've been trying so hard not to let him break me or see me cry but I mean my heart can't take much more. I tell myself that I am not in love with him but it hurts so badly." I said through my sobs.

"It's going to be alright, Ressie. Taniqua and Lauren were talking about coming over next week and staying through the holiday. You should come early too. Take some time away from the stress. You know that good ole' girls' night out stuff always works for them."

My dad laughed his usual congested laugh and my tears of pain instantly turned to tears from laughter.

We continued to talk; I was totally relaxed and calm. Then he sent several kisses over the phone and wished me a good night's sleep. That night, for the first time in months, I slept peacefully.

಄಄಄಄಄಄

QUINTON

The kids were moving like snails around the house preparing for school. Meanwhile, I was running late for work. Imani offered to take the kids to school but I knew she had to get herself together and that would make everyone later than we were.   As the kids went to the kitchen to eat breakfast, I began collecting my things.

"Imani, have you seen my wallet?" I hollered as I prepared myself for work.

"No, did you check the dresser?" She replied from the girls' room.

"Never mind. I found it." I responded as I checked the pockets of my sports jacket.

I took a final look at myself in the hall mirror before making my way out the door. I felt like going for a more casual relaxed look today hoping to stay in that same frame of mind, relaxed. My camel colored pants blended perfectly with the neutral colored striped shirt I chose. No tie. Imani did suggest I wear a tan blazer, saying it was the style and made me look modern. It was a classy look. Something I would like to do more often. After polishing my cognac and beige Stacy Adams, I had the perfect ensemble, cool, confident, and relaxed.

Bryan, Jahlek, and Kai-Aja carried individual containers of orange juice and bagels to the jeep while Imani was upstairs getting Naadira ready for her doctor's appointment. Normally, I wouldn't let them eat in my car but we didn't have time to argue. I collected my briefcase, coat and headed out the door. I was running late for an early morning appointment with Bryan's biological grandparents regarding the money his father left him. Personally, I wanted nothing to do with the money or that family but it seemed they were determined to make their presence known. Of course, all this would happen after all the big college recruits began making a fuss over Bryan playing for their school. Bryan felt I had some jealousy or resentment toward them and that was why I tried to keep them apart. He did not understand that I was trying to protect him from those money-sucking leeches that six years ago did not give a damn if he even had a roof over his head.

Silently I prayed that his grandparents and I would be able to come to an agreement. After some time, I wanted him to be able to know his family but I also wanted to make sure their intentions were honest. Sandra called a few days before and mentioned that if I didn't agree to the meeting that Bryan's grandparents would seek legal advice and have Bryan removed from our home. Although I knew that with their background that could not happen, I also knew that dragging Bryan through that unnecessary drama would only make him pull further away from Imani and me.

When I reached the car, Bryan was helping Kai with her uniform tie while Jahlek was sleep.

"Kai, you sure you're going to be warm enough with that skirt on?" I said as I sat in the driver's seat and buckled my seat belt.

"Daddy, I have on these thick tights. Trust, I am very warm. Plus, those school pants make my legs itch." She said as she pulled her seat belt across her chest.

"Alright, it's cold out here." I said in a warning tone. You could have worn a longer coat."

"Dad, I'm fine." She replied curtly.

She wore her copper hair in a bun with curls falling free from the center. I wasn't ready for my little girl to grow up but she was already there. Bryan checked himself in the rear view mirror, brushing his hair and adjusting his shirt collar. Jahlek was passed out in the passenger seat, half his shirt tucked in his pants and face ashy as hell. He was one of those kids that did enough to get by. The other two were into their looks and being apart of the 'In-Crowd'.

"Dad, is Diamond moving in? She don't seem like she wants to go home anytime soon. You know she is making plans for her boyfriend to visit her out here." Bryan said with attitude.

"She needed a couple of days to regroup. I doubt she'll be staying long. Oh, and don't worry about her boyfriend. He isn't staying. He can visit but that's about it. Your mother already told her." I replied.

We pulled up in front of Bryan's school, which was down the road from their school. Sierra was standing outside in front of the school, looking around. Bryan slowly exited the jeep with this silly puppy look on his face.

"Bryan, I want you to invite her over for dinner tonight. We still have that matter to discuss." I said referring to the baby Sierra brought in the car the other day.

So much has gone on over the last couple of days; I totally let it slip my mind.

"Dad, the answer is no. It's not her kid." Bryan answered before slamming the door closed.

Jahlek jumped from his seat and immediately wiped the side of his face.

"What the hell?" I mumbled as I continued to stare at Bryan as he hugged Sierra.

"Dad, Sierra is helping her mom and dad with her nephew. Her older sister ran away and left the baby with their parents." Kai explained trying to get me to calm down.

"And what was the problem with Bryan telling me without slamming the door?"

"He doesn't think you respect him enough or trust his decisions." Jahlek answered while returning to his resting slump. "That's what he say's anyway."

I put the car in drive and continued to the kids' school. Heat began to rise from my collar so I turned down the temperature in the car.

"Daddy, please calm down." Kai begged.

"I am okay, Baby." I replied.

"Then why are the veins bulging out your head?"

"And you're sweating." Jahlek added from the back seat.

"I'm fine. Thanks for the concern." I replied.

Kai-Aja looked at me then twisted her lips to the side and looked out her window.

"And then you and mom say lying is not an option." She said.

I looked at Kai-Aja and thought twice about slapping her for her fresh tone but she was only telling the truth. I was lying. The fact was that I was passed angry but I didn't want them to know.

"Sometimes Kai its better to let things be. Yes, I'm angry with Bryan but your persistence isn't making the situation any better." I said.

Parking was hard to find, so I double-parked in front of the school. Kai and Jahlek took their book bags from the trunk then began to walk towards the school. Kai turned to blow a kiss and Jahlek attempted to tuck his shirt back into his pants before entering the school.

I reached the office about nine-thirty and Bryan's grandparents hadn't arrived. There were no messages from them indicating whether they decided to cancel or not, so I had the secretary order some bagels and pastries, make a fresh pot of coffee, and set up a table with mugs, plates, and condiments such as cream cheese, butter, and jelly. While I waited for Mr. and Mrs. Knight to arrive, I made several phone calls and reviewed some cases. About a quarter past ten, the secretary buzzed and let me know they had arrived. She showed them into my office as I cleared my desk and prepared to give them my full and undivided attention.

"Mr. and Mrs. Knight, it is nice to finally meet you. Would you like something to drink or perhaps a snack?" I asked trying to be as hospitable and cordial as possible granted the circumstances that brought us together.

"No thank you, Mr. Banks." Mr. Knight responded.

His stance of authority and assurance was as false as his run down gators that he tried to pair with what could have been his best suit in the sixties. Mrs. Knights appearance also spoke in tones of poor and desperate. I recognized the two piece green pant suit she wore as one the outfit I bought Trina in our days together. She probably thought she could snag my sympathy but it only made my head ache more.

"Quinton. You can call me Quinton." I offered trying to ease some of the tension.

"We prefer to keep this business, Mr. Banks." He said.

Mr. Knight's breath reeked of alcohol and tobacco.

"Well, let's get down to it then. Imani and I are willing to relinquish any funds and assets left in Bryan's name to you and your family as well as weekend visitation."

"Excuse me, Mr. Banks but this isn't about the money. We thought you understood why we asked to meet with you. We want Bryan to live with us."

"Sandra said that you wanted to discuss the money. She never said anything about custody. Why now? After six years, why are you seeking custody now?" I questioned.

"You must understand that we never liked Bryan. We believe he's the reason Trina was killed. Therefore, we didn't want anything to do with him. However, over the years we have come to realize that Bryan is our only link to his mother. We loved our daughter and we love our grandson." Mrs. Knight said through a cracking voice.

"What makes you think that Bryan would want to stay with the same people that turned him away years ago? Bryan remembers everything. We have had to take him to therapy because of this." I replied.

"We hoped that over time he would forgive us so we can be a complete family again." Mr. Knight answered.

"Bryan has a complete family. His custody is not for bargaining. The money and assets are all that we have to discuss. If you wish to discuss custody, I suggest you seek an attorney. I can't let him go like that." I said with determination.

"Well then, Mr. Banks. I guess this meeting is over. We will be contacting our attorney so expect to be hearing from him soon." Mr. Knight added as he helped Mrs. Knight from her seat. "Sandra warned us that you were going to try to keep Bryan from us. We will not give up."

'*What is Sandra getting from this?*' I thought as they exited my office.

"What about Jahlek? Isn't he Trina's child? Are you going to try for custody of him as well?" I asked as they were about to close the door.

Neither one answered as they continued to the elevator. I couldn't understand why they were so desperate to snatch Bryan from our home. If it was truly about family then why not ask for Jahlek as well. The mystery of the situation filled my heart with rage and determination to find the root of their intentions.

I returned to my desk and flipped through my Rolodex, searching for Sandra's number. After finding it, I put on the speakerphone and dialed. An automated voice response stated, '*the number you are trying to reach has been temporarily disconnected.*'

My gut feeling was telling me this was deeper than I could have imagined. Instinctively, I called Rodney, let him know what was going on, and told him to keep an ear to the streets.

CHAPTER 9

IMANI

Naadira sat on my lap as I answered emails and worked on finishing my project. Every now and again, she would type a letter or two, making her feel like she was doing big things. Normally, she would be in school but the doctor confirmed with the school nurse that she had chicken pox. Therefore, for those couple of days she was home, Naadira would be my personal assistant.

We programmed the CD player to play three hours of our favorite artists – Jill Scott, Alicia Keys, Luther Vandross, and Usher. My foot was tapping out the beat to *Confessions* as my fingers raced across the keyboard. Naadira tilted her head back to look into my face whenever I would semi-sing and I would return her look with a big wet kiss on her forehead.

It was about three o'clock when we finally took a lunch break. Naadira requested the usual peanut butter and jelly so I decided to join her and have one too. We were enjoying having the house to ourselves. No fighting between Kai and Jahlek, no arguing between Quinton and Bryan only, our music and us. Days like these were rare so I planned to enjoy it to the max. Since it was Friday, I decided not to cook a big dinner. It would be take-out night and since Reese and the kids were coming over, we were having pizza.

"Naadira, do you want to watch a movie?" I asked my little girl while she finished her sandwich.

"What movie do you want to watch?" She replied.

"I don't know. What movie do you like to watch with daddy?"

"Daddy watches BLADE. But I don't wanna watch that because it's too scary. I wanna watch...umm...Bee Movie."

"Okay, let's get the movie and go watch TV in my room. We can lie in my bed."

"Okay." She replied before running into the living room to get her movie.

I cleaned the table and dishes while I waited for her to return. She ran back through the swinging kitchen door with the look of horror on her face.

"What happened, Naadira?"

She pulled her hands from behind her back with the broken halves of Quinton's crystal elephant. Naadira handed the pieces over to me as tears began to well in her eyes.

"It's okay. Don't cry. It was an accident. Next time walk, don't run." I said as I placed the halves on top of the refrigerator.

"Is Daddy going to be mad?" She asked.

"No, I don't think so. Did you get hurt?"

"No." She replied while she played with her fingers.

"Alright, come on. Let's go lay down." I suggested as I reached for her hand.

She placed her tiny hand in mine and I could feel her shaking. When we reached my bedroom, I pulled back the comforter and helped her into the bed. When I laid beside her, she snuggled close and within minutes, she was sleep. Shortly after, Mr. Sandman took me under his spell as well.

Bryan raced up the stairs and into my bedroom. I knew he was coming before he opened my door because of his loud thunderous steps. He sat on the bed beside me and began tapping my shoulder.

"Yes, Bryan." I said to acknowledge his presence.

"Sierra is here. She's down stairs." He replied with excitement.

"That's great. Now go downstairs with your company and let me get myself together. Did you offer her something to drink?"

"Yes, Mom. She's watching videos. Did Dad tell you that he wanted me to invite her over tonight?"

"He hasn't called all day." I said realizing that I hadn't spoken to him, which was unusual.

Naadira began to squirm and moan as if she was fighting in her dreams. I rubbed her back until she went back to a peaceful slumber. It was a little after five so I knew the house would be filling up soon. Kai, Jahlek, and Quinton were on their way home. Charisse and her family weren't far behind. Diamond normally didn't make it in until eight. I wanted to let Naadira sleep for a while longer so I told Bryan to lower his voice while we continued talking.

"Do me a favor. After Kai and Jahlek come in, order pizza. Make sure you get enough for Aunt Reese and her kids."

"Alright. When are you coming down?" He whispered.

"In a few. Let me freshen up and change my clothes."

I showed Bryan that I was wearing an old t-shirt and sweats and he frowned up his face. I knew he didn't want his company to see me like that.

"Can I take Naadira down with me then?"

"Bryan, she's sleeping. What's wrong with you? Are you nervous to be alone?" I laughed at his silliness.

"Nah. I wanted her to meet Naadira. Forget it. I'm going down stairs."

He leaned over to kiss my cheek before jetting out the door. After he closed the door, I laughed at his silliness some more.

Looking through my closet, I realized that even my new wardrobe was beginning to fit snug. I recently went to Old Navy and the GAP to purchase a new wardrobe because of my recent weight gain. No one seemed to notice it though but the scale doesn't lie. I loved Old Navy's Sweetheart jeans so I decided on the dark jean pair. Then I went through Quinton's closet for a pullover sweater to hide my bloated stomach.

"It must be getting close to that time of the month." I said to myself as I removed the pins holding my hair in its wrap.

When I was done, I let down my shoulder length hair and admired myself briefly in the mirror. Kai-Aja loved my new haircut. She said it made her want layers too. Once I was completely dressed and ready, I woke Naadira and dressed her. She was still a little nervous about Quinton's elephant but I assured her that everything would be alright.

The doorbell rang twice before Bryan opened the door. Kai-Aja and Jahlek came through the door arguing until they saw Sierra sitting in the living room. They put their bags in the closet with their coats then rushed into the living room to sit between Bryan and Sierra. I greeted Sierra with a hug and gave her a smile of approval. She was a very pretty girl with an innocent face and sweet voice. Bryan excused himself to order the pizzas while we continued talking.

"You have a very beautiful home, Mrs. Banks." Sierra complimented as she looked around the living room.

"Do you want to see the rest of the house?" Kai asked.

"If that's okay with your mom, sure." She replied.

"Of course. Kai, change your clothes while you're upstairs. Jah, you too." I said.

"Alright." They responded.

Naadira followed Sierra and Kai-Aja throughout the house. I waited by the window for Quinton's car to pull into the driveway but Charisse and her family rolled up instead.

"Bryan, go outside and help your aunt." I said feeling a mix of upset and happiness.

Charisse was always welcomed in our home however I was disappointed that Quinton hadn't even called to let me know if he had a change in plans. I picked up the cordless and dialed his cell. He answered on the first ring as if he were anticipating my call.

"Q, where are you? Is everything okay?" I asked.

"Hey. I was a little tied up with this case. I'm on my way home now. I should be there in about ten minutes." He replied.

"How did everything go with Bryan's grandparents? I had been waiting for the results of that meeting since morning." A nervous knot had formed in my stomach as I waited for the answer.

"We need to talk about that later. It wasn't good, Baby." He replied somberly.

"No, Quinton. Don't tell me that." I felt the urge to scream but resisted.

"Baby, we'll talk when I come home."

"We have a house full of company. Bryan brought Sierra over and Charisse is here with the kids."

"Well, we will find time to talk. Right now, I'm trying not to think about it. Tell the kids to put the laundry downstairs. I'll be home in a few. Love you."

"Love you, too."

My mind went blank as I returned the phone to its base. Bryan noticed my vacant expression, put his arm around my shoulders, and again kissed my cheek.

"Dad has to work late?" He asked.

"No, he's on his way. He wants somebody to put the laundry downstairs. Can you and Jahlek handle that?"

"Yeah. Is that all? Is that why you look lost?" Bryan asked.

"I'm okay, Sweetie. Go take care of that before your company comes down." I said while rubbing his back.

Charisse had put her things in the guest room while I sat in my rocking chair and collected my thoughts.

"What's up, Diva?" She asked as she walked into the living room.

Christian found Naadira and made their way to the paint table while Damien tailed his mother as she carried Alaire on her hip.

"Nothing, Diva. Look at you beautiful lady." I said trying to mask my envy.

Charisse was still slim and sexy after three babies. Yet my darling girls wrecked my thighs and abdomen. Charisse looked as if she stepped out of a magazine. Her casual attire put my wardrobe to shame. She strutted her slender frame in front of me wearing a tri-color cable knit sweater with a thin brown leather belt around her waist representing the beauty of autumn. Paired with the orange gaucho pants and brown suede boots her outfit complemented the new auburn highlights in her hair.

"Thank you, Sweetie. I found this sweater in the boxes at my apartment. Myra pulled it out." Charisse said.

She must have noticed my unresponsiveness and asked, "What's wrong?"

"Quinton had the meeting today. I think they want to take Bryan."

"They can't do that. Can they?" Charisse replied.

"Girl, you know as much about this as I do. But I do know they will have to go through hell and high water before I let him go."

"I hear you, Sis. Where's Quinton?" She asked.

"He should be here any minute."

"Well, don't stress. Quinton will handle everything, Girl."

Charisse placed Alaire in her playpen and sat on the arm of my chair.

"Sis, you know he ain't going to let nobody take that boy from you."

"I know. I can't believe this shit is happening."

Sierra and Kai-Aja walked into the living room. Kai introduced Charisse to Sierra and then they made their way to the basement.

"Kai, tell Bryan not to play the music too loud down there. You know your father will have a fit if he hears that bass thumping."

"Okay, Mom. Can I take some soda and stuff downstairs?"

"As long as you keep it clean down there."

The basement was the hang out whenever the kids had company over. We first designed the basement for when Quinton and I had guests but the kids took over, as they got older. We didn't mind because it kept them out of our face. Normally, I would send Christian and Naadira down with them but I decided not to spoil their fun. Besides, they knew when Diamond came home she would put them out the basement since she practically lived down there.

The telephone rang and Naadira jumped to answer it before anyone else stole her job as my secretary.

"Mommy, it's for you." She said as she brought the cordless.

"Hello."

"Yes, is this Imani?" The female caller asked.

"Yes this is." I replied.

"Hi, my name is Sandra. I'm not sure if you know me but I remember you. Listen, I'm not trying to break up your happy home and shit but Bryan's grandparents want to talk to him. I told them that I would ask you first, if it was okay to give them the number." She said.

"Hell no, it's not okay. You're not even supposed to have my number and you're calling me like we are friends. We are not friends so stop fronting. This matter has nothing to do with you and we would appreciate it if *you* would mind your business. Quinton is handling everything. Tell them to call him."

"This is my business. That's my kids' brother and as long as he wants to talk to them, it is my business. Now I'm warning you, if you don't want no problems let Bryan be with his family."

"Oh, there's not going to be any problems, Sandra. Bryan is with his family. Now like I said, if they want to speak to Bryan tell them to call Quinton on Monday. As far as you and me, don't call here. Just because we left the 'hood don't mean I have gone soft. That's a warning." I stated before hanging up.

I placed the phone on the base and looked at Charisse with disbelief. Anger caused me to loose my composure and go somewhere I have not been in years. I needed a few minutes to regroup.

"You'll be in New York next week, right? We can handle this if you want." Charisse said.

"Reese, we are too old to be beating down somebody for no reason." I replied.

"Oh, you have plenty of reason. She's the one that started all this bullshit. Fucking crack head. What the hell does she get out of this?" Charisse asked.

"Who knows?" I replied. "You know misery loves company. She wants somebody to be hurting with her broke ass. I am not about to entertain her, though. By choice or by force Sandra will mind her business. Trust!"

There it goes again. The ghetto was rising inside of me, dying to come out.

For the first time since we moved from New York, I felt the urge to go back. However, I couldn't risk playing into this woman's game. I knew something or someone was putting pressure on Sandra to destroy my family. There was desperation in her voice. Nevertheless, I would be damned if she succeeded.

Charisse and I sat there briefly contemplating what we were going to do and then we decided to let Quinton handle it the legal way. However, we knew if she called again or showed up, we would handle the situation the Brooklyn way.

മൽമൽമ‍ൽ‍ൽ‍ൽ

RODNEY

"Quinton, there ain't nuthin' buzzing around here about Bryan. All his hype faded after he died. I have no idea what Trina's family is up to but I will try to find out." I tried to assure Quinton as I drove full speed towards Sandra's block. "Try to calm down. Go home and do your Friday family-bonding thing. I'll handle Sandra."

"Rodney, I don't need you getting involved. Sandra is not your problem. She's the messenger." Quinton explained.

"You think somebody got pressure on her? Is she *really* desperate to get Bryan in New York? Did Bryan ever mention anything to you about that rumor?" I asked.

"What rumor? That shit about him knowing where his father's stash was hidden. Nah, I didn't ask and he never mentioned it to me. Do you believe there really is a stash? That shit sounds so far-fetched." Quinton replied.

"I don't know what to believe. You know that's what Trey was looking for before he got locked up."

After Bryan and Trina's house was hit, rumors spread that Trey – a hustler from the Bronx – was looking for some cash Bryan's father had supposedly stashed. The only time I ever heard of the supposed treasure was when I first met Sandra. At first, I thought it was true being that she was close to Bryan and had brought me inside information before. However, after the hit, Trey's men searched the entire house and only came across a couple of thousands and according to the rumors the stash was something like two million. I was satisfied with having back my regular business and my share of the money but Trey was after more. By no means was he in need of money. He allowed the greed to consume him. That was years ago and the stash was long gone or so I thought. My gut was telling me that I was wrong.

"I don't want to approach Bryan about his father's operation or anything that will trigger bad memories. I know he still has dreams, no, he has nightmares about that night and it's hard enough for him to talk about that." Quinton explained, breaking the silence.

"I hear you, Q. Like I said, I'm going to talk to Sandra. Try to find out what's really going down. Take it easy, dawg."

"Alright, I'm going to get back at you later. I'm pulling up to the house."

"Yo, tell Reese to give me a call. I tried her cell but her phone ain't on. The voicemail is full and I sent like twenty texts." I said, admitting that I was missing my woman.

"As soon as I get in, I'll let her know. Are you trying to work things out with her or are you still too hard to admit you're wrong?" Quinton asked with a slight snicker.

"I'm glad to see you find humor in my misery. I'm out. Later." I replied before disconnecting.

I pulled in front of Sandra's house and dialed her but it was disconnected. It wasn't my style to ring her bell and risk someone seeing me but this was urgent. Swiftly, I walked towards the side of the house then down the stairs leading to the basement. I knocked several times before kicking the door. I knew she had to be home. Sandra never worked. She knew how to make the game work for her. After a few seconds, she called out from behind the door, "I'm coming."

She opened the door while trying to gather her robe.

"Don't worry. You ain't got shit I want to see." I said while brushing past her and walking into her lavish living room.

"It wasn't always like that. There was a time I couldn't keep you away." She replied.

She plopped onto the sofa and looked at me with an inviting stare but I wasn't falling for it. Not anymore. Well, not since Reese.

"I'm going to make this quick and spare both of us the torture. Whoever got you trying to get Bryan let them know that I'm trying very hard not to get involved but shit is getting critical. If I get another call about you or the Knight's contacting Quinton and his family, there's going to be some motherfucking trouble heading your way. Got me?"

"Rodney, please. You ain't God, nigga. You don't have *any* power over here, Boo. Those threats gonna follow you right out that door. Now, if that's all you came for, you should remember how to lock the door behind yourself. I got some business to tend to." She replied as she started towards her bedroom.

"What nigga you got back there that got you feeling cocky?" I asked as I approached her.

She stood with her hand on the knob and a bold expression on her face that said she wasn't backing down.

"You jealous?" She replied.

"Don't flatter yourself, Love." I used my hand to gently cup the side of her face then grabbed her chin between my forefinger and thumb and applied pressure. "Keep in mind; I can still make shit happen. And if you want to protect your family, you'll deliver my message."

Her eyes revealed that I had shaken her with my last threat. She placed her hands on my chest and I was temporarily distracted as her robe opened and displayed her bare breast and the thick curls between her legs. Her skin void of flaws begged me to taste but I fought the urge to comply.

"Please leave, Rodney. This has nothing to do with you. Don't get involved." She begged.

"Quinton is family. I'm already involved. This is not about the money Bryan Junior has; it's about the mystery money, isn't it? Sandra, keep their family out of it." I replied as I released her face.

"And what about us, Rodney? We used to be family too." She said as she pointed to an old portrait of herself, her daughter Sharay and me.

I looked at Sandra who apparently cleaned up since the last time we bumped into each other and memories came rushing back. Sandra wore her hair down and had it colored a dark brown, which complemented her soft, cocoa skin. Her hands were void of the false tips and were freshly manicured with a light peach color. In a matter of a week, she looked like a different person. Well the woman I used to know anyway. Still, the gold-digging aura surrounded her.

"You chose Bryan and destroyed our family. No matter how many times he hurt you and I saved you, you kept going back. You didn't give a shit about us. That's over. There's nothing left here." I said as I pointed to my chest.

"So, why did you help me get Bryan? You did it because deep down you thought it was his fault we didn't work." She walked towards me and attempted to put her arms around my neck but I pushed her away.

"Sandra, don't play yourself. You were always a money chasing whore. I knew that before we got involved but I thought I could change you, help you raise Sharay but you were only after the paper. You left me for Bryan and that was your biggest mistake. When me and Trey got at Bryan that was business, nothing personal. That was my biggest mistake. Now my best friend has to deal with some bullshit I'm positive you're involved in." I said as I began to back away, heading for the door.

As Sandra was about to respond, Sharay and her younger sister, Jasmine walked through the door. I stared at the teenager as she stared back at me. Knowing she wasn't my daughter didn't stop me from loving her any less. She will always be my angel. I raised Sharay as my own when Sandra and I dated years ago. When Sandra took her from me and ran back to Bryan, I felt a void in my life. No one knew my pain, not even Quinton. Sharay is the reason why Sandra never took any of my threats seriously. I could never hurt Sharay and would go to jail if anyone tried.

"Hi." She said as she helped take off Jasmine's jacket.

"Jasmine, how was school?" Sandra asked as she pulled herself together.

"It was good. I got a lot of homework." She replied.

Neither one of the girl's resembled their father. Sharay shared the same cocoa colored skin as her mother and dark hair where as Jasmine was very fair with sandy brown hair. It was hard for me to believe that Jasmine was Bryan's daughter. Bryan and Sharay share some features that she does not. Like Bryan Junior and Sharay have their father's nose and until Sharay started getting her eyebrows waxed, they were thick like her father and brother's. Sandra swore Jasmine was Bryan's daughter and personally, it really didn't matter. I knew she wasn't mine and that was all that mattered at the time.

"Well, let's go in your room and look at it. Rodney, I'll talk to you. Thanks for visiting." Sandra walked into the girls' room as Sharay and I stood in the living room.

"So, how are you?" I asked.

"Fine and you?" She replied.

"I'm okay. How's school?"

"Good. I graduate this year. I already was accepted to three Universities. I'm trying to go as far away as possible. You know, get away from this..." She stopped and looked around at the house that crack built.

"That's great, Sharay. I'm sorry I haven't been around for a while. You know you can call though. We used to talk all the time and then you stopped calling. Whatever happens between your mom and me has nothing to do with our relationship."

"I have tried to call you. It seems like you are always so busy. It's hard to catch up to you. You know my mother found out that I was still talking to you and punished me, took away my phone for a month. She doesn't want me around you or your family. I don't know why she's bugging. Then the last time I tried to call you, your wife answered so I hung up. You know, I still see Aunt Keisha and Grandma. As a matter of fact, Grandma said she wants to buy my graduation dress." She stated referring to my family as her own.

The fact was my family and I swore to always be a part of her life. I was the only one that forgot to hold onto my promise.

Sharay walked into the kitchen and grabbed two cans of soda from the refrigerator. She passed one to me then took a seat on the countertop.

"Are you alright? Do you need anything?" I asked as I went into my pocket.

"No. I didn't ask grandma for money, she offered. But I'm fine. My mom actually took the money that she got after my father died and opened accounts for me and Jasmine. Plus, I'm working so I'm good." Sharay replied.

"Your mother opened accounts?" I asked surprised that Sandra had enough sense to handle the money responsibly. We swore she had exhausted their money on drugs for herself. *'Then why is she after Bryan's money?'* I thought.

"Yeah, she's trying to do the right thing. She's cleaning herself up one day at a time." Sharay smiled as she talked about her mother.

"I'm glad to hear that. Listen, I have to run but give me a call.

Maybe we can go to lunch tomorrow." I said as I tried to remove the plastered smile from my face but it was hard because I was so proud of Sharay.

"Okay." Sharay jumped down from the counter to walk me to the door.

As we approached the door, she tapped my arm and I turned towards her.

"You know Diamond, Bryan's cousin, and me are best friends, right? Well she gave me Bryan's cell phone number and we've been on the phone everyday. Talking and laughing. I even told him about you, me, and my mom's situation. I told him that even though Bryan was our father, I only consider you my dad. He told me that he felt the same way about Quinton and I felt relieved that someone understood and related to how I felt. So I wanted you to know that even though this whole situation is way awkward, I love you anyway and you'll always be Daddy to me."

Immediately, I hugged Sharay then whispered, "You never stopped being my angel. I'm so sorry that things turned out the way they did but I want you to always remember that I was never ashamed of you. The reason I never told anyone about you is that your mother wouldn't let me. I respected her wishes but I never wanted to leave you. These last few years have been hard for me but I never forgot you."

We stayed that way for what felt like forever. She looked up at me and had one of the most beautiful smiles I ever saw.

"I gotta go, Sweetheart. Give me a call tonight about eight and maybe you can come by my house. We'll probably catch a movie or something. You can bring your sister too."

"Okay, I will. Oh, Daddy do you think you can talk my mother into letting me go to Pennsylvania with Diamond so I can meet Bryan. Diamond said she was going back tonight but I asked her to wait until tomorrow so I can go with her but my mother won't let me go." She said.

"I'll talk to her tonight when I come to pick you up. I can't make you any promises that she'll say yeah but if she says no, I'll sneak you down there. My kids are there too so you can spend time with them." I said.

The thought of explaining our situation or relationship to Quinton and Charisse never dawned on me until after I made the promise to bring Sharay to Pennsylvania. Nevertheless, the happiness that glazed her eyes was worth any consequence.

As I sat in my car, flashbacks of the years I spent with Sandra ran across my mind. The only time I remember experiencing pure happiness was when I was with Sharay until I met Charisse. I realized I didn't want to lose that feeling again. It was Sandra that caused me to have insecurities and that was the reason I held back from giving Charisse everything she wanted for us. What I should have realized was that Charisse was a real woman and didn't want me for what I could give her, but for my heart, my soul, and my love. The love I held back for too long.

My cell phone began to ring and Charisse's number flashed on the screen.

"Hey, Baby." I greeted.

"Hello, Rodney. You've been looking for me." She replied flatly.

"Reese, I love you and more importantly I need you. I know you heard this before but baby I ain't never feel like I do now. Today was the first day where I could honestly see that I am wrong Reese. Help me be a better man."

"What do you want from me, Rodney? I gave you everything I had and then some but that wasn't enough for you. So now what? You want me to forget everything and take you back. I told you…"

"Reese, I'm not taking no for an answer. I'm willing to work twice as hard to get you back. I know it's hard to forgive and forget but Reese I promise I can make it go away." I interrupted before she could completely turn me away.

"Rodney, it's not going to work. There are still things I don't know about you and we've been together too long for it to be this way. I can't continue to be with a mystery man. I want to know the good and the bad about my man. That way if ever something or someone from your past happens to pop up, it won't shock the hell out of me or worst threaten our family."

"If that's what you need, you got it. Tomorrow, I'm coming out there and we are going to talk about everything. Reese, remember nothing in my life has been honest and I can guarantee there may be some things you may dislike and some that may hurt you." I explained.

"Let me worry about that. If I'm strong enough to open the jar of worms, I got to be tough enough to eat them." She replied. "So, we'll see you tomorrow?"

"My mother asked me to take her shopping in the morning so I'll be out there about three. Trust me, I promise never to hurt you again. No more deception; no more games. I love you, Reese."

"I know." She replied.

CHAPTER 10

QUINTON

Imani and Charisse were in the kitchen helping the younger children with their pizzas while our teenagers were in the dining room laughing and playing around. To my surprise, Sierra was sitting at the table with them. Imani waved, acknowledging my presence as I walked towards the office. My head was throbbing from the day's meetings so I was in no mood to play family man. All I needed was a few minutes to rest and collect my thoughts before joining our family but time was not on my side. Before I could sit in my massage chair, Naadira came crashing through the office door, face full of pizza sauce. She jumped onto my lap and gave me a huge hug and sloppy kiss on my cheek. Then before I could ask her how her day was, she was gone. That was like her. She loved to be around me but if Christian was around it was, 'Daddy who?'

After checking my voice mail and sorting through the bills that Imani left stacked on my desk, I decided to get a slice of pizza and talk with the kids. Imani had a thousand and one things on her mind but as long as we had company, I knew she would wait until the time was right. Bryan stood from his seat to greet me meanwhile Kai and Jahlek continued to stuff their faces.

"Hello, Mr. Banks." Sierra said after wiping sauce from the side of her mouth.

"How are you? Are you enjoying yourself?" I replied.

"Yeah, I'm cool." She said while looking at Bryan and smiling.

"That's good. How was school Kai, Jah?" I asked as Kai-Aja and Jahlek continued eating their pizzas.

Kai replied through a stuff mouth, "It was okay."

Jahlek nodded his head in agreement.

"Bryan, what's going on? Everything's alright? I see you brought your friend over." We shared a man's handshake and then a strong hug.

"Everything is good. Sierra has to go home about nine. Can you give us a ride?" Bryan asked as he returned to his seat beside his girlfriend.

"I'll see if your mom will take you. I'm not really feeling well." I replied.

"Alright." He said then returned to the conversation at the table.

After taking two slices of pizza, I walked into the kitchen to greet my wife. Charisse was on the phone and on her way out of the kitchen as I approached the open door. I waved at her as she slid past me towards a quieter place. Imani leaned against the sink as she watched the kids eating and playing at the table. Alaire was snuggled in her arms drinking from her bottle. I put my plate in the microwave, set it for thirty seconds then went to the refrigerator for bottled water.

"Baby, *she* called our house." Imani said as she looked at Alaire.

"Who called?" I asked oblivious as to whom she was referring to.

As I twisted the cap, it dawned on me who 'she' was.

"Really? What did *she* have to say?"

"She threatened our f-a-m-i-l-y." Imani whispered, trying to keep our conversation between her and me.

"She must be out of her fu... mind! That woman is out of control."

"This whole situation is getting out of control." Imani said before placing Alaire against her chest to burp her.

"I'm beginning to get a sick feeling about this. This isn't about money anymore, is it?" She asked.

"We'll talk about this after the kids go to sleep, Imani."

"Quinton, give me a clue. All day I've had this feeling pitting in my stomach and I can't take it much more. Tell me something." She begged.

I looked around to make sure no one was listening.

"Yes, this has gone beyond the money. They want full custody but I still feel there's more. I don't know exactly what so I decided that I should go to New York for a while. When we go up next week for Thanksgiving, I'll stay behind. Hopefully I can get some hint as to what's going on. I'll ask Mama and James to come back with you to help out with the kids if you want."

"Quinton, you know how I feel about you going to New York even for one day. It's not safe, Q. I can't let you stay out there." She replied as she began to walk away.

Naadira and Christian were finished with their pizzas and left the table, anxious to return to their fun. Bryan, Sierra, Jahlek, and Kai-Aja left the dining room and by the bass from below, I knew they were having a good time but the music amplified the pounding in my head. Aggravated, I knocked heavily on the basement door and instantly the music was lowered to a more reasonable volume. I followed Imani into the family room wanting to comfort her but I also needed her to know it wasn't about her or me. We always promised to protect our children. No matter what Sandra or anyone else said, Bryan was our child and he needed us.

Imani sat on the rocking chair in the corner and looked out the window.

"Imani, this is not about what you can or can't let me do. This is what I have to do. The only way I am going to get the information I need is to hit the streets myself. I've tried doing it by the books but now it's time to do it my way, Baby." I explained.

"Q, you have a family now. You are not a thug anymore. You are my husband and a father. I think you should really rethink this." Imani said through tightly clenched teeth.

"Imani, I already made my decision."

"Another decision made without me. I am your wife, Quinton. Doesn't that mean anything to you? Can't I get that much respect?"

"Imani, I respect you. But there are some things that go without discussion and this happens to be one of them. We are not going to lose Bryan to anyone and it is my job to make sure of that. I'll only be gone for a few days. As far as Sandra calling, I'll take care of that first thing in the morning. Don't stress, Baby. Tonight is not the night."

I returned to the kitchen, removed the pizzas from the microwave, seasoned them, and headed back to the family room.

"What movie did you get for the kids today?" I asked.

At first, she was hesitant to answer. I knew she would be

unhappy but this has gone out of our hands. I'll be damned if someone would take *my son* from *me*.

Naadira, Christian, and Damian rushed through the dinning room straight into the family room as if they heard my question and had the answer. Naadira picked up the remote and turned on the TV and DVD player.

Imani looked towards the kids then replied, "Charisse brought over *The Incredibles* and *Underworld*. Let the kids watch the cartoon first, and then we will watch *Underworld – Evolution* after they go to bed." Imani replied.

She didn't say another word throughout the movie but we did exchange glances. None of which expressed pleasure or understanding. Charisse returned to the family room and sat beside me with a blank expression. She sat quietly for minutes before I noticed the tears well in her eyes. Rodney found a way to hurt her once again. I knew it was best to let her be and Imani must have felt the same. Imani placed Alaire in her playpen, placed a hand on Charisse's shoulder, and then left the room

"Why didn't you tell me, Q?" She asked in almost inaudible whisper.

"Reese, what are you talking about?" I responded hoping it wasn't one of the secrets from Rodney's *Pandora's Box*.

"You knew he had another family. All these years, you played along. Let me look like the fool all the while he's hiding his double life." She stared at me as if she was attempting to read my mind.

"Rodney doesn't have another family besides you and your three. Where did you get that? That is something I would never have lied to you about." I replied, clueless.

"After you gave me Rodney message, I decided to call. He told me he was coming down this weekend and we were going to try to fix our relationship. We talked for a while but he must have accidentally hit the talk button because it dialed my phone back and I heard him telling someone that he was going to pick up his daughter tonight so they can come here tomorrow. Alaire is already here so who the fuck is he referring to? I knew he had secrets but none like this."

Charisse's expression turned from confusion to pure hatred.

"Reese, I swear I have no idea what you are talking about? Rodney and I have been like brothers since we were kids; I'm telling you he doesn't have any other kids. Maybe, he was talking in codes. We both know that he is still hustling as much as he lies and say he isn't. Did you try calling him back?" I asked.

"I can't. My gut is telling me something ain't right, Q. Maybe, he's hiding something from the both of us. How am I supposed to move on from this? How can I trust someone that doesn't acknowledge his children? We've been together too long for this kind of thing to pop up now. I imagined the worst but this is beyond expectation."

Reese looked at me, her eyes filled with pain. Both of us lost for words. Maybe there were no words left. Not knowing what else to say, I decided to take Sierra home after all.

Before leaving, I decided to check in with Imani. I knew she had been upset with the way the things that had been going on with Bryan and the custody battle but I needed her to trust me and know that my intentions were solely to benefit the family. Imani was in our room folding clothes that were lying across the chest at the foot of our bed. She looked towards me as I entered the room then immediately looked away. I knew she had been crying and I wished I wasn't the one to blame. Imani continued to put away the clothing as I walked closer to her. She was determined not to look my way so I stood in her path and continued to block her as she tried to walk around me. Frustrated, she blew an exasperated breath, sucked her teeth and stood before me with folded arms, tapping her foot.

"Quinton, I'm not in the mood for your games tonight. Please go back down stairs and let me finish what I was doing. Let me clear my head." She said as she pressed her hand against my chest.

"Baby, we are supposed to be there for each other. I understand how you feel about me leaving but you have to understand how I feel. I can't let them take our son, Imani. I need to find out what's really going on. I can't do that from here." I tried to explain.

"How can we be there for each other when you never talk to me? You know going to New York is only going to bring more drama. What are the kids and I supposed to do if something happens to you? Have you taken that into consideration?" She asked as tears streamed down her cheeks.

I grabbed Imani and brought her to me then wrapped my arms around her. We stood embraced until she backed away to look me in the eyes and say, "I can't lose you now, Q."

"You won't. I'm coming back, Baby. Nothing's going to happen. No one will even know I'm there." I continued to comfort her as I tried to assure her that everything would turn out fine.

Gently, I held Imani's chin between my forefinger and thumb to turn her face up so I could look into her eyes. We kissed with intensity, then passion. My hands wandered over her body as she explored mine. I started towards the bed as I began to disrobe, our lips still never losing contact. She followed my lead as she began to unbutton her jeans. I held her hands, preventing her from continuing.

"Let me take care of that." I said as I pulled off her sweater and unsnapped her sheer pink bra.

"Quinton, I..." She began but I quickly placed my finger against her lips.

"We'll talk later. Let me love you." I whispered as I trailed wet kisses from her neck to her navel, removing her jeans and then her matching sheer bikini underwear.

As she lay across the bed, I took time to admire her. Imani knew I liked to be teased so she turned around and put her ass in the air, moving erotically across the bed. I spanked her the way she liked as she continued to entice me with her moves. I attempted to enter her from behind but she had other ideas.

She easily slid off the bed and walked around me as I stood butt-naked and rock hard. Imani turned on the stereo and programmed Toni Braxton's *Tell Me* to play repeatedly while she entertained me with the moves she'd been learning from her pole-dancing exercise classes. She stood before me only wearing pink lace thongs and black stilettos as she began to gyrate, grinding against my manhood. Using me as her pole, she placed her arm around my neck, lifted her right leg, wrapped it around my waist and grind some more. Initially, my mission was to please her and ease her fears but I assumed all was thrown to the wind as passion built stronger and the temperature in the room rose.

As she slid down on her knees, I fought against the urge to pick her up, throw her on our bed and take control. When her mouth encased my manhood, tingles shot up my spine. I knew if I didn't stop her soon, I would erupt.

"You okay, Baby." She asked.

That minute was all I needed to pull her up and hold her close allowing myself time to calm down. We kissed passionately as I laid Imani on the bed, wedged myself between her legs, placed her legs on my shoulders as I began to taste her. Her sweet nectar flowed onto our peach cotton sheets as her body continued to dance. Her release left her panting yet begging for more. I entered her slowly, allowing her body to greet me. Her warm, moist cavern encased me as I gently stroked her. The rhythmic pulse of her approaching another orgasm brought me into an alter state as my strokes doubled. The headboard shook and the springs creaked as we neared an explosion leaving us weak and sweaty.

Imani smiled as she rested her head on my chest, trying to catch her breath.

"What's up?" I asked, breathlessly.

"We have company. What if they heard us?" She asked with a huge smile plastered across her face.

"Nah, I doubt it. Everybody was into what they were doing when I came upstairs." I replied.

"Good." Imani replied as she attempted to move from beside me.

"Where are you going?" I asked as she headed for the bathroom.

"In the shower. I want to show my face before Sierra leaves." She replied.

"Oh shit. I totally forgot that Bryan asked if one of us could drive her home before nine."

"Well, it's fifteen minutes to nine now. You want me to take her." Imani offered as she wrapped herself in her plush lilac bathrobe.

"No, I'll take her. Besides, I think it'll be better if you stay with Reese." I stated before grabbing my towel.

"It's that bad, hunh?" Imani asked.

Without a response, I headed into the shower.

On the way to Sierra's house, Sierra and I were able to talk and get to know each other better. I did not want to seem intrusive but I was curious as to why she was caring for her sister's child instead of her parents who she claimed she lived with. It didn't make any sense why her parents would push a responsibility like that on another person, above all their younger child that works and goes to school. Without seeming obvious, I led Sierra into the subject with simple questions.

"Would you like to bring your nephew to play with the kids?"

Shock crossed both Sierra and Bryan's face.

"Umm, I think my parents are going to keep him this weekend?" She replied.

"Well, whenever you come by you are more than welcome to bring him along." I stated nonchalantly.

"Her parents keep him most of the time. That day she was doing them a favor." Bryan added.

"Oh, I'm sorry. Kai-Aja made it seem as if he was your sole responsibility. I knew she had to be mistaken. There is no way a girl like you could handle all of that alone. No offense."

"Excuse me, Mr. Banks. But, I am totally capable of raising Isaiah by myself while working *and* going to school. I've been doing it this long without my parents and I can continue another eighteen years without them." Sierra countered with pure attitude.

"All I'm trying to say is you should not be held responsible for someone else's mistake."

"My son is not a mistake."

Her front finally caved in as she lost her composure. The car was silent as Sierra's last words sunk in.

"Dad, I told Kai that was Sierra's nephew. I didn't want Kai or Jahlek to tell you or mom before I had a chance to explain." Bryan said, apologetically.

"Do you care to explain now?" I asked Sierra as she looked at Bryan.

"Mr. Banks, I had no idea Bryan hadn't told you or Mrs. Banks about Isaiah. He is definitely my son. I had him when I was seventeen.

Also, I am not a full college student. I had to repeat my twelfth year due to my absences but they are allowing me to take some college courses. I live with my grandparents and younger sister. My mom died last year from Cancer and my dad is in and out of jail." Sierra paused as she wiped her tears. "I am not proud of my life, Mr. Banks but I am not ashamed of my son. I am a good mother and I am not looking for anything from your son but his companionship."

"What about your son's father? Is he still in the picture?" I continued to interrogate the young woman as Bryan tried to comfort her.

"He's in New York. My grandparents had him arrested and when he was released he moved there." She replied.

"Dad, please drop it. This was a lot for her to go through, don't make her relive her past." Bryan pleaded as he held her hand.

"Mr. Banks, You're a lawyer, right?" Sierra asked.

"Yes, I am. Do you need my help concerning this situation with your baby's father?"

"Kind of. I wanted to know what would be the maximum sentence for a repeat sexual offender."

Her question threw me off. I was expecting her to ask something concerning child support or custody.

"It depends on the circumstances surrounding the case. Do you mind if I ask you some questions?" I asked suddenly feeling a need to protect Sierra and her son.

"I can handle it." She replied.

"Were you raped?"

"Yes."

"Was this person older than you?"

"Yes."

"How can you classify this person as a 'repeat offender'?"

"He molested my sister, too. That's when my grandparents had him arrested again. And now he's trying to get visitation to see my son."

Bryan's head hung low as he listened. My heart raced as anger replaced compassion.

"Sierra, one more question. Outside of these incidents, have you ever seen this man before?" I asked, gathering enough information to give a more precise answer.

"He was our father." She replied.

My expression went blank after her final response. Child custody cases with circumstances such as sexual abuse crossed my desk every so often and I wondered what became of the victims and their families. I would have never imagined having a situation hit so close to home. My mind spun a thousand thoughts but none of which could have properly expressed my sympathy. Rage began to build inside as I thought of the possible outcomes of such a case in which no sentence could ever measure the amount of pain this woman will live with.

"Sierra, I can make sure that it will be a very long time." I said before pulling in front of her house.

If it were up to me, the bastard would be serving his sentence in a grave.

ကလလလ〜ကလ〜ကလ

<u>CHARISSE</u>

All night I tossed and turned, trying to clear my mind and find enough peace to fall asleep but it was an effortless fight. Even the soothing sounds of Vivian Green's *Emotional Rollercoaster* couldn't help me out of this funk. Probably because her words hit home. Who ever said, '*the truth hurts*' never lied. Rodney had finally managed to fuck my head up. Several times, I dialed his number only to hang up before the first ring. Years I put up with his lies only assuming what he was hiding but I would have never imagined that he'd have another child let alone ever been in another serious relationship. It's not like it's impossible. After all, Rodney is the whore of all whores. He never lived a day faithful to anyone or anything but his money and his business. Maybe he had been faithful to that other woman and she was the reason for his ways, his inability to trust or express love. She left me with damaged goods. Too bad I can't get a refund.

As my body began to give in and sleep finally began to creep through, my cell phone began to vibrate. Instinctively, I checked the Caller ID before answering. At two o'clock in the morning I didn't expect it to be anyone other than Rodney. Unfortunately, I was right. Anger pumped through my veins, giving me the fuel to pick up the phone and rip Rodney a new asshole. Still it wasn't enough, I wasn't ready. The phone rang three more times before it went to voicemail. Seconds later the phone indicated I had received a message and without second thought I turned off the phone, closed my eyes and waited for sleep to take over.

"Mommy, mommy. Aunt Imani said to pick up the phone." Christian yelled as he vigorously shook my arm.

"Who's on the phone?" I asked as I checked my watch for the time.

"It's Daddy!" Christian exclaimed with pure excitement.

After reaching for the phone, I pulled back and decided to let Christian speak to his father for a while so I could collect my thoughts. Christian was full of smiles as he answered the phone and began telling Rodney about all the fun he had the night before. Damien and Alaire were still sleep so I continued to rest while Christian talked with his father. By the time Christian finished, I found a new strength to carry me through this call and possibly the largest obstacles yet to cross our paths.

Holding the phone to my ear, I listened and waited for Rodney to initiate the conversation.

"Reese, are you there?"

"Yes. How can I help you today?" I peevishly replied.

"What's the matter with you? I called last night. The first time your phone rang until I got the voicemail, then when I called back it kept going straight to voicemail. Is everything cool?"

"No, Rodney. Everything is not cool. Your phone never disconnected from our conversation yesterday. I heard you tell someone you had to pick up your daughter before you head out this way. The thing that struck me as odd was that Alaire is here with me. And don't give me any shit about talking in codes. What's the fucking deal, Rodney?"

Rodney took a deep breath before he replied. "I thought we established the fact that we have a lot to talk about. I told you there are some things in my past that you may not like."

"So, you have another child? Another daughter? Is she the reason why you abandoned our family? When..."

"We will talk when I get there! Don't start this shit now. We are already on our way. I was calling to tell you to expect me a little earlier than three; we should be there in a little over an hour." Rodney stated before I could finish my questioning.

"We? What do you mean by 'we'? I know you were not planning to pop-up with the little girl, Rodney! What is wrong with you?"

"Charisse, I am not about to argue about this. I'm trying to do things the right way... for us. I'll be there shortly." He said before hanging up.

As I placed the phone on its cradle, tears began to fall freely onto the pillow. My first thought was to pack up the kids and leave but I couldn't continue to run from the truth. Instead, I continued to lie in bed, assuming the answer to my unanswered questions. Damien woke shortly after the phone call, providing me with a distraction from the torment. I resumed regular morning activities while waiting for Rodney to arrive. Quinton and Imani were up and busy like any other Saturday. The boys, Jahlek and Bryan, were in uniform ready for karate class, Kai-Aja, equipped with gym bag and water bottle was snacking on a Pop Tart while she waited to be dropped off to her dance class. Naadira and Christian were at the kitchen table eating cereal. I put Damien in a booster seat beside Christian and fixed a bowl of cereal for him. Imani entered the kitchen, still in her housecoat and began rummaging through the refrigerator.

"What's up, sis?" She said, still searching the fridge.

"Good morning. What are you looking for?" I asked.

"Quinton wants a Vitamin Water. I told him we don't have any more but he's convinced he saw one last night. Do you see a damn Vitamin Water in here?" Imani asked as she held the refrigerator door wide open.

"Nope." I replied after thoroughly checking each shelf.

Imani opened the kitchen door then hollered, "Q, there are none left."

There was no response, only the sound of the front door closing and the chirping of the car alarm disarming. Imani slammed the refrigerator door and released an exasperated sigh.

Naadira looked up to her mother shortly before returning to her cereal.

"So, since Quinton is taking the kids, what are our plans for the day?" I asked, hoping to calm Imani and forget my rude awakening.

"Quinton said we are having a family meeting. He was on the phone late last night arguing with *your man* then woke up talking about a damn family meeting. I'm not in the mood for this today." She replied.

"That would explain the change in Rodney's schedule. What were they arguing about?"

"Reese, I have no idea. I think they were talking in riddles. Quinton obviously didn't want me to know."

I wanted to tell Imani what I knew. But the fact was I didn't know much. I could only assume that their disagreement had to do with Rodney's secret. Still, how would it affect Quinton and cause them to argue. Again my mind was having its own "Questions & Answer" session and my stomach was doing somersaults. The faint sounds of bare feet slapping on the wood floor heading towards the kitchen caught my attention. Before I could question Imani as to who it could be, Diamond walked through the kitchen door carrying a saucer and empty bottle of Vitamin Water.

"Good Morning." She said before yawning.

"D, did you take the last Vitamin Water?" Imani asked as Diamond deposited the plastic bottle in the recycle bin.

"No, I brought that one in with me." Diamond replied while washing her dish.

"Okay. Just wanted to know." Imani stated then collected both Christian and Naadira's empty bowls and brought them to the sink.

"Hey, Diamond. I didn't hear you come in. What time did you get in?" I asked.

"About three, I was waiting to see if my home girl was going to ride back with me but she made other plans last minute. So I wind up driving back by myself."

"Did you stop by your mother's yesterday?" Imani asked.

"No. I called when I got out there but she didn't answer so I went by Uncle John's house. Oh, Aunt Mia sent a bag of clothes for Naadira; most of the outfits still have tags. She said Amber is growing taller and shapely over night." Diamond giggled.

"I know. I spoke to them late last night. Mia said the doctor's wanted to put Amber on a diet. John wants to put Amber in the YMCA so she can be more active." Imani shrugged her shoulders and said, "Personally, I think Amber is fine the way she is. She has that Amazon build. She's not overweight just thick. When she gets old enough it will be sexy."

Diamond nodded in agreement. "We all suffer from the thick thighs and wide, round bottom. It's in our genes."

Diamond ran her hands over her prize assets and added, "And they look great in jeans."

We all laughed at Diamond's silliness. It actually was refreshing to have some laughter in a time of craziness.

"So, ladies, what is on our agenda for today?" Diamond asked, changing the subject.

"Quinton called a family meeting. For what? I have the slightest idea. But he said that everyone has to be here. That includes you, Miss Diamond. Rodney's on his way here as well." Imani stated as she started for the kitchen door.

Diamond's eyes widened, "What's the problem? Aunt Imani, is something going down with the family, again? I thought we were through with all the drama."

"There's always some drama in the Bank's & Wright's families." I added with a playful wave.

"Don't forget the Bennett's and Nettles' family." Charisse added with slight sarcasm.

Imani added in agreement, her favorite line, "You ain't ever lie."

We all laughed and continued about our morning routines.

Rodney arrived about two hours later. I looked past him trying to catch a peek of his surprise guest but his tinted windows shielded her. We didn't so much as say hello before the boys ran into his arms. Rodney showered them with hugs and kisses as if it had been years since the last time he had seen them. The look in his eyes as he admired them was as if he really was seeing them for the first time. His eyes sparkled as Damien played with his locks and Christian ran down a list of toys he saw on Nickelodeon. I continued to hold Alaire as I watched Rodney and realize that there was a change in him. His face displayed relief and his eyes beamed a new life. After a few more seconds with his sons, Rodney finally came to greet his baby girl and me. Rodney kissed her a hundred times before even looking my way. Obviously, I was on his shit- list. Rodney carried Alaire into the living room placed her in the playpen.

The boys were first to follow, then I shortly after. I continued to wonder about the mystery guest. Rodney turned on the television and instructed Christian and Damien to sit still until we returned.

"Reese, can we go outside for a minute?" He asked.

"Hold on. Let me ask Imani or Diamond to keep an eye on the kids."

Imani and Naadira were on their way into the family room so as they entered we left. I grabbed my coat then followed him out the door. Rodney and I stood out front and tried to find a way to ease into the conversation but there was no easy way so I jumped right in.

"Is your daughter in there?"

"Yes."

"How old is she?"

"Seventeen."

"Seventeen! How could you keep this from me? Did she pop-up recently or have you been lying to me and yourself for the past seven years?"

"I wasn't always apart of her life, Charisse. My own foolishness kept me away from her when she needed me most. I never lied to you. I never mentioned it. Reese, after you left I realized a lot of things. First, I realized that I missed you. I missed the kids and us feeling like a family. To be honest with you, it wasn't my intentions for things to turn out this way, with me abruptly entering her life but circumstances brought us together and I don't want to lose her or you again."

"Circumstances? Circumstances like what? What about her mother? Is her mother back in the picture, too?"

"Her mother made it clear that she and I weren't supposed to be together in the first place. She left me, Reese. In return, I neglected my child trying to pretend they didn't exist so I wouldn't have to deal with the truth."

"And what was the truth? She hurt you, didn't she? So you turn around to hurt me and our kids. How many times did I ask you to talk to me? Tell me what you been through so I can get to know you better. Instead you chose to treat me like I was your enemy. Now, too much time has passed and I have endured too much pain. It's really hard to forgive the Rodney I know."

"You're not giving me a chance, Charisse."

"I gave you too many chances, Rodney."

"So that's it. We're not going to talk. You never really wanted to work things out. You wanted me to beg."

"Don't turn this into something it isn't. Right now, I don't have the heart to do this. I'm going inside with our kids."

"Can I introduce you two first? She's been anxiously waiting to meet you and the kids. For years she has been trying to be a part of my life, a part of our lives but I continued to shun her away. I felt that as long as I made sure she was taken care of I did enough. Now I see that money can't replace time. I wasted years trying to build an empire when I should have been trying to build a family. Give her a chance, Charisse?"

I agreed by nodding my head but in my mind I was thinking, "Do I have a choice?"

Rodney jogged to the jeep and opened the passenger side door. Once the young woman stepped out of the jeep, my jealousy burned deeper. I studied her face searching for any resemblance to Rodney but there were none still it was obvious that he loved her as he held her hand with a light in his eyes.

"Charisse, this is Sharay. Sharay, this is my wife."

'Wife.' Where did that come from?' I thought as I continued to stand there feeling awkward and confused.

"Nice to finally meet you. I have heard so many good things about you." Sharay offered her hand. I hesitantly accepted.

"Thank you. I'm sorry I haven't really heard much about you but since we are here, we might as well spend some time getting to know each other better. Have you met your brothers and sister yet?" I asked as cordial as possible.

"Yes, I've seen the boys a couple of times when I stopped by Grandma's house. But I haven't seen the baby yet. Only in the pictures." She replied with a huge smile on her face.

Rodney's expression was a mix of confusion and happiness. Obviously, he wasn't aware of the fact that Sharay had met the kids.

"Let's go inside so we can properly introduce you to everyone."

"Is Diamond inside?" Sharay asked as she looked up to her father.

"You know Diamond?" I asked.

"Oh, she's my best friend? As a matter of fact, she's the person that introduced me and Bryan?" Sharay replied.

As we entered the house, my mind spun. *'This world is really small.'* I thought.

"So you have an interest in Bryan?" I continued to inquire hoping to gain as much information as possible trying to make some connections.

'Somewhere this has to make sense.'

Sharay quickly turned and said, "No way. Bryan and I are blood."

"We'll get into all the details later. Right now, let's enjoy the moment." Rodney interrupted as we entered the living room.

Imani stood and greeted Sharay in her normal matter, a huge hug, and kiss on the cheeks. Thoroughly aggravated and disgusted, I decided to leave everyone in the house to get better acquainted without me. I needed to breathe. Without saying another word, I gathered my keys and pocketbook, exited the house, jumped in my car, and headed for the highway.

CHAPTER 11

__IMANI__

After Charisse's car screeched off the block, it seemed as if time stood still.   No one spoke, moved, or even breathed.   Rodney immediately began trying to call her but was unsuccessful every time. Diamond suggested trying to follow her but we all knew she was long gone. The young woman that came in with Rodney stood there with a worried look across her face. Diamond put her arm around the young woman shoulder and said, "No stress, Sharay. Everything is going to be alright."

"You two know each other?" I asked.

"Auntie this is my girlfriend, Sharay.   Sharay, this is my aunt, Imani."

"So this is the friend that was supposed to come... hold up...Is this the same Sharay, Bryan's sister Sharay?" Finally, I was able to put the face to the name.

"One and the same." Diamond replied.

"Wait! Why is this not making sense to me?"

"Auntie, it's really a long story. Let's concentrate on finding Aunt Reese and then we'll straighten everything out." Diamond replied before I could get the answer I needed.

Rodney continued to try to reach Charisse while I thought about her possible whereabouts. Charisse was quick to go home to her parents but considering the circumstance I doubt that would be the first place on her mind. Plus, she would never go too far without her kids.

Almost two hours passed and we still hadn't heard from Charisse. Rodney and I must have searched all the nearest parks and the mall but she was nowhere to be found. It wasn't like Charisse to go longer than fifteen, maybe even twenty minutes without checking on her kids and never without letting someone know where she was heading.   The anxiety was beginning to show on Rodney as he continuously ran his hands through his locks.

"I tried calling her phone at least a hundred times already. She's not answering. She'll be back, give her a minute to collect herself. You are throwing a lot on her at once." I said as Rodney continued to pace in front of the living room window.

"I'm sorry. If I would have known I would cause so much trouble I would have stayed home." Sharay stood beside me as we both tried to calm Rodney.

"It's not your fault, Baby. I should have told her a long time ago. I should've told everyone. This isn't the end, it's only the beginning." Rodney replied.

He finally stopped pacing and took a seat on the loveseat.

The kids were in the dining room snacking on peanut butter and jelly sandwiches as Diamond supervised. The expression on Diamond's face when Charisse walked out the door and her impulsiveness to change subjects earlier let me know there was a whole lot more to this story.

"Rodney, you know I normally try not to get into your business but what could have possibly pushed Charisse overboard? Sharay, I'm sorry you have to be a part of this, Honey. But can someone please tell me what the hell is going on?"

Sharay looked over to Rodney then back at me before she began her story. "Well, you see, it's really a complicated situation."

"Sharay, go in the dining room with Diamond. I'll handle this." Rodney said.

"But Daddy..."

Daddy!

"Go on! I got this." Rodney demanded.

"That's your daughter? How? When?" I asked as my brain tried to compute the shocking information.

"Imani, it's really hard to explain. She is my daughter, not biologically though. Her mother and I use to date on and off in junior high and high school. Sandra always had her eyes on the money though. So when Bryan's business started taking over she went following behind him. Bryan had no intentions on making her his wife. He treated her as another one of his whores. I tried to get her back but after she started using drugs, I knew she was lost forever. After graduation she showed up at my door, really beat up and pregnant. She hurt me when she left but I still loved her."

Rodney's lost expression led me to believe there was a moment in his life where he allowed himself to be vulnerable and hurt. They say *'young love dies hard'* and I know this as true all so well. Fortunately, Quinton and I found our way through those trying years.

Rodney continued his story.

"I helped her get back on her feet but I never told anyone, not even Q. I kept her and Sharay hidden for years from the outside world but we were a family at home. When Sharay was about three, Sandra ran out on us and I was left to raise her alone. Back then Quinton and I were hustling hard so I couldn't really take care of her by myself and that's when I told my parents and sisters the whole situation and they helped me raise her until Bryan made Sandra take her away from me just before her tenth birthday." Rodney sat on the ledge of the bay window and kept his head hung low as he relived the most painful memories of his life.

"Did you know that Trina and Sandra were friends?" I asked with a sick feeling circling in my stomach.

"We all met at the same time. Q knew I was dating Dee-Dee, that's what they called her then. But he also knew she left. That's pretty much all he knew. When Trina left with Bryan I thought everything was forgotten and my secrets were safe. With Sandra and Trina out of the picture I thought we could move on and leave the past as that. When she took Sharay from me, my life seemed to collapse. So much happened that year, I snapped. I never meant for anyone to get hurt... I wanted my family back."

"Rodney, if I remember correctly you were never a one woman man, when the hell was you *in love* with this woman? This had to have been before I came into the picture. And why now? Why wait all these years to spring this on Reese? You know this is tearing her apart."

"That's not exactly true. After Sandra left me, I did my dirt but before then I was faithful to my woman like I was to Charisse when we first met. It seemed that the more Reese pressured me to get married, the more I was reminded of the last time I was truly committed to someone and how she shitted on me. I never meant to hurt her or anyone else that was involved. The coward in me forced me to run away and act as if they never existed but the memories replayed in my dreams, haunting me until fate and consequence brought me and Sandra face to face again." Rodney paused to regain strength.

"Yesterday I went to talk to her about the situation with Bryan Junior and then Sharay walked through the door and the years came rushing back. The last time I saw Sharay was at Bryan and Trina's funeral. We tried keeping in touch over the years. We spoke now and again but the pain of the past tore us apart. It's been years since I've seen her and I couldn't take another day not being with her, Imani. You got to understand." Rodney pleaded as if he were begging for his life.

"It's not for me to understand. You need to explain this to Charisse. When I thought the worst has taken its course, more drama finds its way into our lives. Did Sandra have anything to say about Bryan junior? Does she know anything about why his grandparents want to have custody?"

"That's for me and Quinton to discuss? Actually, that's the purpose for the meeting and the reason I brought Sharay with me. After I talk to Quinton and we straighten things out, we will let the family know. Listen, I need to find Reese. Do you think you can watch the kids? I have a pretty good feeling I know where she went."

"Yeah, I can handle the little ones. Go find Reese." I added before placing a gentle hand on his shoulder.

Rodney stood up with a new stance in life. The courage to accept the past and look forward to the future fueled him as he headed out the door in search of his love.

It never dawned on me that Rodney had so much drama in his life. But I guess that's the way he chose for everyone to see his life. His carefree life as the outside world saw it was a façade.

Shortly after Rodney left, Quinton returned with our kids. It slipped my mind that he hadn't returned after dropping them to class. I guess he needed to clear his mind before meeting with Rodney especially after dropping a bomb like that.

Quinton spoke briefly with Sharay after he introduced Kai-Aja and Jahlek. Kai-Aja and Jahlek did not act surprise when Quinton said, "Bryan's sister." Knowing my kids the way I do, Bryan had probably told them before he told Quinton. They were close like that, never any secrets.

Quinton greeted me with a kiss and an apologetic look in his eyes. We walked into the kitchen as he put away the groceries he brought in with him.

"I'm sorry about this morning. I had a lot on my mind and needed to release so I went to the gym until the kids were finished with class. I was going to call you but I left my cell phone in the office." Quinton held me in an embrace as he ran through his story.

He must have finally noticed the worried look on my face as he asked, "What's wrong?"

"Rodney showed up with Bryan's sister, whom I found out happens to also be his daughter. But before he could get to explain to Charisse, she picked up and left. It has been long but we can't reach her. Rodney left a few minutes ago to look for her again after he thoroughly explained the situation to me. At first, I had no idea that was Sharay; I thought it was one of his relatives until Diamond properly introduced us. I can't believe he hid this from you for so many years."

"So he told you too. He is the closest I have to a brother, Imani. I never imagined he had so many things going on and so much rage and vengeance bottled inside. It was only a matter of time before he erupted, I only wish his repercussions didn't hit so close to home. If he would have told me I'm sure we could have handled things differently. If I had known he had his own personal riff with Bryan I would have helped him keep a cool head. But instead he handled things his own way and now everyone's life has changed. I don't regret anything that has happened to us in the last six years but it could have all been different if Rodney hadn't interfered."

"Quinton, this had nothing to do with us and our family. Well, outside of the fact that it may be a little awkward to have Sharay and her mother in our lives but everything will work its way out. Once we fix this situation with Bryan's grandparents, everything will be okay."

"Imani, we would never have had to go through this had he not organized the hit on Bryan's father. If he had let things play out the way life ordered, we would not have this problem with Trina's parents. Eventually, Bryan's father and Trina would have fallen to the life they created. Instead, he snatched Bryan's father and those boys' mother from them in the worst way imaginable leaving us to clean up his mess. I love the boys, no doubt but I can guarantee Bryan would be a lot less defiant had he still had his parents or had they been separated differently. We already had Jahlek and I'm positive Bryan junior would have still been apart of our lives. Now the men that hit the house are after some money that supposedly only Bryan knows about. Not the money he got after his father died, a whole lot more than that. That's what all this shit is about. It's about money!"

"Rodney caused the fire. Oh my God, Quinton! Why? What the...what the hell was he thinking? So that's what that tramp is after. That's what Sandra is stirring up all this drama over. Does Sharay know about this money?"

"Don't know. But we will straighten out everything as soon as Rodney comes back. Imani, I am so sorry, Baby. I really tried to keep our family out of drama but it almost feels inevitable."

"Quinton, it's not your fault. We've done all we could to protect the kids, now it's time for us to be stronger than before for them and for Charisse. Do you think we should send the kids to Georgia with your Aunt Katherine for a while? Until we can get this taken care of." I paused for a moment to collect my thoughts before continuing.

"Are you and Rodney all right? I mean you don't have any hard feelings knowing now that he had a part in Trina's death."

"I don't know what to say about that right now. I mean this really has more to do with the boys, Bryan and Jahlek. We have to bury this deep. As far as sending the kids, we can send Kai, Jahlek, and Naadira but we have to keep Bryan close. Sharay and Bryan are the only ones that can help us finish this. I believe Sharay knows more than Rodney thinks. She's been adamant about keeping in contact with Bryan and he doesn't seem interested at all. Even if her intentions are harmless, she is after Bryan for something." Quinton said as he leaned against the fridge.

ഇ൝ഇ൝ᄗᄗᄗᄗ

<u>RODNEY</u>

It should not have been a surprise that Charisse would run to the one place no one would expect, church. No one thought of her as the religious, God-fearing woman she actually was. Charisse and I visited this church once Quinton first moved to Pennsylvania. We talked of having our wedding there. A promise that was well overdue to be fulfilled.

When I walked into the church I immediately spotted her in the first pew. Hesitantly, I approached her all the while contemplating what to say that would make her listen to me.

Before I was able to say a word, she held up her hand and said, "Not in His house. Please don't come to tell me anymore of your lies."

"Reese, you said you would give me a chance to explain. Please let me tell my side. I promise, Baby, no more lies. I'm ready to bare it all to you." I pleaded.

"After all these years you are finally ready. What happened? Did your daughter give you some morals? I've been by your side, Rodney. Why now? Why are you trying to break me down? What did I do for you to treat me this way?"

Tears ran freely from her eyes and my heart felt as if it were swelling with her hurt and disappointment.

I sat beside her in the pew and took one of her hands in mine. "Can we talk, Reese? Please I need this one chance to show you that I have changed. I've hurt so many people with my lies but none of them mean as much to me as you do. You are my wife, Charisse and I want to make this forever."

"It's too late, Rodney. You have finally taken me to a place I don't think I can come back from. If I sat here and told you that there was a chance, I would be lying to you and myself. Do you understand what I am saying?"

"Charisse, Sharay is not my biological daughter but she is my daughter nonetheless. And yes, Sharay is Bryan junior sister but there is so much more to this situation. It is a very long and complex story but if you let me, I will tell you everything and you will see that I was really trying to do the right thing. And if you feel like leaving me after, then so be it."

Charisse stared at me as if she were lost in decision so I began to take the trip down memory lane. With each ugly detail, her body language changed. But by the time I got to the part about having someone take care of Bryan, she turned her head.

"So, it was personal. You had Bryan killed because of jealousy, not business. How could you live with that all these years?" She asked as she placed her hand on my thigh.

"I tried to convince myself that it was all about the business, I told myself that since I hadn't done the actual robbery or set the fire that I had nothing to do with it."

"But you did. You told those men where to find him..."

"They already knew..."

"But you were the one that told them he was holding all the money in his house. How did you know about that anyway?"

"Sharay's mother told me. But when the guys hit the house they never found the money so I assumed it was another one of her lies. A few weeks ago, I ran into her and she only mentioned the money Bryan Junior received after his father died. She never mentioned this stash."

"So, where is the money?"

"According to the rumors, only Bryan Junior knows about it."

"And that's what this is all about? Does Sharay know anything about it?"

"I haven't asked her yet but that's part of the reason I brought her with me. With her and Bryan together we should be able to piece together the whole story. I was beginning to believe this is another one of her mother's ploys to get Bryan Junior's share of their father's money until I found out her daughters had money she won't touch. But, *this*..."

I said referring to our relationship. "...is not about her, Reese. This is about us. Do you understand now? I never lied to you; I wasn't sure how to tell you. Reese, I need you to help me get my life in order. Can you help me?"

Charisse waited several seconds before responding, "Let's work on repairing some of the things from your past and then we will try to work on us. I love you, Rodney. The kids need us to be a team. You have to be willing to be there for us and be ready to sacrifice your lifestyle."

"I'm ready to do that now. I love you and I can't risk losing you or my kids." I said determined to make her believe my sincerity.

Charisse leaned over and placed one of the sweetest kisses on my lips then said, "In all of our years together, I never heard you say 'I love you' until now."

I pulled her into me and held her tightly as the pressure in my chest began to lighten and I was able to breathe again.

"Let's go fix this mess." She said as she looked lovingly into my eyes.

When we got back to the house, all was quiet. Christian jumped from his seat and ran to meet us at the door. As if she knew it was us, Alaire began to wail at the top of her lungs. Quinton looked at me then rose from his seat and went into the kitchen. Sharay seemed to be the only one happy to see me. Charisse rubbed my back as she noticed the distress that masked my face. Quinton immediately returned to ask Kai-Aja and Jahlek to take Christian, Naadira, and Damien into the basement so we could speak freely. Meanwhile, Diamond took a seat between Bryan and Sharay. We gathered in the family room and the meeting began. Quinton started with the fact that the Knight's want full custody of Bryan Junior. Quinton stated that he was prepared to sign over the money to Mr. Knight and allow them weekend visitation but that was before they requested full custody.

Imani's jaw almost hit the floor.

"We never discussed visitation." Imani said as she looked at Quinton with a look to kill.

"He wants to meet them, Imani. We can't deny him that." Quinton retorted.

Sharay raised her hand and asked, "Can I say something?"

"Go ahead." Quinton replied.

"When I first started calling Bryan it was because my mother was so determined to keep me away from him and any one else related to our father and his past. One night I overheard her arguing with some man about some money. That is when *she* started calling about the money. But when you took too long to respond, she got the Knight's involved. She promised them his portion of the inheritance if they could get you to New York to help find the stash. She always knew there was a stash but never worried about it until recently. Until she found out that I knew about it. It's not my business, I know, but I don't feel that Bryan grandparents are interested in anything more than the money. Sorry, Bryan." Sharay looked to Bryan apologetically.

"I knew Sandra had something to do with them showing up. Sharay, do you know anything about this money?" I asked while praying she said no.

Sharay looked to Bryan who wore an expression of disappointment then to Quinton before replying, "We both do."

Bryan stood up and attempted to leave the room when Quinton demanded he sit beside him.

"I told you, I don't know what you are talking about. Bryan never told me about the money!" Bryan shouted.

"Calm down, Bryan." Imani said as she held his hand. "It's okay. You don't have to be afraid to talk to us."

"Mom, I don't know what she is talking about. She's lying. My grandparents want me because I am family and they love me not because of money that doesn't even exist." Bryan stated as he looked coldly at Sharay.

Sharay began to cry as she spoke. "Bryan, I hate being in this situation as much as you do but this man is threatening to kill my family and yours if he doesn't find the money. My mom has done everything she could to keep us out of it. Trust me. But he keeps finding her and now he won't leave us alone until he gets the money."

"What man, Sharay? Why didn't you tell me this before?" I asked.

Charisse sat beside Sharay and laid Sharay's head on her chest.

"I tried to tell you but Mommy said she don't want to get you involved. He was at the house the day you stopped by. I have been trying to tell Bryan hoping he would tell his parents but he wouldn't listen to me."

"Because you're lying!"

"No, I am not and you know it! Think about it Bryan. You don't want to remember but this is only going to get worse if you don't tell the truth." Sharay sobbed harder with each sentence.

Bryan looked to Quinton as he absorbed Sharay last comment.

"Bryan, is there something you need to tell me and your mom?" Quinton asked.

Bryan still didn't answer.

"Sharay, who is this guy? Do you know his name?" I asked.

"His name is Trey. Mom convinced him that I didn't know anything about the stash because I lived with you and never really got to know my father. But Trey knew Bryan lived there with his mother and our father."

Quinton and I looked at each other as we both recognized the name. It hurt to hear Sharay refer to Bryan as her father and Quinton's expression told the same story. No matter how true it was, we owned these children as our own and purged the fact that we didn't have the same blood.

"What do you know about the money?" Imani asked.

"Before our father died, he told me and Bryan where the money was and how to get it. He said in case he wasn't around when we got older; he wanted to make sure we were taken care of. He said he couldn't trust my mother or Trina. He gave me a charm bracelet with a gold locket, inside my locket is the combination."

Sharay held out her wrist and displayed the locket.

"Bryan has the address and the box number inside of a bear that our father gave him. My mother recently found out that Bryan and I knew where the money was when she overheard me telling Diamond."

Quinton again looked at Bryan who now had tears in his eyes. "Bryan, is that the same bear that's in your closet?"

Still, Bryan didn't answer.

"If this is true Bryan, please say something. Our families can be in real trouble if you don't tell us the truth." Imani said as she tried comforting him.

"Trina and Bryan took me to make that bear. It was the only time we ever spent time together as a family. When we got home, that's when he told me and Sharay about the money. After her mother came to get her, me and my mother was about to go to McDonald's when some guys came rushing in the house screaming and showing their guns." Bryan began to cry harder as the memories came back.

"My mom took me to the back door and told me to run to my grandma's house. She was supposed to meet me there. But she never came."

Quinton put his head in his hands as Bryan cried. Pain erupted inside my heart as the guilt filled my soul. I was responsible for tearing their lives apart. Bryan and Sharay will have to live with the pain forever because of my jealous actions.

Charisse noticed my expressions, took my hand, and then whispered, "It's not your fault. You didn't mean for it to happen that way."

"I'm not giving up the money, Dad. Bryan made me promise to take care of my family with it and I want to keep that promise. Not for him but for my mom, for Trina." Bryan said after wiping away his tears.

Quinton looked at me and his look said one thing, 'We got to handle this.'

"So, what are we going to do?" Charisse asked as she continued to comfort Sharay.

"First, we are going to continue as planned. We are going to New York on Wednesday and while we are there, we are signing over the bank money to the Knight's. Then Imani and I are sending the kids to the Georgia. Bryan, you are going too. Charisse, you, and your kids should to go to your mother's for a little while. I'm going to talk to Sandra and arrange to have her and her girls sent somewhere until we handle this. Seeing that it's Sharay and Bryan he is after, we have to make sure he can't find them. Then he'll come looking for us." Quinton stated.

Quinton looked to me then said, "We'll be waiting."

"No, we are not doing this again. You are putting our families at risk for dirty money. No! Quinton, this is not going to work!" Imani yelled.

"Imani, we might not have a choice." Charisse said.

"We have a choice. Bryan is giving up the money." Imani countered.

"Mom! I can't do that." Bryan stated.

"How much money is it? I want to know how much you are willing to lose your family for." Imani asked.

"It's about three million dollars, Mrs. Banks." Sharay answered.

"Listen, Imani. We all want to keep our families safe and I would rather give up the money than go through this but you have to understand this is about principle. He made a promise to Trina and Bryan." Quinton responded.

"Some promises are meant to be broken. This can't be the only answer." Imani said.

"Mom, the money is for everybody. For Sharay's family, Uncle Rodney's Family and ours." Bryan stated.

"Bryan, do you understand where that money came from? It is not worth it. I can care less about the money." Imani tried reasoning with Bryan but he was not giving in.

"Imani, let us handle it. Everything is going to be alright. You should know I would never let anything happen to our family." I interjected feeling even more guilt than I have experienced in my life.

The look on Imani and Charisse's face was full of worry and despair but it was a done deal. Quinton and I were going to handle this for the last time.

CHAPTER 12

QUINTON

Sharay called her mother to let her know she was in Pennsylvania and she was safe. She told her mother that she told us everything and that Rodney and I would handle the situation. Rodney took the phone when she was done and continued to assure Sandra that Trey would not harm her or her kids. Charisse was cool and had even asked to speak with Sandra. They spoke briefly, no harsh words. Only words of compassion and understanding. Sandra agreed to help us in taking care of Trey and his peoples and offered to ask the Knight's to cease their custody suit. Sandra cried over the phone as she thanked us for helping her.

Imani left us in the family room as she went into the kitchen to begin dinner. It was strange for Imani to cook on a Saturday but everyone knew she retreated to the kitchen as a way to cope with stress. Charisse followed behind to offer her help and comfort. Diamond and Sharay helped Kai and Jahlek with the younger kids in the basement. Bryan, Rodney, and I went for a walk down to the creek. I wanted to help Bryan understand what was happening and assure him that this would not cause us to love him any less.

Once we got to the creek, Bryan allowed the tears to flow as me and Rodney talked to him about accepting his past and using it as a step towards the future. Bryan understood that how his biological father acquired the money was wrong and how he treated Sandra, Sharay, and Trina was wrong as well. Bryan felt that the money would make everything right for everyone. He was concerned that something would happen to me and Rodney but I promised him that we would be alright.

"I understand that Bryan put you in a really awkward and painful position but believe me, your mom and me will do everything in our power to make sure you never have to go through anything like this again." I said.

"Dad, is Mom going to be angry with me?" Bryan asked.

"No. She may be a little angry with me but she understands how you feel and loves you too much to be upset. She doesn't want us to get hurt." I responded.

"B, you aren't doing anything that I'm sure me and your father wouldn't have done. You concentrate on school and ball. That's all you have to worry about." Rodney added.

"And sticking by your girl." I added remembering Sierra's tragic situation. "Remember, me and your mom always got your back. We are going to help you and Sharay get through this."

"Thanks Dad." Bryan said.

Later that evening, we returned to the house and were greeted with the aromas of good ole' soul food. Imani was putting the last dish on the dining room table as we hung our jackets. Charisse had a sleeping Alaire in her arms as the other children gathered around the table. I followed Imani into the kitchen for some alone time. She tried to avoid any contact with me for the first few minutes. Ultimately, I grabbed her arm and turned her towards me but before I could apologize or even try talking to her she started swinging.

"You don't give a shit about me or our family! Not everything can be settled by fighting or going to war, Q. Someone is going to get hurt. Haven't you learned already? Haven't we lost enough?" Imani hollered as I held her hands.

I motioned her to a kitchen chair for her to sit. I kneeled before her and attempted to comfort her but she swatted my hands away.

"Imani, please don't do this. We can handle this. Nothing is going to happen to Rodney or me. However, I need you to be in my corner or else I am not going to have the strength to do this. Now I know this is not your type of situation but Baby, I swear to you everything is going to be alright."

Imani used a paper towel to wipe her red nose then replied, "And how can you promise that, Quinton?"

"You have doubts in your man now, Imani?" I asked.

She sat quietly and searched my face for another option but found none and cried some more. I stood before her and retrieved another piece of paper towel. Allowing me to hold her, she laid her head on my chest and released her fears.

Charisse and Rodney entered the kitchen. Charisse tried to calm Imani but her efforts were futile.

"Listen, Imani. I stand to lose as much as you do but now is not the time to lose faith. What happened to Q's 'ride or die' chick?" Charisse joked.

Imani let out a small laugh and the tears stopped. "I was never his ride or die chick."

"But you always had his back." Charisse said. "I got my man's back. What are you going to do? Are you going to sit here and make yourself sick or are you going to be strong for your husband?"

Charisse was a tougher breed of a woman than Imani was. Rodney admired the fighter in Charisse. If Charisse could, she would follow behind Rodney packing heat and all.

"Trey isn't stupid, Imani. He knows your man is serious. He'll probably change his song when he realizes who he's fucking with." Rodney added.

Imani looked up to me and the clouds of hurt slowly began to dissipate.

"It would have been so much easier if I hadn't known any of this." Imani stated before rising from her seat.

"Then we would be lying to each other. This relationship isn't built like that." I added.

Imani wrapped her arms around me and whispered, "You know I always got your back."

Love couldn't explain how I felt for Imani. She was so much more than words and holding her moved something inside me.

"Let's go eat." Rodney announced as he exited the kitchen grabbing Charisse by the waist.

The night crept upon us as the house became full with laughter and fun. Bryan thought it would be a good time to pull out homemade movies and he was right on target. We laughed until our stomachs hurt as we watched Imani going into labor, Kai-Aja's dance recital, and many more recorded memories. I think the one that brought tears was when I caught two-year old Naadira using lotion to paint Kai-Aja's face while she was sleeping then tried to hide the bottle when she realized I was watching. Our family had been through the best and the worst of times together and nothing, not even the drama which lie ahead could break our bond.

Charisse was one of the first to fall asleep then Imani shortly after. Rodney and I got the kids ready for bed as Sharay, Diamond and Bryan got dressed to go riding around. There wasn't much to do in our area after midnight so they must have been heading to Imani's nephew, Steve's house. From where we lived, it was only about thirty minutes away with no traffic. After Rodney and I put the kids to bed we sat in the basement, had a couple of beers, and formulated our plan. Rodney and I decided to use our connects to get Trey before he got to us. Rodney knew his enemies and his base for business. We just had to make sure he was in the right place at the right time.

The next morning, Rodney and Charisse packed up and headed back to New York. Sharay stayed behind with Diamond. Imani was in the office editing her manuscript which was due to be published by Christmas. Meanwhile, Naadira, Kai-Aja and Jahlek were on their usual Sunday morning chores. Bryan left early that morning to get Sierra and her son.

"Dad!" Bryan called from the front door.

"In the kitchen." I replied as I unloaded the dishwasher.

Bryan ran into the kitchen with Sierra in tow. Her eyes were red and swollen as if she had been crying.

"Is everything okay?" I asked.

"He's here, Mr. Banks." She cried.

Immediately, I knew she was referring to her father. "Did he try contacting you?"

"He was at her house when I got there. He was waiting at the front door like he was a friend. When he saw me he tried to act like he was ringing the bell. I knocked on the door and when someone came to the door he ran." Bryan stated.

"Okay, well let me call some people and we are going to get you another order of protection and maybe even some security. Calm down. Everything is going to be alright." I said as I held Sierra's shaking hands.

We went into the family room where her sister and son were waiting and I began making calls. I called an old affiliate, Shawn and asked him if he and his men would mind doing me a favor. Within minutes three diesel-wrestler-type men showed up at my door. I introduced them to Sierra and briefly described the situation and they agreed to help. Next, I called the police, told them the situation and immediately they notified Detective Michael Liggins, another one of my partners.

When Mike arrived he began gathering information to put out an APB.

"What's his full name?"

"Tremell Isaiah Storms." Sierra replied.

"Does he go by any alias or nickname?"

"His friend used to call him Storm but most people called him Trey."

"About how old would you say Mr. Storms is?"

"He should be about forty."

"Could you give me a description of Mr. Storms? Does he have any distinct marks, scars, or tattoo?"

"He is about five foot ten, umm; he is fair skin like me with reddish brown hair. He had braids last time I seen him, two piercing in his left ear and he has a tattoo on his right hand. It's a lighting bolt."

Alarms began to blare inside me head. The same man she described was the same man Rodney and I were after. The world was very small.

"He didn't have any braids when I saw him today." Bryan added.

"Did you get a close look at him?" Mike asked Bryan.

"Yeah, he was standing right next to me for like two minutes before I knocked on the door. At first he didn't even look my way but after I knocked and said my name he stared at me until someone came to the door then he ran." Bryan replied.

"Alright, thank you both for your cooperation." Mike said as he closed his pad. "Q, let me talk to you a second."

Mike and I walked into the dining room. Sitting at the table, Mike began to run down a list of things he has to do before he was able to get the order of protection.

"I'm going to run a check on this guy and see if he has any priors and last known addresses. I want to put an order against him for Bryan too since this guy got a good look at him, to be on the safe side. You know me and the boys don't respond well to sexual offenders so when we catch him..."

I interrupted, "It's going to be ugly."

Mike nodded his head in agreement. Meanwhile, I was thinking that this was too close to home. *'I have to get them out of here.'* I thought.

"Quinton, what's on your mind man? You look like something is up."

"Nah, concerned for Sierra. That's all."

"Well, don't stress yourself. We're going to take care of this guy." Mike stated before gesturing for a handshake.

We shook hands then I showed him to the door.

"Tell Mrs. Banks I said hello."

"Will do, Mike. Thanks."

"I'll give you a call later on tonight." He said before getting in his car and backing out the driveway.

Sharay was standing in the doorway of the basement staring in my direction. The faint sounds of *Floetry* played in the background. When I finally made eye contact she asked, "Is everything okay?"

"Yeah. Everything is fine. Feel free to make yourself something for breakfast. Bryan is in the living room with his girlfriend and her sister, if you want to meet her." I replied.

"No. I'm cool. Is Mrs. Banks awake?" She asked.

"She should be in the office. Why? If you need anything you can ask me, Bryan or Diamond."

"Oh, I don't need anything. I wanted to apologize for bringing problems into your home."

"It wasn't your fault. As a matter of fact, if you wouldn't have come we would still be in the dark about a lot of things." I said.

"When all of this is over, I hope your mom will continue to allow you and Bryan to keep in contact. Maybe he can even meet the little one. What's your sister's name?"

"Jasmine. She wanted to come with me but my mom didn't even know I was coming out here. Next time I visit, I'll bring her." Sharay smiled then returned to the basement.

When I was sure she was out of earshot, I called Rodney and gave him the update.

"Are you serious?" He asked.

"That's the same thing I was thinking."

"Alright, let me drop by Charisse's house real quick, go by my crib to change my clothes, see what's the word in the 'hood and I'll be on my way back out there."

"I got to get Imani and the kids out of here by morning. I don't want the kids around if this dude decides to come looking for Bryan. Give me a holla' when you're on your way."

Rodney agreed then we disconnected.

ଞଠଞଠଞଠଓଓଓ

CHARISSE

The boys were playing in their room while I fixed lunch. I ran a mental note of all the phone calls I had to make first thing in the morning before going to my parent's house for the week. My agent left three messages on our home voicemail. Each message was marked urgent. Sunday was my down day so all business had to be postponed until Monday. Plus, I still hadn't found a way to tell him that once again I had to cancel. He told me that modeling with kids was not going to work but I had to pay the bills somehow and modeling was all I knew. Money was definitely looking stretched since Rodney swore he was going to stop hustling. Which was still hard to believe but there was something in his eyes that said he really wanted to make things work.

My heart was all for a reunion but my mind thought better.

Rodney was due to come by and spend time with me and the kids, something we all looked forward to. Honestly, I missed him even with all his bullshit. Still, I wasn't about to jump back into an unhealthy relationship. We agreed to take things one day at a time. Maybe the distance will help heal old wounds and move us into the right direction.

The doorbell rang and Christian quickly ran to see who it was. He looked out the window, ran to the front door and began to jump in excitement.

"Mommy, Daddy's here."

"Okay, I'm coming, Sweetie." I replied as I turned down the heat under the pot of beef stew.

Alaire was in her walker watching everyone moving about around her. Myra wasn't due back until Tuesday, which was a blessing. Although she had been extremely helpful and generous, her jealousy was beginning to work me.

'Prayerfully, it would only be a matter of time before she has this house to herself again.' I thought as I opened the door to find an extra fine Rodney standing on the other side.

He wore a black leather jacket that I could swear made his broad shoulders stand out. His locks were in a bun and his face was freshly shaven. When Rodney entered, he slipped his arm around my waist, drew me nearer to him, and greeted me with a passionate kiss. Like a scene from a movie. Christian and Damien watched and giggled. He took off his jacket and hung it in the hall closet as I went back to check on the food. The biscuits were turning a golden brown and the stew's aroma filled the kitchen. It was Rodney favorite meal.

His heavy footsteps against the wooden floors were an unfamiliar sound in this house but welcomed all the same. The boys continued to run around as Alaire babbled and cooed along in enjoyment. Rodney entered the kitchen staring at me as if he was seeing me for the first time.

"Can I help you?" I teased.

Rodney stepped behind me and kissed the nape of my neck. In that moment it felt as if my body went limp. I tried to act as if he didn't have any effect on me but my body told a different story as rhythmic beat began between my legs and a fire spread throughout my body. He wrapped his arms around my stomach, holding close and very tight.

"You smell good." He said as he kissed the sweet spot behind my ear.

"It's the stew." I joked.

Rodney pressed his rock hard penis into my behind and I knew food was the last thing on his mind.

"Why don't we have lunch? Then we can put the kids down for a nap and share some quiet time together." I offered as I became lost in his touch.

"Do you know how long I've waited to hold you like this? These past two weeks have felt like years." Rodney replied.

"The longer we take to feed our kids, the longer it will be before you get to sample desert."

I turned to look in Rodney's eyes and see the man that I fell in love with nearly seven years before. Rodney kissed the tip of my nose and ran his hand over my hair.

We fed the kids and put them to sleep in my bed. Christian was resistant but after Rodney bribed him with a new remote control car, he fell right to sleep.

Rodney and I went into the living room and sat on the futon, snuggled and watched television. Lunch had caused both of us to feel tired but didn't dull Rodney's urge to be intimate. I decided to change into something more comfortable while he reclined the futon into a bed. Toni Braxton's *Tell Me* played on repeat and a bottle of J. Rogét sparkling wine sat in an ice bucket. When I returned he was stripped down to a pair of black silk boxers and me in a red lace thong with a matching red lace corset with satin trim accessorized with four-inch pumps and handcuffs. We closed the curtain that hung in the entryway, shielding us from our children and began making up for lost time.

Rodney took his time kissing and caressing every inch of my body. His kisses caused my body to tingle in ways I never experienced. After removing my pumps he massaged my feet before sucking my toes. My body craved to have him inside of me but he took his time as he made love to every inch of my body. Rodney spoke in a low husky tone, describing his love for me and his promises for tomorrow. He trailed butterfly kisses from my foot, up my leg, inside my thigh until he hit my spot. I threw my head back in delight as he parted my lips with his fingers and began to feast as if he hadn't eaten in years. Ravenous yet sexual. Once I released, Rodney turned me around, undid my corset, and trailed small kisses up my spine.

"Rodney, baby. Please..."

"Shhh. Don't tell me how to do this!" He demanded.

He entered me from behind as he switched between his thumb and his forefinger to play with my asshole. I was a feign for anal sex and he knew how to tease me. Once he felt I was juiced up he pulled his finger out and easily inserted his thick penis. At first the shock caused me to jerk but once we got into the groove, it was on. Rodney's thrusts became more powerful as he neared his on climax. He withdrew his penis and allowed the cum to drip onto my back. One session wasn't enough for him. We found different positions as we satisfied each other repeatedly. When we thought we had enough, we showered and then sexed like high school kids in the shower. After hours of hardcore loving, Rodney and I laid on the futon and found sleep, him in a wife-beater and boxers and me in a black satin robe.

The loud sound of keys clashing against the hard wood floors startled me out of my sleep. Myra stood at the entryway with the curtain pulled back and her mouth wide open. Instinctively I took the throw from the single seat and covered Rodney, *like she would be interested*, and then ushered her out of the living room.

"What are you doing here?" I asked as I tightened the belt on my robe.

"I live here. What is he doing here?" She countered.

"He's visiting. Is there a problem?"

"You think? What the fuck is going on, Reese? I thought you two were over."

"We are trying to work things out."

"Well, you and Rodney are going to have to work things out

somewhere else."

"What the fuck do you mean *somewhere else*? I live here, too. If I choose to have company that is my business."

Myra didn't listen to anything I had to say. She put up her hand and walked off. I followed her into the bathroom.

"He has to go!" She hollered as if she were trying to wake everyone in the house.

I pressed my finger against my lips signaling for her to be quiet then whispered, "Wait a minute, Myra. He's my kid's father, if nothing else and he has the right to visit when he pleases."

"He is not welcome in *my* motherfucking house, Reese! He has to go!"

"Let's get this straight, *Myra*. Technically, this is *my motherfucking house*. You are renting. Now I understand you may feel a little disrespected and I apologize but as long as I live here he is going to come by."

"I love you, Reese. How are you going to let him come between us like that?" Myra pleaded.

"Myra, there is no us. I am in love with, Rodney. I'm sorry if you got the wrong impression but there will never be anything between *you and me* again."

"Well, then I think you and your kids need to move. Go back to your fucked up man and let him continue to ruin your fucking life."

"Like I said before, Myra. This is my damn apartment and if anyone is going to leave, it will be you. Now, you can sit back and fucking relax, or start packing your shit. I'm going to get dressed and then I, *my man,* and my kids are going to spend the rest of the day lounging in *this* house."

Myra stormed out of the bathroom, picked up her keys and marched out of the house. The front door slammed behind her waking the kids and Rodney. Anger and embarrassment both filled my head as my nosey upstairs neighbors looked out their window.

'*I should have bought that apartment too when they offered. Then I wouldn't have to deal with assholes in my business.*' I thought as I locked the front door to my apartment.

Rodney jumped from the bed and grabbed his jeans, where I am sure he was hiding his piece. He never left home without it.

"Reese!" He yelled.

I opened the curtains then replied, "Yeah, Baby."

"What the fuck was that noise?"

I didn't know whether to lie or tell the truth so I simply replied, "Myra."

He shook his head then continued to get dressed. I attended to Alaire who was now screaming at the top of her lungs and sent Christian and Damien into the living room with their father. After calming our baby girl, I got dressed in my usual jeans and fitted shirt, pulled my hair up into a bun and joined the rest of my family in the living room.

"Reese, I think you need to move back into the house." Rodney said as soon as I entered the room.

"Not right now, Rodney. We just started working things out. I know *this* is a bit of an awkward situation but it's better for both of us to take things slow remember. You still got a lot of business to handle." I placed Alaire in his arms then put the television on for the boys.

"I don't like this at all, Reese."

"Well, how about this? Since me and the kids are going to go to my parents for a few days when I get back, if you got yourself together, we will come back home."

I felt an attitude erupting and I did not want to ruin our perfect day so I tried to calm down.

"How long is a few days?" He asked.

"Well you know me and the kids always spend Thanksgiving with my parents so we will be gone the rest of the week. I was planning on leaving probably tomorrow night. Is that good?" I replied.

Rodney was hesitant to answer. He looked at me with disbelief. "Like that you're going to move back in?"

"Just like that. And then we can work on making me *Mrs.* Rodney Bennett."

A slow smile crossed his face then he replied, "This is going to be our last holiday separated. You hear me?"

I approved with a kiss.

Rodney and I watched Sponge Bob with the kids for a while before his cell phone began to ring. He answered the call but made it short. Then he looked at me and I knew that our day was done.

"Reese, that was Q again. He called me earlier and had some shit going down so I told him that I was going back out to Pennsylvania tonight. I know I promised you we were going to spend the day together but you know the situation. I got to see some people on the block before I head out there. Ma, you know if it were under different circumstances I would put it to the side." He explained as he began to collect his things.

"You don't have to explain. I understand. Please make sure you call and let me know what's going on. Let me know you're okay." I said.

He hugged and kissed the kids before he walked to the hall closet to get his jacket. I followed with Alaire in my arms.

"What time are you leaving to go to your parents?" He asked.

"I was thinking to be on the road by five in the evening."

"Call me." He said.

We shared another lustful kiss before he smacked my behind then headed down the steps. I stood at the door until he got in his car then closed the door and joined the boys in the living room.

Myra returned two hours later with more attitude than before. She had her sister, Maggie with her and two frail, hungry looking dudes. Maggie kept staring at me from the corner of her eyes as Myra collected some of her things, destroying the house as she went along. I put Alaire in her walker and instructed Christian to watch her and Damien while I helped *Aunt Myra*. As I approached the bedroom, Maggie stood in front of me and began riffing.

"You know this is real messed up, Reese. How you going to dog her like this?"

"Mind your business, Maggie. Me and Myra had a misunderstanding and need some space."

"I told her to leave your trifling ass alone a long time ago. Thank God she kept her apartment since you don't give a damn about putting her out in the dead of winter."

"If she had her own apartment, why the fuck is she still here?"

Myra ran out of the room and into my face, "Isn't it obvious? I wanted to be with you, Reese. All these years I waited, knowing that one day you would come back and this is how you repay me."

"Are you serious? Myra we spoke about this. I told you years ago I moved on. You..."

"And every time I spoke to you, you talked about leaving him and how you wished you never met him." She cut me off before I could continue.

"But it is what it is, Myra. Rodney will always be here and I will always love him. Believe me, Myra, I never meant for things to work out this way."

"Then why can't we work things out. Why can't you be with me? Reese, I can help you raise the kids and we can be a family."

"Come on, Myra. Don't beg her for shit. She's not worth it!" Maggie shouted.

"Watch your mouth! Don't get fucked up in front of company." I retorted.

One of the two guys finally spoke up and said, "Myra, get your stuff and let's go."

Myra looked at me one last time, her eyes begging for acceptance but instead I turned my head away. Maggie picked up two of the four bags that were at the front door and began down the steps as the two men picked up little things Myra had instructed them to collect.

"I'll be back Tuesday to pick up the rest of my things." Myra said as she stood by the door. "Hopefully by then you'll have a change of heart. Charisse, I promise you I will take care of everything if you let me."

"Okay." I said and with that she was gone.

'I am so glad I won't be here on Tuesday.' I thought.

I knew deep down in my heart that her words were pure. If I let her, Myra would make sure I would never want for anything again. But it would only be a matter of time before my thirst for Rodney returned. There was no way for her to handle that need. It was an untamable thirst that no one but Rodney could quench and I loved it.

CHAPTER 13

IMANI

Naadira crept into my room and climbed in my bed while her brothers and sisters were finishing their chores. It was time for her nap and time for me to spend some time with my family. All morning long, I had been up and down between the office and my bed trying to find a comfortable place to work.

"Naadi, where's daddy?" I asked as I removed my papers from the bed.

"He's downstairs talking to Bryan and the girl?"

"Who? Sharay?"

"No, the other one. The one that was with them when Bryan got the earring." She replied.

"Sierra?"

After I cleared a space, Naadira got underneath the blankets and puckered her lips for a kiss.

"Yeah." Naadira replied then laid her head on the pillow and was sleep within a wink of an eye.

Quinton walked into the bedroom as I prepared to get in the shower. He was still in his favorite Bobcats jersey and matching shorts, his leisure wear as he called it.

"Hey, I was coming upstairs to see if you wanted anything?" He said.

"No, I'm fine. Naadi told me we have company so I'm going to go show my face and find something for dinner."

"Before you go down, we need to talk."

"Quinton, I am really not in the mood for any more talking. Whatever it is, give it to me flat out."

"Remember when I told you Bryan picked up Sierra and her nephew the other day. It's not her nephew, it's her son."

"Her son! Then why did she lie. I'm going downstairs to have a talk with her and Bryan. I hope she don't think Bryan is going to play daddy. They are too young...he is too young for that type of relationship, Q."

"Imani, you might want to relax before you jump down her throat." Quinton wasted no time getting to the point. "She was raped...by her father. You know how we always say it's a small world, her father is Trey, and he saw Bryan this morning at her house."

I cleared a space on the chest and sat down while I digested the information.

Quinton continued, "I already called some people to watch over her and Mike has the information for his boys at the precinct but I don't feel safe with you and the kids here. This man is in our neighborhood. So I made arrangements for you and the kids to leave first thing in the morning."

"And where are we supposed to go, Q? This is unreal!" I shouted.

"I'm going to take you and the kids down to the airport in the morning. I spoke to my aunt and she can't wait to see you and the kids."

"Quinton, I am not going to Atlanta! Are you out of your mind?"

"Do you have some where else in mind?" He asked sarcastically. "Kai and Jahlek have already started packing. I told them we were going on vacation and I am going to meet y'all down there."

"This ain't no damn vacation! Enough is enough already, Q. The kids are missing school and on top of that we're lying to our kids. What about Thanksgiving? We are going to spend our holiday on the run. I feel like we are under some witness protection program."

"Imani, we are not about to go through this today. Our safety should be your first priority. The kids can make up the lessons. Their break starts Wednesday anyway." He countered.

"You know what, Quinton. You are right." I cynically complied.

It was effortless to continue arguing therefore I surrendered. Quinton went to the closet and pulled out both of our suitcases. My mind wasn't set on packing right away so I continued into the bathroom to freshen up. After a quick shower, I felt more relaxed.

By the time I exited the bathroom, Quinton had finished packing his suitcase. He stood by the dresser acting as if he was searching for something but I knew he was waiting for a way to ease into a conversation. My heart went out to Quinton even though I didn't agree with what was going on, I knew it was in his best intentions for me and our family.

'Get yourself together, Imani. Your husband needs you.' I thought.

Confused emotions caused me to pace back and forth between the closet and my suitcase that lie on my bed. With each trip, I returned empty handed as I continued to move about the room as if I were absent-minded, attempting to pack my bag. Quinton turned away from the dresser as I turned away from the closet and we silently stood face to face, still like a photograph.

Quinton's hands said what his mouth couldn't as he grabbed my shoulders and brought me close to him, smothering me with his love and in return I offered understanding. He gently kissed the top of my head then ventured down and covered my lips with the sweet taste of his lips. The tension put us in the mood for some passionate, stress-relieving sex but our baby occupied our space. With both of our minds filled with thoughts of tempting, tasting and touching each other, Quinton decided to take Naadira to her bed as I lit vanilla and jasmine scented candles. By the time he returned, I was on my knees in the center of the bed, wearing a sheer black baby doll and thong, using my forefinger to call him to me. Quinton locked the door behind him and waited there momentarily as he let his imagination run wild. A sly smirk crept across his face as he slowly strolled towards the bed. He offered his hand, I accepted and he gently pulled me to him and continued to intoxicate me with his kisses. Impatiently I began to tug at the drawstring to his shorts but he pushed my hands away.

"Don't rush me!" He ordered then slowly removed his jersey.

Quinton's taut muscles and smooth chocolate skin enticed me. I ran my hands over his muscular pecks then over his ripped abdomen fighting the urge to tear off his shorts and taste him. He turned his finger in a circular motion instructing me to turn around. I complied. Quinton didn't know how much he was turning me on. It was so bad that I knew as soon as he stuck his penis inside, I would explode. I was on my hands and knees waiting for what was too come as I felt his hands caressing my ass then removing my thong. He pushed the sheer material of my lingerie around my shoulders and told me to take it off. As I removed the thin material, a warm liquid dripped onto my back. The bottle of strawberry flavored massage lotion dropped beside me then his strong hands spread lotion all over my back and even on my bottom. Using his tongue, he trailed down my spine until he reached the crack of my ass. He slapped each cheek and watched it jiggle before spreading them wide, kissing his way down to my sweet spot and began to sample my honey. He wet his finger with my juices then played with my clit as he continued to eat until I reached an ultimate orgasm. My body and mind went weak, simultaneously.

"Are you ready?" He asked as I lay on my back, staring at him as he stood at the edge of the bed.

"Baby, you know I am ready for whatever." I replied, breathlessly.

"That's what I'm talking about." He replied then removed his shorts and revealed his rock-hard penis.

"Now, that's what *I'm* talking about!" I exclaimed as he climbed onto the bed and began to position my legs around his neck.

I tried to keep my moans and cries under control but when the loving was that good, it was useless. Quinton grabbed the remote and turned on his stereo set and the serenading sounds of Mariah Carey came pouring out. Tears of joy, streamed down my cheeks as we switched positions over and over until ecstasy left us sweaty and breathless. I lay on top of Quinton's sweated chest and played in his tangled curls as we both tried to catch our breath.

About a half hour later, I headed to the shower again. The warm beads of water massaged my body while the chamomile and lavender body wash relaxed me. The faint sounds of a ringing phone cut into my tranquil moment. The sound was then replaced with Quinton's heavy voice. I spent a few more seconds in the shower before I turned off the water and stepped out. After drying off, I wrapped my towel around me and exited the bathroom. Quinton was sitting on the edge of the bed, deeply engrossed in his conversation. As I got closer, Quinton looked up to me then switched the phone to speaker.

"According to our records, he jumped bail and been on the run for the last year. Still no leads on where he could be hiding but we're still working on it. I have a feeling he won't be going back to New York though. Something's telling me he's going to stay close." Mike stated.

Quinton shook his head then said, "I got the same feeling."

"Q, listen, Man. Don't worry about Sierra. I got a patrol car circling her block now and we are going to have an unmarked sitting close by at night."

"Thanks, Mike." Quinton replied before ending the conversation.

There was nothing for me to say at that moment, so I placed my hand on top of his and waited for the moment to pass.

"I'm going to finish packing then I'll go check on the kids. Why don't you take a shower and try to relax?" I offered hoping it would help.

Quinton waited a few seconds before he replied, "Thanks, Baby."

Quinton rose from the bed and headed for the bathroom while I began to massage my body with baby oil. As I put on my jeans, a loud crashing sound came from downstairs followed by the sound of screeching tires. I hurried into my top and rushed down the stairs to see what was going on. Bryan met me at the bottom of the steps holding a brick with something scribbled on it. After turning it several times, trying to decrypt the hand writing I finally manage to read the message. *'Gotcha, motherfucker.'*

The house was full of detectives and police officers as the kids and I loaded our suitcases into the back of the van. Bryan looked scared and confused, I prayed for him more than I prayed for anything or anyone. There was no disguising the fact that I was shaken to the core as I rubbed my stomach which began to feel queasy due to stress and nervousness. Thankfully, no one was hurt considering Sierra, Bryan, her sister and her son were sitting right beneath the window. Sierra's grandparents came over as soon as I called. Quinton and I wanted to update them on the situation. We suggested that they let Sierra, her sister and son go to Georgia with us and they agreed. Rodney pulled up to the front of the house as the last police car rode away. He jogged from his car to the front door as Quinton and Mike stood on the porch talking. He waved acknowledging me and Kai, who stood beside me, then engaged in conversation.

Although it was turning five o'clock, the sky was dark. The kids I was sure were starving, I knew I was and since we had company, I figured it was time to start dinner. Naadira was coming down the stairs as I walked into the kitchen and the men from the window company had walked through the door. She looked at them with a raised eyebrow then turned to look to her brothers and sister. Naadira wasn't much for socialization when she woke up, so she continued into the kitchen with me. Sierra's grandmother, Mrs. Kelley, came into the kitchen to offer her help. You know I never turned away extra hands so I passed her an extra apron asked for any ideas, and then we went to work.

Bryan asked if it was alright for everyone to go into the basement to watch television since the men were in the living room and it was still really cold on the first level. Mr. Kelley did not mind hanging with the kids while they played in the basement. I assumed Diamond and Sharay left while Quinton and I were upstairs because the basement was empty. I prayed it was clean.

In less than two hours, Mrs. Kelley and I had fixed enough to feed an army, which was exactly what we had. Once Quinton and Rodney finished cleaning the shattered glass pieces, everyone was called into the dining room for dinner. Diamond walked through the door in time to join us. The thirteen of us could not fit at the dining room table so after everyone fixed their plates, the teens went into the kitchen taking Sierra's son with them. Diamond stayed with the adults and helped Naadira and Sierra's sister, Jessie with their plates. Quinton sat at the head of the table, Rodney and I sitting at his sides. Mr. and Mrs. Kelley sat opposite each other, Mrs. Kelley sat beside me, and Mr. Kelley sat beside Rodney.

The food kept everyone busy so there was no room for talk but as bellies got full conversation eased its way in. Despite the reason that brought us together, we laughed and joked until we were tired. Quinton instructed our troop to clean up and put the food away and Mr. Kelley volunteered Sierra to help them. He took his sleeping great-grandson in his arms and carried him into the family room where we continued to enjoy the rest of our night. As it neared midnight, we began to say our good-byes.

"Kai-Aja and Naadira hit the shower." I hollered as they ascended the steps. "Bryan, Jahlek. That means you too."

"About what time are you leaving in the morning?" Mrs. Kelley asked as she put on her long black wool coat.

"We will probably leave here about five. So if you want, we can pick them up on the way to the station." I offered.

"No, that's okay. We'll meet you there. I want to see y'all off." She replied.

"I understand. So, we'll meet about a quarter to six then."

"That's good." Mr. Kelley added before kissing my cheek and then shaking Quinton's hand. "Thanks again, Quinton."

"Its fine, Mr. Kelley. I only wish we could have met under better conditions." Quinton stated.

"Me too." Mr. Kelley agreed.

"Good night, Rodney." Mr. Kelley said as he escorted his wife out the door.

"Good night, Mr. and Mrs. Kelley." He returned.

We watched until they backed out of the driveway. Quinton shut the door and put on all the locks. Rodney checked the windows, the back door, and then his gun. My stomach dropped as he put it back in the waistband of his pants.

"I'm going to ride with y'all down to the airport in the morning." Rodney said as Quinton and I began to ascend the stairs.

"Why don't you stay here with Diamond? She normally would leave about eight. Then we can go down to my office and do some of our own work, you know." Quinton suggestively responded.

"Got it. Alright. Good night, y'all." Rodney said before heading to the guest bedroom.

Quinton took my hand and led me to the bedroom. It took everything in me to stay calm but I managed to find sleep without uttering a word of concern or worry. Solely an 'I love you.'

১৩১৩১৩৫৩৫৩৫৩

<u>RODNEY</u>

"Quinton! Behind you!"

Sweating poured down my face as I jumped out of my sleep for the fifth time. All night the same nightmare played repeatedly. Each time I stood by and watched as Trey shot Quinton in the back. It was if I was trapped in a shatter and soundproof plastic room watching as everything went on around me.

When I checked the time, it was after seven. I couldn't believe I slept through everyone moving about the house. I looked at my cell phone and saw that I had two missed calls. One of them was Charisse and the other was a private number. I checked my messages then returned Charisse's call.

"Good morning." She said in a soft whisper.

"Hey, Mama. What's up?" I asked.

"I was calling to let you know that Sharay is here with me. She and Diamond stopped by yesterday then I got a call from Sandra asking if Sharay could stay here for a few days."

"What? How did she get your number? What's going on? Let me speak to Sharay. Is she up yet?"

"I gave Sharay my number yesterday and I guess she told her mother. She's still sleep, though. Rodney, I don't mind. She is a good kid. We sat up last night and talked until one this morning. She's good company."

"Did Sandra say why?" I asked as I loosened the band that held my locks and allowed them to drop freely. "What did she say to you?"

"Does it matter? I'm going down to my parent's today so you know she'll be safe." Charisse said.

"Thank you, Mama. I'll wire you some money when you get there, okay? How are the kids?"

"Rodney, we'll be fine. The kids are fine. We miss you, though. Hurry and meet us."

"I will. I don't know what I would have done without you. You know that?"

"That's why I'm your better half."

We shared a laugh and spent a few more minutes talking then ended our call.

Diamond knocked on the door shortly after.

"Come in." I said after I got out the bed and put on my sweatpants.

She walked in with a plate of food in one hand and a cup of coffee in the other.

"Aunt Reese asked me not to let you starve. She also said she wanted to make sure Imani had a house to come home to. Guess you can't boil water, huh?" Diamond said as she set the plate on the nightstand.

"Thanks, Diamond. When we get our mansion you can be our maid." I joked.

"If your guest house looks like Steadman's, I'm there." She replied.

We both fell out in laughter. Her cell phone alert sounded and she flew out the door yelling, "I'm coming, Boo."

Quinton came through the door and was almost knocked down as Diamond ran past him. I took my breakfast and coffee into the living room to watch the news. Quinton joined me with his newspaper and a cup of coffee. I hadn't seen Quinton look so stressed in years. Twice in one lifetime, he had to fight to keep his family. Yet he remained calm as he collected his thoughts. He sat in his favorite recliner, kicked off his boots and a loud thud followed. He exhaled as he sat back and finally found a moment to relax. Quinton took a sip of his coffee then rested his head on the plush headrest.

"I need a vacation. After this shit is over, you and I need to hit up one of those five day cruises to the islands. You know Imani and Charisse have been planning to go on one of those for the longest."

"It's different for women to go on a cruise together. For two dudes it doesn't sound right." I joked

"Well then I'll enjoy watching all the women that travel together all by myself." He countered.

I looked at Quinton then smirked, "Married and all, you still my nigga."

Outside of Diamond's occasional giggle coming from the dining room and the chatter from the television news reporters, the house was quiet.

"Imani gave you hell all the way to the airport?" I asked before biting into the toast.

"Yeah. Can't blame her though." Quinton replied absently. "You know, I had this fucked up feeling ever since Bryan said that Trey got a good look at him yesterday."

"You think Trey knew it was him?"

"Besides the fact that Bryan looks exactly like his father, Trey heard Bryan say his name."

Quinton eyes said that he did not want to take any chances waiting around for Trey. He wanted to find Trey before he found us. He took another sip of his coffee and returned to his resting position.

"I think he's back in New York, Q." I stated.

"What makes you say that?" He asked.

"Sandra called Reese and asked her to take Sharay for a while. Something isn't right with that. Sandra despises me, why would she let Sharay be with my girl and my kids?" I replied.

"Then what about the little sister? Why didn't she ask Reese to take her too?"

"Maybe because Reese never met Jasmine? Maybe because Sharay is more of a help than a burden? Honestly, I have no idea. My gut is telling me there are more secrets; my mind is telling me not to question Sandra's actions."

"You finally chose to follow your mind. Reese must have really put some good shit on ya'. Got you thinking and shit." Quinton joked.

"Fuck you, Man. On some serious shit though, when I call Reese later, I'll ask Sharay what's going on in her mother's world. I don't have the energy to think on Sandra's level."

The thought of me trying to be as shiesty as Sandra annoyed me and the thought of her bringing two girls up in that environment, infuriated me.

"What time is Reese supposed to be heading out?" Quinton asked as he rose from his seat.

"About five. I told her to tell Sharay to call me but they will probably be busy getting the kids together." I replied.

I picked up my dishes from the coffee table and attempted to pass them to Quinton since he was on his way to the kitchen but he ignored me and continued on his way.

"I ain't your maid." He commented as he passed.

"It's like that now, nigga." I said as I turned off the television and started towards the kitchen.

"You're *my* son. Remember nigga!" Quinton replied as he threw the dishcloth at me. "Now wash my dish, *Son*."

"Q, suck my di..."

Diamond walked into the kitchen as I was about to reply to Quinton's last comment. She had her hands covering her ears as she walked over to the refrigerator.

"Watch your mouth, Rodney." Diamond chastised.

Quinton broke out into a hysterical laugh.

"Aren't you going to be late for work?" I asked.

Diamond ignored me as she tried to pluck a lint ball from the orange and tan turtleneck sweater she wore over a pair of tan pants which she styled up with a pair of construction Timberlands. She accessorized her ensemble with a gold Hugs and Kisses earrings and necklace set. By the way she was dressed, I knew she was not heading to her internship at the publishing company.

"Nah, I got the week off. Me and my dad made plans to go to Virginia to see his peoples for Thanksgiving." She replied.

"You say *his peoples* like they're not your family too." Quinton stated.

"Honestly, I barely know them folks. I met my grandmother before she passed and that might have been the first and last time I met his peoples." Diamond said.

"Damn. In nineteen years, you only met his side once?" Quinton asked.

"In nineteen years, that was the only time he went home to visit. You got to remember my father had problems and family was not his first priority." Diamond looked at Quinton as if she was telling him something he should have already knew.

"How long y'all going for?" I asked.

"Four days. After dinner on Thursday, we are driving back. If he doesn't get here soon I might change my mind." She huffed then pulled a bottle of water from the refrigerator and exited the kitchen.

Quinton followed Diamond out of the kitchen and left me with the dishes.

Quinton was in his office handling business as usual while I made a couple of business calls as well. I had showered, shaved, and dressed for the day wearing my burgundy and tan striped Ralph Lauren Polo knit over black Ralph Lauren Polo carpenter jeans and matching burgundy and tan Timberland field boots. The outfit said comfortable and ready to hit the street for business. While I was on the phone with my main partner, Sharay was calling on the other line. I quickly ended the conversation and answered the other line.

"Hey, sweetie. What's going on?" I greeted.

"Nothing. You wanted me to call you?" She asked.

"Yeah, what's going on with your mother? All of a sudden she's cool with you being around Charisse. Is there something I need to know?"

There was a pause before she responded.

"Trey called mom with all kinds of threats saying she better have some information for him when he gets back in town or else he'll find another way to get it. She thinks he was referring to me so she sent me over here?" Sharay replied half-heartedly.

"What about Jasmine?" I asked.

"What about Jasmine? I told you he knows she doesn't know anything. He wouldn't hurt her anyway. Trey wouldn't hurt any of us he is just trying to scare mom. " She stated.

"Do you know this man, Sharay? He will do whatever he feels necessary. You know that, don't you?"

"I know he had something to do with what happened to Bryan and Trina. But he and Jasmine are like how you and I are. He is always there to spend time with her."

Immediately, alarms sounded and lights blared.

"Sharay, has he ever tried to touch you in any way? How about Jasmine? Has he ever tried to...?"

Sharay cut me off. "Daddy! He never touched me or Jasmine.

Where *did that come from?*" She asked.

"Quinton had his background checked and found out that this guy has some child molestation and rape charges. Is there any way I can get in contact with your mom? She needs to get Jasmine and herself as far from Trey as possible." I replied.

"Are you serious, Daddy? But he loves Jasmine so much. He would never hurt her. He is the only father she knows."

"Baby, listen to me. I need to talk to your mom. Where can I reach her?"

Sharay sighed as she digested information.

"This is getting worse and worse. Everyday it's something new. I'm tired of this, Daddy. I want everything to be like it was before. Mom deserves a better life." Sharay said with deep compassion in her tone.

"It's all going to end soon and I'm going to make sure your mom and Jasmine are safe."

"She might be at the Knight's. She said she was going over there to talk to them. I think she is going to try to lie about the money. I wish none of this stuff ever happened. No money, no lies, and no drama." The anger in Sharay's voice tore a hole in my heart.

"Me too, Baby. Trust me. Daddy is going to take care of it." I promised my baby girl. "Listen, I want you to go with Charisse and the kids and try not to think about this. I know that's hard because this is your mom and sister but I need to know you are not stressing yourself out about it."

"I'll try but I can't promise that I won't be worried." Sharay replied.

"Tell Reese I will call her in twenty minutes. I want to catch up with your mom. Alright?"

"Yeah." She solemnly responded.

"I love you, Angel." I said.

"Love you, too." She said then hung up.

Hurriedly, I searched my wallet for the number. When I finally came across it, I fumbled with the phone in a rush to dial the number.

Mr. Knight answered; we exchanged greetings and small talk before he handed the phone to Sandra.

"Hey." She answered.

"What's going on, Sandra? I spoke to Sharay. She said Trey called you. Why didn't you call me?"

"Hold on." She said for a brief second then returned. "For what? I took care of it." She replied in a hushed tone.

"What the fuck do you mean ' *for what*'? If someone threatens my child, I should know."

"He didn't threaten her, Rodney. We had an argument but it had nothing to do with Sharay."

There was something in Sandra's voice that told me she wasn't telling the truth. The fact that Sharay has no reason to lie added to the feeling.

"Why are you lying for him? She told me everything already. How much longer are you going to play this game, Sandra? You are putting yourself and your girls in danger. Did you know that Trey got locked up on rape charges?"

"He told me, Rodney. He didn't *rape* the little girl. She accused him..."

"He molested both his daughters! His oldest daughter has a son by him. Is this the sick motherfucker you want around Jasmine?"

"You're lying. You're jealous because I finally got someone to take care of me and mine. Listen don't call me with your bullshit. Me and my girls are going to be alright. When Trey comes home, I'll straighten everything out. I'll get him to understand that the money was a lie to get rid of Big Bryan so all this commotion can come to a fucking end."

"The money is real and if it were that easy, then why is Sharay with Charisse. Do you even know where your man is?" I asked.

"He's in Philly." She replied with assurance.

"He's in Pennsylvania but not in Philly. In fact, Bryan ran into him yesterday. This shit is getting too deep, Sandra. Too many people's lives are being jeopardized for some shit *you* started. I know you don't want to continue living your life looking over your shoulder wondering if your past is catching up to you. Now do you want me to get involved on your behalf or not? I can make sure you and Jasmine are safe until this is over." I said.

"And what am I supposed to do? How am I supposed to live?"

"Sandra, take a minute and think about this. Is all this drama going to be worth the trouble in the end? Don't put your girls through it. They don't deserve it. You don't deserve it."

Sandra began to cry, "Rodney, what have I gotten myself into? He promised to take care of us and no one would get hurt. Then he calls yesterday, screaming and making threats. He told me that I had better have the money whereabouts or else he would find a way to do it himself. I had no idea he meant, Bryan. He was convinced that Sharay had nothing to do with it but he is stuck on Bryan. Did Bryan ever mention that he saw who shot his father?"

"Calm down, Sandra. No, Bryan never mentioned it. Bryan said he wasn't in the house when his mother and father were shot. When they ran into each other yesterday, Bryan did not remember him so that seemed to be true. Listen to me. I know you have money in accounts for the girls. I want you to take the money out and buy tickets for you and Jasmine to visit your brother in California and get yourself set up out there. Don't worry about your apartment or your things. I'll have that taken care of. Leave tonight. Get a cell phone when you get there and call me. We'll keep in touch like that until this situation is dead."

"Rodney, it's not that simple. He is going to find us. He always finds us."

"Just do as I said and keep Jasmine away from the phones. She maybe the reason he keeps finding you. No matter how much you told Sharay to stop calling, she would always call. That's the father-daughter bond."

Sandra inhaled deeply. "I never thought about that." She whispered.

"So can you do it? Are you ready to make that move?" I asked.

"I guess I have no choice." She replied.

We exchanged good-byes then ended the call.

Before Quinton and I began our mission, I wanted to let my crew in New York know what was going down and to keep their eyes open for anything that may seem out of the ordinary. I also instructed them to keep an extra close watch on Charisse's place until she and the kids made it safely out of New York. Jamal, my main partner, assured me that he would get the crew together and handle business. I knew his terms of handling business meant to go after Trey and his people so I told him to sit low and be alert. Jamal was the type who always had the upper hand, sitting back wasn't his style, but he understood that my family was involved and agreed to wait.

"How long before Charisse heads out?" He asked with the sound of a clip being loaded into a gun echoed in the background.

"Couple of hours. Follow her to the highway then give me a call. Thanks Jay." I replied.

"Anytime, Brother. Do you need someone to watch over your mom's place?"

"She's supposed to be visiting family in Delaware with my sisters. Pass by the block and make sure it's quiet until she leaves. I'll call to find out when they plan to head out."

Trey wanted a war and was about get what he was looking for. My gun was loaded and waiting. Quinton had his men, legal and illegal, organizing and patiently awaiting to take Trey out. It was time to hunt his ass down.

CHAPTER 14

QUINTON

Imani's voice expressed pure anger and agitation. She complained about everything from the delayed arrival to the long line at the car rental. Things that she could normally tolerate pinched her last nerve but I knew it was because of the situation surrounding the last minute trip to Georgia. My aunt Katherine did everything she could to make Imani feel at home but nothing seemed to change her mood. Katherine showed the kids to their rooms—the rooms that once belonged to her own two children—then offered the recently renovated basement for Imani, Naadira and Sierra's son. It was still early and Imani insisted that it would not be any trouble to go to a hotel but thankfully, Katherine wouldn't allow her. It wasn't like Imani not to be cordial even under extreme circumstances. When I asked her if she would feel better at home, she would suck her teeth then play silent.

"Imani, I understand that you're upset but please don't make everyone miserable. If for no one else, do it for the kids. They know something is wrong and you know we normally try to shelter them from drama." I stated.

"Well, they're getting too old to continue living in a plastic bubble. Eventually they will have to step into the real world and deal with real issues. They have to learn that the world is not always sugar coated." Imani replied.

"Are you listening to yourself? These are our kids. We have to protect them until they can protect themselves. Since when has the game plan changed? The Imani I knew world revolved around her kids and their happiness." I countered.

"And who's concerned for Imani's happiness? Who's there to protect me and make sure everything is okay? My husband? Quinton, I really don't feel like talking much less arguing so I'll call you another time." Imani said weakly.

"Imani, Baby this is not an argue..."

The dial tone let me know Imani was no longer listening.

Imani's mood swings were getting worse. Hopefully she would calm down before she took out her frustration on the kids. I thought about calling her back but I doubt she would have answered. I slammed my cell phone on the computer keyboard then left the office. Rodney was sitting on the couch talking on his phone when I entered the family room. We were waiting for Mike to come by so we can figure out a strategy. Although Mike was a detective, street rules always applied, more so when the case came too close to home. He knew more dealers, runners, and under-handed thieves than the average thug. Those were his peoples and his connections for instances such as the one we were facing. One of his connects used to run large orders for Trey from New York to Philly and gave us an address to where he operates in Pennsylvania. The informant also mentioned that he had recently received a called from Trey's right hand man and asked for some information on me. That gave us reason to believe that he was still in the neighborhood or not too far from it and had intentions on popping up.

Mike finally arrived just as my patience began to wear thin.

"Quinton, I have some undercover officers going to check out Trey's spot in Philly." Mike said after ending his phone call. "I think this guy is waiting for you to make a move, Q. We need to go to New York and disrupt his business. That should force him out of hiding."

Rodney immediately ended his phone call and focused in on our conversation.

"We can leave out tonight. My boys in Brooklyn have been looking for a reason to hit the Bronx. They will never see it coming." Rodney added.

"Will Sandra and Jasmine be safe? Trey might try to hide out in her house." I asked.

"Sandra will be in California with Jasmine. I had the locks changed anyway." Rodney replied.

"Then I guess it's a go. I'll call Shea and ask him to meet us with the box." I said referring to the metal box where I kept my guns stashed.

"What about your parents?" Mike asked.

"My mother and James will be leaving to meet Imani and the kids in Georgia. They should be packing up the car right about now." I replied.

"I had to beg my mother to go help Imani. My mother and my aunt Katherine haven't seen each other in over twenty years and started speaking a few years ago when my aunt Karen got sick. If it wasn't for her grandkids, she wouldn't go."

"Imani's peoples should be safe, right?" Rodney asked.

"I don't see why not. Trey's main focus is on you, Quinton and Bryan." Mike replied. "I'm going to go get some things together at the office and pack up for the trip. We can meet up at about seven at the bar."

I escorted Mike to the front door and thanked him for his help. Rodney and I already ran through our list of acquaintances. We figured if this got real ugly we were going to need an army. Rodney's clique was deep and down for the task. We invited a couple of guys that I used to roll with when I was in the game, whom also had problems with Trey and or his men.

Rodney and I began lowering the shutters over the windows and securing all the doors. From the outside the house looked like a fortress. The house was completely ready for whatever storm or war that came its way. In the basement behind the bar there was a floor safe where I kept a 9mm stashed for emergencies. I loaded the gun and placed it in the waistband of my jeans. I readjusted my jeans, fixed my sweater to cover the weapon, and began up the stairs. Halfway up the stairs, I came across one of Naadira's flower printed socks and a rush of anger came over me. I wanted my family home but I knew it wasn't safe. The more I thought about Imani crying or Bryan having to live in fear, the more rage built inside. When I reached the dining room the phone began to ring. My anger had elevated to a level beyond control so I wasn't in the mood for conversation. Without thinking, I ripped the phone out of the wall and stormed up to my bedroom.

I tried everything to calm down but it seemed as if nothing worked.

I changed into a t-shirt and shorts and headed for the garage to our mini gym. I figured a couple of rounds with the punching bag or a couple of miles on the treadmill would eventually tire me out but instead it seemed as if the feeling had become more intense. As I started for the weight bench, Rodney entered. He was also dressed to workout.

"That was Imani on the phone. She said to give her a call when you had a chance." Rodney said as he warmed up.

With that the fury had begun to calm. Sweat poured down my face and coated my skin as I sat on the bench trying to collect my thoughts. The sound of Rodney's fist making contact with the leather bag matched the pounding in my head. I decided to head back in the house and call Imani and the kids.

"Hey, Baby. How are you feeling?" I asked Imani as I peeled out of my sweated clothes.

I searched for a towel to cover my naked bottom then opted to remain bare remembering no one was home.

"I am fine. I was calling to apologize. Q, I know this isn't easy for you either and I really don't want to add any extra stress to the situation. I love you and miss you."

"I love you too, Imani. I know how you feel. After this is over Baby, I promise to give you all the individual attention you need. We'll take a vacation, wherever you want to go, your choice. As long as it's just us two, I don't care where we are."

"What about the kids? They deserve a vacation too." Imani asked.

"When school is over we will take them on a road trip. They'll enjoy that. Right now, we need to concentrate on us. We have been at each other throats lately and I don't like how it feels. It feels like we are arguing for little things and that's not like us. I think we need a break from reality."

"We might need a break from each other. I told you before. You stopped talking to me and started talking at me. We are a team, Quinton. We make the decisions together. I try to talk to you about the kids but you handle things on your own. If you can't start giving me the respect I deserve we might not have anything to talk about except separating for a while. The kids cannot be around us like this. They notice it too. Kai came to me about it recently."

'*Damn.*' I thought as I sat on the side of the bed.

"When I get out there I want to have a talk with the kids. Maybe I have been a little hard on you and them but it's only because I want to see them do good, Imani. It's so easy to fall under the wrong influence. And sometimes I get so wrapped up in being the man of the house I forget the woman that helped me build it."

"Try thinking before you act. With the kids and *with me*. Guide them with love and not with an iron fist. Sometimes if we are too strict, we can push them away. I got your back even when we don't agree; I need to know what's going on in my house before the final decision is made. If you can promise to share the responsibility a little, I can promise things will get better."

Imani and I fell silent for a brief moment. She sighed then continued, "They know you love them, Quinton. They love you too. We have good kids, Baby."

"I know." I replied. "How are they now? Do Kai and Jahlek know what's going on?"

"Not that I know of. But you know the kids share everything with each other. No one has said anything to me. With the exception of Naadira, she asked if we had to leave because somebody broke the window. I told her yes. That's what I told all of them. I doubt if Bryan told them the whole story."

"Where are they? Can I talk to them?" I asked.

"Your aunt took them to see your cousin Takiyah. I have Sierra's baby here with me. I am not ready to be a grandmother. The diaper and bottle days are way over for me." She replied.

"So we're not going to try for our little boy?"

"Quinton, we are getting too old for babies. In a couple of years our kids are going to have their own. We are going to need our energy for them." She said.

"Imani, that's ten or more years from now. I thought we had agreed to try one more time."

"Quinton, let's talk about that another time. Let's get through this situation first. I am about to put the baby down for a nap. I will tell the kids to call you when they get back. It's almost three now. So they should be back in the next hour or two. You know your country ass family has dinner early. Katherine had these black-eyed peas soaking all day. She got ribs sitting out, marinating. I didn't know how to tell her we don't eat pork. I offered to fry some chicken instead but she said we can have both."

Imani laughed and everything was okay. It was good to here her laugh again.

"Well if they went over to Takiyah's house then they will probably eat over there. Takiyah is like her mother, she can cook her ass off."

"I know. I remember. She cooked Thanksgiving dinner by herself last year when she came up to Pennsylvania. Your mother tried to help but Takiyah shut her out the kitchen." Imani fell out in laughter.

"If I remember, she shut you out too." I joined in the laughter.

"Well, Takiyah needs to slow down on some of that good cooking because she and her husband have gained some weight. Katherine got a picture of them and the kids upstairs. Wait until you see them." Imani said.

"Don't let them stuff our kids." I stated jokingly. "You know you can't cook like that. We can't afford for the kids to take trips out here on the regular."

"What? Do you know who you are talking to? I can do my thing in the kitchen."

"You do your thing. No doubt. But that southern cooking is hereditary and let's face it, you're not black." I joked.

"Then what the hell am I?" She questioned.

"I don't know but I love you anyway."

Imani and I talked for a few more seconds as I gathered my things for the shower. After she hung up, I jumped in the shower and scrubbed off the layer of sweat that had dried into my skin. I used Imani's lavender and chamomile wash, which brought me closer to her. The thought of her aroused me. I wanted to call her back and try phone sex. But I knew that wasn't her style. Then again Imani was down for whatever so I grabbed the cordless and dialed her back. I started right into the fact that my body was ready and needed her. She gasped and then returned with some dirty talk of her own. Her voice was enticing and the thought of touching her was exciting me more. The thought of diving deep inside her while she called my name between deep breaths made me stiff.

"I want you to put your finger inside of me while you flick my clit with you tongue. Ohhh, Quinton baby, it feels so good. I'm so hot and so wet. I'm sliding my finger in and out. Want me to taste it?"

"Imani, you are good, Baby. You taste so good. I want you to cum for me."

"I'm getting there Baby. Ooh, Quinton. I'm cum..." She was speechless as she reached her orgasm.

I followed right behind. Imani remained silent as I regained my composure; the warm water ran over my back. The sound of a baby crying filled her background.

"Quinton, I gotta go. Jason woke up. Call me when you're done. I should be free by then."

"Talk to you later, Baby." I replied.

Rodney and I were heading for the bar in his car. I parked my car by the office. We packed light; two change of underwear, an outfit, and our guns. We knew we would be spending most of our time in the streets trying to find Trey before he found us. As we pulled up to the front of the bar my cell phone began to ring. *Private Number* flashed across the screen. Curiosity urged me to answer.

"Hello." I greeted.

"Hey, Quinton." The woman replied.

"Who the hell is this?" I asked.

"You don't need to know me. I'm calling for Trey. He said you have what he needs. If you don't have it for him by Thursday morning, he'll get it another way."

"Tell Trey to confront me face to face and stop handling his business like a bitch!"

"This is a warning, Q. If you don't want him to bite into your Georgia peach you'll get him the money."

Then the caller hung up.

Rodney noticed my expression and knew I was livid.

"Q, what's good?" He asked.

"He knows where Imani is. I gotta get on a flight now."

"You can't go out there by yourself.   Damn! It's like this motherfucker got eyes everywhere." Rodney replied.

"It's better that we split up. You stay up here and see if you can draw him out of hiding. I got to be with my family in case his punk ass tries to pop up out there." I stated.

Mike arrived as we were about to get back into the car.

"Yo, Q. Where y'all going?"

"He knows where my family is. I gotta go."

"What did he say?" Mike asked.

"It was a woman; they threatened to hurt Imani if they didn't get the money by Thursday morning." I replied.

"Why Thursday? Why not tomorrow or Wednesday?" Mike thought aloud.

"Don't care, Mike! The nigga threatened my fucking family." I said.

"Hold on,,,Hold on. We might be able to catch this guy tomorrow morning. I got a lead to where Trey may be hiding in New York. Let's check it out. If it ain't legit, we'll get you on the next flight out."

I looked at Rodney who was shaking his head then back at Mike. Mike noticed Rodney's expression and asked, "What's up?"

"Friday is Sharay's eighteenth birthday. He's thinking she's going to get the money and run. That got to be why he gave us a deadline." Rodney replied. "And Sandra was convinced he had no idea Sharay knew about the money. He was playing cool and close. Mother fucker!"

"Let's get this bastard." I stated.

We jumped back in our cars. Rodney and I were making our phone calls updating everyone on the new plan. Mike called his boys who met us a few blocks from the bar and then we hit the highway.

ଽୠଽୠଽୠଔଔଔଔ

CHARISSE

My mother had taken the kids to the park and left my sisters and me behind to start dinner. My sisters, Taniqua and Lauren were doing most of the cooking. I was sitting with Sharay at the kitchen table, arranging then rearranging the condiments. Sharay blankly stared at the television that sat on the kitchen table. If the television were on it would have seemed as if she were engrossed in whatever program but instead she chose to stare at the black screen. Our minds were both occupied with the drama that drove us here. For the kids it was a routine trip to grandma's house, for Sharay and I it was seclusion from all the madness back in New York. I had originally planned to make the most out of this trip. *'Relax to the max'* was the motto we had developed on the drive up but it seemed as if we were getting off to a bad start.

"Reese, what's on your mind, Sis?" Lauren asked in her usual heavy southern drawl.

"You don't want to know." I replied.

"I thought you and Rodney were doing well." Taniqua interjected.

"We are doing very well, now. There is just some outside interference right now. Everything should boil over soon." I replied while spinning a straw on the table.

"You know you can talk to us, Reese."

Both Lauren and Taniqua stopped what they were doing and directed their attention to me.

Sharay placed her hand on top of mine then whispered, "Everything's going to be okay, Charisse."

"Thanks." I replied.

Sharay rose from her seat and started for the basement. When we first arrived, my mother had given Sharay a tour of the house and Sharay immediately became fascinated with the art studio my mother had set up in the basement. Sharay and my mother talked for over an hour about the passion for art. My mother requested that Sharay make a painting for her collection before we left.

Sharay must have found her inspiration.

"Charisse, come help us with these greens. You know nobody makes greens like you. You got Nana's touch." Taniqua said as she pushed the bucket full of chopped collard greens across the counter.

The three of us put together a dinner that was sure to be leftovers for the next two days. Our father had come in as we put the last piece of fish in the draining pan. My mother had returned with her vanload of grandchildren. There were times when I would have liked to pull my hair out with my three and yet this woman has the patience to take seven kids to the park; my three and Lauren's group of four. Lauren's children were older than mine, her youngest being eight. Daddy began running down the rules as they ran into the house. Lauren instructed her kids to wash and get ready for dinner. Christian followed behind them as if he were apart of that troop. Mama took Alaire and Damien into her bedroom to wash and get them ready for dinner. I insisted on taking Alaire but my mother ignored me. This had actually been Alaire's first visit to my parents. My mother had intended on taking full advantage of having her daughters and grandchildren home for the week. Meanwhile with Daddy nothing changed. Taniqua fixed his plate, Lauren gathered his drink and hot sauce, and I began setting the table for the rest of the family like when we were younger.

The doorbell rang. No one moved because we were all shocked as to who the visitor may be and what could be so important to disrupt our dinner. Sharay offered to answer the door but I told her to finish her food and I would handle it. Daddy thought to leave the visitor at the door until dinner was done, normally I would agree, but my curiosity had the best of me.

I looked through the peephole then backed away then checked again to make sure I was seeing right. When I opened the door, Myra stood boldfaced before me with a large bag beside her.

"How may I help you?" I asked.

"Is Mrs. Nettles available?" Myra's nonchalant act was going to get her punched.

"Myra, I didn't know you were into stalking. That is something new."

"Bitch, please. Your mother asked me to come up." Myra countered.

"And you couldn't decline the invitation?"

"For what? For you? You're not that special, Baby. Get over it."

"That's the same thing I am about to tell you. Get over it. We are never going to happen so making nice with the family is not necessary. Now if you'll excuse me, we are having dinner. I am trying to keep my appetite." I retorted.

As Myra was about to respond, my mother came to the door in her June Cleaver persona.

"Oh Myra dear, come in. I am so glad you could make it." She greeted as she pushed me aside.

"Thank you, Mrs. Nettles." Myra rolled her suitcase inside and began to unbutton her tweed pea coat.

"Is she staying?" I asked.

"Yes, Charisse. Why is there a problem?" My mother questioned as she took Myra's coat and scarf.

'Yes, a big problem!' "No, Mom. No problem at all." I said then returned to the kitchen.

My father was the first to question but his answer followed directly behind me.

"Myra. Girl I haven't seen you in years. Come give Poppa a hug." Daddy exclaimed as he rose from his seat.

Taniqua nudged her elbow into my side and mouthed, "What's up with this picture?"

I shrugged my shoulders and returned my attention to Alaire who was still gumming cornbread. Myra walked over to Christian and gave him a kiss on his forehead, which he immediately wiped off, and then she ran her hand over Damien's curls. She looked over to Alaire then at me and said, "Reese, I know you're not giving her table food."

Trying to ignore her was harder than trying not to punch her in her face so I elected to take my daughter and our plates into the living room.

"Myra, you can have my seat." I said as I walked past her.

My mother tried to strike up conversation but no one had anything to say. The rest of dinner was quiet. Sharay brought Damien into the living room when they were finished with their plates.

"Charisse, is everything okay?" Sharay asked.

"It will be." I replied.

A little after ten, everyone was settling into their beds. Myra tried every chance she found to be alone with me but I was always one-step ahead. After dinner, I was washing dishes and she offered to help. So I left her to wash the dishes while I bathed my kids. After I put them in bed, I decided to take a dip in the indoor pool that was built where the guesthouse used to be. Lauren and I were into our third lap when Myra came strolling through the door. Lauren looked at me and began to laugh. I playfully slapped her arm and we began to splash water at each other.   When Myra thought we weren't paying attention, she got undress and jumped in. Lauren and I left. Then when I thought I was finally rid of her, I snuck downstairs to dip into the peach cobbler. After warming it enough to take the chill off, I took the cobbler to the enclosed porch, sat on the cushioned bench and looked out into the sky as I enjoyed the warm, sweet filling as it hit my taste buds. With my grandmother's shawl wrapped around my shoulders, I began to find peace in my tranquil surroundings.

"Can I join you?" The voice said, interrupting my moment.

"Not really." I replied.

"Reese, can we talk?" She asked as she moved closer.

"Can't you let me have my peace for one night? Damn, Myra. What the fuck do you want from me?" I asked as I attempted to rise from my seat.

"It's obvious, Charisse. I want you. Why can't we be together, Reese? Rodney can never love you like I do." Myra pleaded.

"Myra, if you really love me, you would let me be. Move on with your life. There is nothing left here for us." I said as I pointed to my heart.

Myra stood in front of me wearing only a button down pajama shirt. Her thick thighs peeked from underneath. Her skin remained flawless and had a golden shine. Myra let her hair drop to her shoulders and began to unbutton her pajamas. As she got to her fourth button, the lace material of her black bra was revealed along with a set of perfect plump breasts. I tried to act unfazed but when she placed her freshly pedicure foot beside me; I couldn't fight the urge to run my hand up her leg. The sweet smell of rose oil permeated the air as she drew closer.

"I knew you couldn't resist." She whispered as I traced my index finger up her thigh, tempted to go further.

"Myra, this ain't right." I said as I placed my hands on her waist and attempted pushing her away.

She placed her hands on top of mine and said, "Don't fight, Reese. It's hot and waiting for you."

She took one of my hands and placed it on the thin material that covered her vagina. I cupped it and watched as her body reacted. I removed my hand and pulled her closer, motioning for her to straddle me. She complied without second thought. I cupped her breasts and kissed the top of them. She held my face in her hands as she pulled me in for a kiss. I turned my head and said, "No kissing."

She looked confused for a brief second then quickly changed her attitude when I ran my thumb over her erect nipples. I unbuckled her front close bra and allowed her breast to sit bare. I took one into my mouth and licked the nipple before sucking it. I forgot how sweet she tasted. Myra moaned in delight as she ran her hands over my hair. She began to gyrate her hips as the passion between us heightened. Myra pushed my hands away and stated, "I control this."

Myra unwrapped my shawl and tugged at my t-shirt until I too was baring my breasts. She began to caress them as I placed my hands on her bottom. My cat was yearning for a tongue bath.

"Let's take this inside." I said as I traced Myra's neck with my tongue.

She hesitantly replied, "Okay."

She held her shirt together as I collected my shirt and wrapped the shawl around me. I turned off the porch light and locked the front door. Myra sat on the couch with her legs spread eagle, waiting. As I was about to join her, I noticed someone coming down the stairs. I immediately put my shirt on and mentioned for Myra to cover herself. Sharay came down the stairs groggy eyed and said, "Daddy's on the phone."

"Thank you, sweetheart." I said.

As I answered the phone, Myra rose from the couch and exhaled an annoyed breath. I sat in the single chair in front of the window and collected my thoughts before continuing.

"Is everything okay, Reese?" Rodney asked.

"I'm fine, Baby. A little tired, that's all." I replied.

"Oh, I'm sorry. I didn't want to wake you..."

"No, I wasn't sleep yet. What's going on?"

Myra walked around turning off all the lights then headed into the basement where her lonely futon awaited her.

"Mama, I am not going to lie to you, shit is getting thick but it will definitely be over soon. I promise." Rodney replied.

"I hope so. Don't do anything stupid Rodney. I miss you so much. I want you in one piece."

"I miss you, too. Don't worry, Reese. We got it under control. How was your day?"

"Strange. But it's better now that you called." I replied.

Rodney and I continued to talk for a few short seconds. I made sure not to mention Myra's unexpected visit the whole time. After our conversation, I was no longer in the mood for nor did I desire Myra. I felt the need to at least apologize to Myra and explain that what we started was a mistake but I knew things were better left alone.

Sharay carried Alaire down the stairs while I held Damien's hand and followed. Christian was still running with his older cousins whom were already sitting at the table for breakfast. Mom and Myra wore matching aprons as they served breakfast. Myra made sure not to make eye contact as she shuffled around the kitchen making sure everyone was satisfied. Dad wasn't a breakfast person so he came in for his cup of coffee then went back into his den.

"Charisse, you want to take a trip over to visit Pop-Pop?" Lauren asked.

"Is he still in a home?" I returned.

"Yeah. He's doing well, too. He loves the nursing home." Lauren replied.

"He loves the nurses." Taniqua added.

"Sounds like a plan. Mom, do you mind watching the kids?" Even though I knew the answer, it was still polite to ask.

"Girl, y'all go on and enjoy your day. Myra brought her equipment with her so we're going to get some shots of the kids for a family collage and then a family portrait. The grandkids only today and on Friday we'll do one of all of us." My mother said as she wiped down the counters.

"Is this family portrait going to include our husbands?" Lauren asked.

"Of course, honey." My mother replied.

"Then when were you going to tell us so we can inform them." Taniqua added.

Mom turned around with a hand on her hip and stated, "I just did."

Knowing my mother the way I did, it wasn't her intention to tell us all at once. She was more than likely going to pull Lauren and Taniqua aside and tell them. Then on Friday surprise me with the news so it would be too late for me to tell Rodney.

Lauren and I had hands full of bags, struggling to get into the front door while Taniqua exchanged kisses with her husband over the phone. Myra was sitting on the porch in my mother's wicker chair wearing a thick navy blue wool sweater and some gray sweat pants with a City College insignia on the pocket, *my gray sweat pants*. She was sipping on a cup of what I assumed was hot cocoa since she never drank coffee and talking on her headset. I tried to ignore her and continue into the house but when I heard my name, my focus was on Myra. I stared at her wondering if she had been talking negatively about me, and who could she be talking to. When I caught myself feeling jealous, I knew it was time to go inside.

Christian and Damien ran to greet me at the door in their matching footed pajamas. Christian tried to help me with my bags as Damien whined for me to pick him up. My dad scooped Damien up into his arms and then assisted me with some of my bags. Lauren and I had lost our minds shopping for the kids. The Children's Place and The Gap Kids had amazing sales on their winter collection.

Once I got everything situated, I went for Alaire and called the boys into our room for a story and some private time. Christian's mouth ran a mile a minute while I breast fed Alaire. Damien sat beside me with my cell phone to his ear, pretending he was talking to his father. With Alaire full and Christian all talked out, it was time to put them to bed and grab a couple of seconds for myself.

Soft jazz played from the living room as I descended the stairs. Myra sat on the couch wearing a pair of boy cut panties and a white tank top. With a glass of wine in hand, she relaxed on the sofa enjoying the soothing sounds of the saxophone.

"Myra, we need to talk." I said as I approached her.

"Talk." she replied.

"What happened yesterday was a mistake. I never met for things to get that far. I really think it's best to keep our distance." I stated.

"You really think it's best for me? Or for you?" She questioned then continued, "Reese, you want me just as much as I want you. Stop fighting. Let yourself love me."

"I don't love you, Myra. I am in love with Rodney. So please let me be." I begged.

"I can't do that, Charisse." She said as she rose from her seat.

Myra walked closer to me and stood in front of me. She went for my hand but I snatched it back. She reached for my pants zipper and I smacked her hand away. She looked at me for a moment as if she were confused then smiled.

"Myra, it's over. I'm sorry." I apologized then started back up the stairs.

She whispered something as I got halfway up the stairs. I stopped in mid step trying to make out what I thought I heard.

You will be.

CHAPTER 15

<u>IMANI</u>

The editors from the newspaper would not stop calling my cell phone. They wanted me to write a story on what was happening in *my* household. They figured that since we have a neighborhood paper, we should spotlight the crime in our neighborhood. What they did not realize was how complicated this situation was, mainly since children were concerned and one of the young was my child. At first, I thought it was a joke from one of my co-workers and if that, it would have been a bad joke. Then the Chief Editor called and threatened my job if I could not give them the story. So I quit. Knowing it would only be a matter of time before they found thirsty interns looking for a break to cover the story, I had to find a lawyer to protect my family's rights and the identities of the innocent involved such as Sharay, Bryan, Sierra, and Jessie. Things seemed to have been getting worse as the week progressed.

Quinton said he knew someone that could handle this and have the newspaper served with a summons before the day was out. That only solved half the problem. We still had a psycho stalking my son and husband. I had a feeling Quinton was in New York. He was adamant not to tell me where he was or what he was up to. He kept assuring me that everything will be okay and he will see me soon. But my gut had a sick feeling. Normally, that feeling was dead on therefore I decided it was time to do a little research myself. I called around to some of my friends who were reporters at other papers to have them start a wire.

Any information that leads to the whereabouts of Tremell Isaiah Storms aka Trey will receive a substantial reward and an exclusive story on the rapist/drug lord at large.

It had been three days since I spoke to Charisse and with all the commotion going on a call was well past due. I tried calling her phone twice but she didn't answer. Quinton's aunt, Katherine invited me to a girlfriend luncheon with her daughter, Takiyah and some of her neighbors. Although my heart was not in place for it, it was a welcomed change. Her husband volunteered to watch the kids and their son, Glen was stopping by and offered to help. As I sifted through my suitcase searching for an appropriate outfit, my cell phone began to ring. Assuming it was Charisse returning my call, I didn't check the Caller Id before answering.

"Hey Girl." I greeted upon answering the phone.

An unfamiliar female voice replied, "Is this Imani?"

"Yes, it is. May I ask whom I am speaking to?" Immediately I thought it was one of the interns from the newspaper and started to hang-up.

"You may not remember me but we ran into each other a couple of weeks ago at the supermarket."

I began scrolling though my memory trying to picture who this woman could be then like a flash the picture cleared.

"Shandi?"

"So nice of you to remember my name."

"How can I help you? How did you get my number?" I questioned.

"Everything is accessible for the right price." She replied.

"What's this about?"

"It's seems as if this world is a very, very small. First, you took Omar from me and now it seems as if my brother is after your husband. My, this world goes in a full circle." She stated.

"Listen here, Bitch. Tell your brother to stay the fuck away from my family or else you'll be attending another funeral." I countered.

"All that tough talk yet your punk ass up and moved to Georgia. Now you listen, *Bitch*. I lost everything when I lost Omar but I'm not about to lose again. You and your husband better come up with the money or else Bryan will be joining his *real* mother and father."

The line went dead.

It all started to make sense. Our chance meeting in the supermarket was not coincidental. Somehow, this woman had tracked me down and had been providing her brother with information about our whereabouts. Still, I could not figure out where she was getting the information.

'How could she know so soon that we were in Atlanta?' I thought.

She knew too much therefore her informant had to be someone close to our family.

"But who?" I said aloud.

Instead of calling Quinton and adding more worry to his plate, I decided to give my brother, John a call. Somehow I knew hearing a familiar voice would take away some of the stress and ease the building headache. Plus, if I didn't call him soon he would come down to Georgia and kick my ass for not keeping him updated. Their phone rang several times before Anissa answered.

"Hello." She greeted.

"Hey girl, what's going on?" I replied.

"Nothing much, Sis. Trying to stay out of John's way."

"What happened?" I asked.

"He's having a fit...again. He thinks it is impossible for me to have any guys as friends without them trying to get some booty. One of my homeboys called here and it got out of control. Mind you he don't let me go out after school, not even if I'm going with one of my home girls and now he's flipping because I have dudes calling the house. What does he want? He wants me to be a hermit?" She stated.

"That's probably my fault." I said with a slight laugh. "Girl, it was drama growing up in that house but Mia has a way of making it better. Give it some time."

"I don't know about all that. I've been thinking about taking a break from this house and spend some time with some of my other family members." Anissa said.

"Like who. You know Jada is one hair from a mental institution, Jordan and Tashii from what I understand are about to break up so they have nothing but drama in their house. Steve never stays with one woman long enough to build a home and although I would love to have you, well you know, right now is not looking too good."

"I have other family. I keep in contact with my father's family. They have been calling me for a while now. My aunt came up here recently and took me shopping and stuff. They are really cool and want me to spend time with them." She explained.

Anissa knew about the secrets of her past. She knew the man that she thought was her brother was actually her father. She also knew how conniving our mother was and had the same insecurities I did as a teenager when it came to trusting people. However, it never satisfied the desire to have someone close to you. I am sure she and Mia had a very close relationship but I knew John had a way of pushing people away. Therefore, it did not amaze me that she was ready to leave. What got me was that she had other family members. As far as I knew, Omar's mother and father had passed and he had no siblings. What aunt could she be referring to?

"Anissa, what aunt are you talking about? Are you talking about your grandfather's sister?" I asked.

"She calls too but no, I'm talking about my Aunt Shandi. Well, she's not really my aunt but she's a close friend to my family. She still visits my aunt in the home and keeps in contact with my cousins and stuff so she keeps me informed on what is going on. She told me that she would take me to visit them but John said he doesn't think that's a good idea."

"Oh Anissa." I cried. "Shandi is not your aunt. She is Omar's ex-girlfriend. I know you may not want to believe me but she was using you to get to me. She may be a close friend to your family but she's trying to hurt mine."

Tears burned my eyes as I thought of how Shandi had taken advantage of my baby sister when she was most vulnerable and needed someone to confide in and trust. However, I was relieved to know where this woman was getting her information from and how to end it.

"Are you serious?" She asked.

"I would never lie about something like that. She called here threatening me. Anissa please believe me. This woman is connected to someone dangerous. I really wish you were not in the middle of this but please don't tell her anything else about our family. She using everything you tell her to get closer to me." I explained.

"Imani, I am so sorry. I didn't know. I'm going to call her and scream on her..."

"No, don't do that. Don't say anything yet. Maybe if you keep cool she might give you something that could help me out. If she asks about any of our family's business, make up something but nothing too far-fetched." I stated.

"I really rather not talk to her. I cannot believe she played me like that. Maybe John is right, no one is really my friend. They were waiting to find a way to use me." Anissa said as her voice began to break.

"Hey! You got family, Anissa. Family that has your back no matter what. You have to learn to read people better. Not everyone is a user. You will have some really good friends, you probably already do. Keep your radar on." I offered hoping I could help her understand.

"I hear you, Imani. It still doesn't feel any better." Anissa sobbed.

"Nissa, when I get back to New York you could come hang with me and the kids for a couple of weekends. Maybe you need a change of environment. Between you and me, Kai points out some decent looking young men. Maybe you might find your little somebody in Pennsylvania."

Anissa giggled, "Thanks, Sis. I think I could definitely use a change."

"Okay, then that's what we'll do." I said. "Do you think you can do me a favor?"

"Depends on what you need. If it has anything to do with John, I don't think so."

"No. Not John. Shandi. Do you think you can give me some information about her?" I asked.

"That's the least I could do." She replied before she started running off at the mouth.

With the list of addresses, phone numbers, and names that Anissa was able to gather, I began to think of ways to make the information work in my favor. Shandi thought she was in the clear and probably never assumed I would find out about her phony friendship with Anissa therefore she never took any precaution around Anissa when chatting or visiting with friends. Whenever Anissa was with Shandi, Shandi continued her normal activities sharing her life with Anissa. Anissa used that to help me find her before she and her brother found us.

Quinton was shocked when I had called him with the story. When I told him that Shandi lived in the next town over from our home he immediately assumed that was where Trey had been hiding.

"I'm going to call Mike and let him know. Mike thought we were going to get him this morning but came up empty. Whether we catch him tonight or not, I'm going to be in Georgia before morning." Quinton said.

"I hope so. Better yet, I want to come home." I said.

"I know, Baby."

Quinton's brother, Shea had entered his room and was asking him a question while I waited on the other line. Quinton replied and then returned to the phone.

"Imani, did my mother get there yet?" He asked.

"About two hours ago. She and your aunt took the kids downtown. They are sightseeing. Sierra took her son today so I could rest before this luncheon but my mind is full with all this bullshit. I can't even think about anything else, much less get some good sleep. My stomach is bothering me too. You know how it gets when I am stressed."

"Why not try a hot shower and relax? Everything is going to be okay. I'm going to call you back in a few hours to check up on you." Quinton said.

"I am supposed to hang out with your aunt and cousin." I stated.

"They'll understand. Tell them you are not feeling up to it." He offered.

"Alright. I'll talk to you then." I replied.

"Imani, I'm serious. Get some rest." He ordered.

"Yes, daddy." I jokingly replied.

"Love you." He said then we disconnected.

I hadn't had a good night's sleep since this ordeal began. As much as I needed to sleep and relax, I could not. Instead, I reached for my laptop and began a new story using the drama for inspiration. Within three hours, I had over sixty pages, aching fingers, and heavy lids. After releasing some of my worries and pain, the tension began to ease and I finally felt relaxed and found good sleep.

When I woke up, five hours had passed. Feeling as if I had slept away my troubles, I was able to finally leave the basement and join the family. Quinton's mother and I ran into each other as she was running to the kitchen to turn off the stove. The house was full of people; by the resemblance, I assumed they were all Quinton's family. Takiyah and her husband, Wil were trying to keep the kids entertained while Katherine and Henry greeted guest as they poured through the door. I never imagined Quinton had such a large family; he never mentioned it. Kai-Aja was the first to notice that I entered the living room and ran towards me. Bryan and Jahlek smiled and waved then continued what they were doing.

"What's up little girl?" I asked as I kissed her forehead.

"Nothing. How are you feeling?" she asked.

"I'm fine. Where's Naadira?"

"She's upstairs in Aunt Katherine's room taking a nap. She fell asleep in the car when we were coming back from the museum." Kai replied.

"Did you have fun?"

"Yeah, you should have come. We went to the Coca Cola store and Nana bought me, Sierra, Jessie and Naadi matching Coca Cola shirts and shorts. Then she bought a bunch of ashtrays, glasses, and stuff to take home. The boys didn't want anything but they picked up like three shirts for daddy. Oh yeah, he called a little while ago."

"Did you speak to him?" I asked.

"We all did. Well Naadi was sleeping but he said he would call to speak to her later."

"Alright, well let me see if Nana and Aunt Katherine need any help with anything before I go check on Naadi." I said as I walked with Kai into the kitchen.

In the kitchen, I was greeted with a surprise. My brother, Jordan was sitting at the table peeling potatoes. Jordan instantly added a sense of security and put my anxieties to rest. They always said God put the right people in your life at the right time.

"What are you doing here?" I asked before greeting him with a kiss to the cheek.

"I was out here on business and ran into your kids at the museum. Your mother-in-law invited me over for dinner. How are you? Looking a little chunky. Expecting?" Jordan asked as he rubbed my belly.

"No I am not." I stated as I pushed his hands away.

"I thought the same thing." Mama J added.

"Mama please. We got our hands full already." I wrapped my arm around Kai and smiled. "My baby is about to be a teenager. I got to keep my eye on her."

"She is beautiful, Imani." Jordan complimented Kai-Aja.

Kai smiled then replied, "Thank you."

"You know I almost didn't recognize your brother. It's not like he has made it to any of my affairs." Mama J said as she took the bucket of peeled potatoes from the table.

"I'm sorry Mama. I have been so busy getting my business off the ground. We opened a new store in Baltimore and it's been a little rough." Jordan said in defense.

"Aren't you supposed to be showcasing at that event back in New York tomorrow night?"

"Yes. I have a flight out early in the morning. Where's Quinton?" He asked.

"He's in New York. He'll probably be here tomorrow." I replied.

"I guess that means y'all won't be making it to the party tomorrow night?"

I shook my head then responded, "I was planning on going, but we had a slight change of plans."

"It's cool. You'll have to make it your business not to miss the next one."

"When is it?"

"Next Wednesday. It is a networking series. They have different host and location every week. I got two weeks because it is brand new and they didn't really have many host lined up. In fact, I need your boy's number. Maybe Rahsaun would be interested in doing something up in Baltimore."

"Definitely. Remind me to give it to you before you leave." I said.

I made my way around the kitchen, trying figure out what I can help with. It seemed as if everything was taken care of so I decided to check on Naadira. As I made my way up the stairs, the phone began to ring from Katherine's room. I ran up the stairs to catch the call but was unsuccessful. When I reached the room, the phone stopped ringing and Naadira was wide-awake.

"Hey, Sunshine." I said as I ran a hand over her loose curls.

She smiled and reached her arms out. With her arms wrapped around my neck, a feeling of warmth filled my body. I prayed it was a sign that everything was going to be all right.

಄಄಄ಢಢಢ

RODNEY

Sandra called to let me know that she had arrived in California safely. I informed her that I had movers pack all the contents of her apartment and sent it to storage until she found housing in California for her things to be shipped. Sandra was relieved that she was able to leave and finally live peacefully. She said that Jasmine asked to speak to her father several times since they arrived. Sandra told Jasmine that Trey was in jail and they had to wait for him to call them. She did not believe Jasmine bought the story. I assured Sandra that before Jasmine could find a way to contact Trey that he would be taken care of. She apologized repeatedly for all the problems she caused in the past and offered to repay me for my help. I told her it was not necessary because I did not do any of it for her, it was for my baby girl, Sharay. With that, she was satisfied. She asked me to give Sharay her brother's number so that they could keep in contact. Then she said the unexpected.

"Rodney, you know I always loved you. In my heart, you were right for me but it wasn't about what my heart said. My mind was filled with fantasies of what the life had to offer. Bryan had promised me all that money could offer and coming up the way I did, where my brother and I had to split peanut butter and jelly sandwiches for dinner and share clothes, it seemed like a dream come true. You wanted to love me and share a commitment. I wish now I would have listened to my heart. I'm sorry if I broke yours. Don't let a good woman slip through your hands for my mistakes. Charisse is a wonderful woman and mother. She loves you. That's forever. Something I am not sure I could have ever given you."

"Sandra, I know there's a good woman inside of you. Sharay and I have been talking and she told me about all the things you've been through and I know how much you sacrificed for your girls. I think it wasn't the right time for us. Now that we've both had time to grow, fate will put the right people in our lives to help us move forward. Like Reese fell into my life, I am positive that your special someone will drop into yours."

"Yeah..." she paused briefly then sighed. "I hope so. Too be honest with you, I was a little jealous of what you and Charisse had and that's partly why I kept Sharay from you. It was foolishness."

"So what was the other part?"

"Excuse me?"

"You said partly. So what was the other reason you tried to keep Sharay from me?"

"In my own little warped world, I knew eventually you would come back for her and that would be my way to get you back." She replied.

I laughed a little then said, "Okay, since we're being honest with each other. The only reason I didn't come around sooner was that I knew it wouldn't take much from you to make me leave Reese. Somewhere deep inside I had this feeling we belonged together."

"Is that feeling still there?" she asked.

"If you would have asked me last month, I probably would have had to think about it. But I realize now that you and I have the same mentality and that's what attracted me to you but that wouldn't have worked for us in the end. You were down for whatever but not for commitment and underneath it all that's what mattered most to me. For years, Reese had been giving me that commitment and I couldn't see that. I felt like I needed more but always came up empty when I really thought, *'what else am I looking for?'* As my sister Stephanie would put it, Charisse is politically correct for me. She will always be there for me, through the good and the bad."

"Wow." She whispered. "I guess I really need to take some time and learn what love really means before I start looking for Mr. Right, huh?"

We both stood silent. I felt awkward and thought to end the call.

"Sandra, go ahead and get yourself together. I got some things to take care of. I'll make sure Sharay gets the number and gives you a call. Oh, when she comes back this weekend do you want me to send her over there to California with you?"

Sandra didn't reply right away. When she did, I was left in shock. "No. I want her to stay with you. I mean legally she is your daughter and I think it's time I start giving you that respect."

"What do you mean legally?"

"Remember the paperwork we started that I said I threw away. I lied. They had been filed years ago. They already had your signature so I took them back to the same lawyer and had it processed. Sharay is your daughter, Rodney. Now she has your last name to match. I'm surprised she never mentioned it. She's been using Bennett since junior high school. A copy of the papers was sent to your mother. Your sister called me when they got there. I can't believe no one ever told you." Sandra said as happiness filled her voice.

"I knew Sharay had visited my mother and sisters over the years. I don't know why she never mentioned it to me though. Sandra, thank you. This is the best news I've heard in a long time."

"No, thank you." She said. "I will talk to y'all soon. Take care."

Quinton, Mike, and I were on our way back to Pennsylvania. Mike was convinced that we had Trey this time so Quinton believed him and again put off his plans to go to his family. His boys had been watching Shandi's house all night and said they saw movement inside the house and no one entered or left. They believed that Trey and his men were inside making plans on moving out. My instincts were telling me otherwise. Trey was not inside that house or this state for that matter. He had already made his move. In fact, Mike was a step behind Trey. My gut was also telling me that Trey was on his way to Bryan junior. If Quinton had not been brain washed by his new suburbia lifestyle his street instinct would be telling him the same.

Quinton and I went to his office, picked up his car and were on our way to meet Mike.

"After this we can get back to our women and the normal order of things." Quinton stated as we pulled in front of the house.

"Q, I think we should have gone down to Georgia. Something ain't right, Man. It feels like we are being given the okey-doke."

"By who? You think Trey got us following bogus breadcrumbs?"

"Not only Trey but your boy Mike seems to be on the wrong team."

"How you figure?" Quinton asked.

"Why is he insisting that you go with him on this sting? He and his boys should be able to handle this without you. Q, let's go get that flight and get Trey's ass."

Quinton sat with a confused look on his face.

"I don't think Mike is on the wrong team but I think you're right. This is a set-up. I don't think Mike's *informant* is on the right team."

Quinton started his car and began to slowly reverse down the block. I guess he figured he could avoid Mike this way. Quinton wasted no time heading for the airport. He called his boy who had been with us and let him know we were heading out and ask him to keep us posted on what was going on. When we arrived at the airport, Quinton headed over to the ticket agent while I phoned Jamal. I gave Jamal the okay to take down Trey's boys and track down Mike's informant, if one actually existed. Once I ended the call, I caught up to Q who was flagging me with the tickets as he headed to the terminal. As we were about to board, Quinton's phone rang.

He put the phone on speaker.

"Where you at, Q?" Mike asked.

"I had to head back to the house. Did you get in the house yet?"

Before Mike could respond, gunshots rang through the line.

"Oh shit!" Mike shouted before his phone disconnected.

Quinton's phone rang again this time it was his boy, Earl.

"Yo, Trey's team took down three of Mike's men. Trey ain't nowhere in sight though. Mike and the rest of his team are engaged in a shoot out with these dudes. Our boys are rolling up now. We are going to end this shit. Go handle yours." Earl said then hung up.

Jamal was calling as he hung up.

"What's up?" I asked.

"Yo, it's empty. Looks like Trey moved his whole operation. We got one of his boys though. According to him, Trey had ordered his boys to hit up Q's house. Nobody knows where he is though. I'm going to keep putting on the pressure see if he keeps talking." Jamal replied.

"Alright. I'm going to get back at you." I replied. "Fuck!" I shouted after I hung up.

"Your boys ain't come up with shit either" Quinton questioned then proceeded with his statement. "Two dead leads and an empty shop. This shit ain't good Rodney. How are we going to find this dude?"

"We might have to let him find us and be ready for war."

"That's putting my family at risk."

"What's our other option? He is after Bryan and Sharay. Sharay...oh shit."

I jumped from my seat and started to exit the plane.

"We gotta split up. Go to your family. I gotta get to Reese."

Quinton threw his car keys to me, "Take my car."

I called Charisse as I sat in traffic. Her phone went directly to her voicemail.

"Hey Baby. There was a change in plans. I am on my way to you and the kids. Do not leave the house! I'll be there as soon as possible."

Unsatisfied, I decided to call her parent's house.

"Hello." A female voice answered.

"Hey, Lauren. Is Charisse around?"

"This is not Lauren." She replied with a tinge of attitude.

"Oh, I'm sorry Taniqua. Is your sister there?"

"Sorry, this is not Taniqua either. And before you attempt to guess again, no, it's not Mrs. Nettles either. Goodbye."

I immediately called back but the line was busy. I continued to redial until the line was clear.

"Hello." The same female answered.

"Excuse me. I know your family has their own judgment of me but you can't keep me from my wife. May I please speak with Charisse?"

"She can't speak with you right now, Rodney. We were in the middle of feeding the kids. Do not call here any more, motherfucker. Stay away from *my* wife." Then the line disconnected.

Myra! What is she doing over there? I knew Charisse didn't have anything to do with her being there. At least I hoped not.

Knowing that everyone would be trying to get out of town for the holiday, I decided to find a hotel and wait out the traffic. Several times during the night, I tried calling Charisse's cell phone and still I was unsuccessful. It was only eight yet my eyes were burning, in need of a rest. I placed my phone on the nightstand, put my gun under my pillow, and headed for the shower. The hot water beat over my shoulder, massaging the tension loose. As I continued to enjoy the moment, I heard my cell phone ringing. I turned off the water, tied a towel around my waist and attempted to catch the call but was greeted with another surprise.

"Hello, Rodney." The strange woman said as she sat in a chair in the dark corner.

"Do I know you?" I replied.

"No." She replied before stepping into the light.

Before I could speak, she struck me over the head with a bat.

CHAPTER 16

QUINTON

The plane landed minutes after seven. I tried to relax and rest during the flight but I was too anxious. My mind was occupied with finding the man who was terrorizing my family and then bringing them home safe. I looked out the window and watched the sun begin to set as we began to descend in Atlanta. The last time I remember watching a sunset was when Imani and I took our children camping over the summer. Reminiscing on the children laughing and carrying on while Imani and I shared intimate conversation helped me find a comfort zone. So much has gone on this year yet I know there are so many more good times to look forward to. As we began to exit the plane, all my serenity was snatched away as I had to watch my surrounding and be careful of who was watching me.

Imani met me at the airport with my stepfather, James and my cousin Glen. I didn't want Imani traveling alone since Trey could have been anywhere. Imani greeted me with a huge hug and a ton of kisses. Every kiss was sweeter than I last imagined and her closeness excited me. She was dressed in a cream pants suit, which complemented every curve, fitting her perfectly. Her hair neatly pinned in a bun added maturity and sex appeal to the package. I could not wait to get back to my aunt's house and steal a couple of seconds of privacy with Imani. I needed her.

James started the car as Glen and I exchanged greetings. Once we were inside the car, Glen asked for an update.

"It's not like I don't love you cuz, but I knew it had to be something serious for you to bring your city ass down here." Glen joked.

"Well, hopefully we won't have any more visits under these circumstances." Imani replied.

"Why didn't you get Shea to come down with you?" James asked as he kept his eyes on the road.

"I didn't even mention it to him." I answered.

"Where's Rodney?" James asked.

"He went to Charisse's parents' house. We thought it would be best to split up. Who knows where this nigga is gonna show up. Plus, it's the holidays. We should be spending it with our families." I replied.

As we neared our exit, a yellow Hummer raced up beside us, blocking us from our exit. James tried maneuvering around the jeep but the driver would give way as a blue van pulled up on the opposite side. James sped up, trying to get from between the two vehicles but they continued to do the same. I told him to put on his hazard lights, keep speeding to give them the impression that we are going to give them a race, then hit the brakes. As James was about to hit the brake, the passenger side window of the van lowered and shots were fired.

"Duck!" Glen shouted.

James hit the brakes and the two cars continued speeding pass. No one was injured inside our car. James pulled to the side of the road to gather his composure as I held Imani and tried to calm her. Surprisingly, Imani didn't look the least bit frazzled. Things had been so unpredictable, I guess crazy became normal.

"What are we going to do now, Q? What if they follow us back to the house?" Imani questioned.

"She's right, Q. We can't risk these guys following us to the house." James said as he pulled out his cell phone.

"Let's go to my house. I'll call Shannon and tell her to stay at Momma's house." Glen stated.

"That's a plan. I need to make a couple of calls myself. How far are we from your house?" I asked.

"About ten minutes on this highway but I know another way, it will take us a little longer, but they are probably waiting for us somewhere along this route. It's safer to go through the streets." Glen replied.

"Alright. James, do you need me to take over?" I asked.

"Quinton now you know I may be old but I ain't no punk. I don't scare easy either. I got this, young buck. Call your people." James replied as he made his way off the highway.

I called Earl and asked if he had any people in the South. I needed to get a crew and some guns, fast. Earl gave me his cousin in Alabama. He said that was as close as he could get, which was close enough. Earl's cousin, Doug agreed to meet up with us at Glen's place.

It was a little after ten, Imani had taken some medication and was asleep for over two hours by the time Doug and his boys had reached Georgia. Three Suburban trucks full with big men with big guns pulled up to Glen's small townhouse. Doug agreed that we should comb downtown Atlanta for any information. More than likely, Trey would be close by hoping to catch an opportunity at Bryan or me. If he had done his research like we assumed he did, he would probably be Downtown. That was where the family restaurant was. We organized two teams— one to watch over my aunt's house and one to hit the streets. Imani rode back to the house with James, Glen and the team that Doug's brother was apart of.

Imani phoned when she arrived home. Meanwhile, Doug and I rode down Peachtree checking out local hangouts. As we turned onto 12th Street, the same yellow Hummer was parked in front of a pool hall. Doug pulled his truck into an alleyway; we loaded our guns and headed for the storefront hangout. Doug kicked open the door and people started scurrying. Four men jumped up from their seats at the bar and started shooting towards us. One of the men I recognized as one of Mike's boys. They started for the backdoor as we returned fire. We followed with shots ringing in all directions. Mike's boy ran through the alley and I followed.

"Officer Simmons!" I shouted.

He continued running then ducked behind a parked car and began firing in my direction. I found shelter behind a van and returned fire. As I changed my empty clip, he started running again, screaming into his radio. I was tired of running, I ran a couple of feet aimed and shot him in the back of his head. The yellow Hummer sped up the street, almost running me over. I jumped out the way as the jeep drove past the officer's body and screeched around the corner.

Doug drove up in his truck and we continued to chase the Hummer. The chase proceeded onto the highway. Two of Doug's boys hung out the window firing at the jeep. Through the lightly tinted windows, we could see two men. Doug shot one of their people back in the alleyway, leaving just them. The passenger leaned out of his window, firing at us. Doug swerved to the right, and then sped up until we were side by side with the jeep. The driver tried to maneuver around us but was trapped by an oil truck on the opposite side. He pulled out his gun; I shot first. The jeep became out of control, Doug slowed down to move out of its way as it headed for the divider. The passenger jumped out and was struck by another speeding car as the Hummer caught fire.

Partially satisfied with the outcome, we decided to grab a bottle of Hennessey and head back to the base—Glen's house—until morning.

Thanksgiving Eve and nothing but drama. Imani called early that morning to let me know that someone called her cell phone asking for Bryan. When she asked for the caller's name, he began laughing and blowing kisses. Then he complimented her on her outfit. She and the family were at the restaurant for breakfast. Trey did exactly what we thought. However, when Doug's brother checked the area and restaurant, there was no Trey. I told Imani to stay there, we were on our way. Doug ended his call with his brother and we headed to the restaurant. When we arrived to the restaurant, everyone was laughing and enjoying their meals as if there was nothing wrong.

Kai and Jahlek were the first to notice me and screamed, "Daddy."

"Hey, what's going on?" I replied as I hugged them both.

I kissed Kai on her cheek and she laughed.

"What's up with the caveman look?" Kai asked referring to my unshaven face.

"It's been a long week, Baby." I replied then tickled her sides.

I took Jahlek into a headlock and walked towards the conjoined tables, where the rest of our family was seated.

Imani rose from her seated and greeted me with a soft kiss on the lips.

"Everything's okay?" I asked.

"Now it is." She said as her eyes sparkled.

"What's everybody laughing about?" I asked as I joined the table.

"Your mother." Aunt Katherine replied.

"Ain't nothing funny 'bout me Katie." My mother replied angrily.

"Mama and your aunt have been arguing all morning. Your mother must have had enough because she kindly got up and snatched the wig off your aunt's head. It was so funny everyone busted out in laughter." Imani said as she tried to stifle her laughter.

Laughter erupted once again and everything was calm for the moment. Doug and his boys took seats along the counter and began enjoying Takiyah's good cooking while her husband Wil continued to serve the hot plates. Naadira sat on my lap acting as if she were feeding me while Imani ran her hand up and down the opposite thigh. Imani's cell phone rang again and all was quiet. She passed her phone and I answered.

"You got what I want. You choose! The money or your bitch." Trey said.

"You want it. Come see me for it, faggot." I replied.

"Feeling big around your family? You don't run shit anymore, Q. If I don't get my money by midnight, it's your wife's ass." He threatened then disconnected.

Heat rose up my spine. Bryan noticed the rage in my eyes.

"Dad, let's take a walk."

ഇഇഇരുന്ന

<u>CHARISSE</u>

Rodney hadn't called and I became worried. I asked Lauren and my mother to watch my children while Taniqua and I took a drive to calm my nerves. I contemplated driving to New York. I thought Rodney might have been back to his old antics and forgot to call like many times before. By the time Taniqua and I reached the highway, I thought better and turned around. Now was not the time for Rodney to play games.

"Charisse, where's your cell phone? Maybe he's trying to call you." Taniqua said as we pulled up to the mall.

215

"My battery is dead and I left my charger in New York. I'm about to buy one now." I replied as I reached for my pocketbook and exited the car.

Taniqua and I were in the Sprint store looking around until my name was called. Remembering that the phones on display were working phones, I decided to check my voicemail.

'You have fourteen new messages and two saved messages.'

'First message received today at seven seventeen p.m.': "Hey Baby. There was a change in plans. I am on my way to you and the kids. Do not leave the house! I'll be there as soon as possible."

I checked my watch. It was almost nine.

'Rodney should have been here by now.' I thought.

'Next message received at eight twenty three p.m.': "Reese, I don't know what fucking kind of games you're playing. This is my second time calling and your phone is still off. I called by your mother's house earlier and Myra picked up. What the fuck is going on? Call me!"

"Myra! That bitch!" I said after deleting the last message.

'Charisse Nettles.' The young female customer service representative called out.

"I am going to handle that bitch when I get back." I said aloud.

Customers looked in my direction as I approached the customer service desk.

Traffic was so thick it felt like we would never get back to the house. A twenty-minute ride turned into an hour. The longer I sat in traffic the more frustrated I became. My anger was at its peak after calling Rodney's cell phone ten times and each time getting his voicemail. I tried my mother's house, he wasn't there yet. I tried calling his house, no answer.

Taniqua begged me not to fight Myra in our parents' house but that wasn't a promise I could keep. As soon as we stepped in the door, she was the first to greet us.

"Hey, Reese. I put the kids to sleep and ..."

Before she could finish, I channeled all the strength I had into my hand and slapped her to the floor.

"Reese!" Taniqua shouted as I lifted my foot to stomp on Myra's face.

Lauren ran across the living room and tackled me into the sofa.

"That's not how we get down, Reese." Lauren said as she pinned me to the cushions.

"Get off of me. You are only making me angrier. Even if I don't handle her today, she is going to get hers." I said as I tried to free myself.

Myra stood, holding the side of her face and walked towards us.

"I don't know what got into you but if you ever lay a hand on me again, it will be the last thing you do." Myra threatened before walking away.

"Don't try to act innocent, Bitch. Why didn't you tell me Rodney called? What did you say to him?" I shouted.

"I don't know what you're talking about." Myra replied.

"You don't know what I'm talking about? He left messages on my phone, Myra. He spoke to you and you never told me. Don't lie."

"So what, Reese! He called and I told him *we* were busy with the kids. He doesn't care about you, not like I do. Where is he now?" She said as she returned to the sofa.

Lauren released her hold and Taniqua moved back.

"Face it, Charisse. He is probably out fucking one of the many bitches he's *been* fucking." Myra shouted in my face. "And you're sitting here looking like an asshole."

I pulled my knees into my chest and then released them with all my might, kicking Myra in her abdomen. Again, she fell to the floor and this time no one was holding me back. I pounced on top of her and commenced to kicking her ass. Each blow to her face was more powerful than the last. My father came running down the stairs, hollering at the top of his lungs.

"Charisse! Charisse, get off that girl now!"

He grabbed the back off my coat and pulled me off her.

"Why are you two sitting there watching? You know this is not acceptable." He shouted at Lauren and Taniqua.

Myra stood up with a bloody nose and bruised face. My father stood between us facing my sisters and me, still chastising us while

Myra reached for her bag and pulled out a small black gun.

"Poppa, move!" She shouted as she pointed the gun at me.

"Myra put the gun down, Baby." My mother said as she stood on the staircase.

"I love you, Reese. Why you gotta do this to me? Why you gotta do this to us?" Myra cried as she waved the gun back and forth, using it as a pointing tool.

"I told you, Myra. It is over. I will always have a special place for you but I can't love you, I can't be with you." I explained.

"Put the gun down, Myra. You and Reese need to work this out without all this craziness. Fighting and carrying on like strangers is not going to fix anything." My father said as he moved closer to Myra.

Sharay was standing in the doorway, which led to the basement. Myra continued her rampage, threatening to shoot who ever came close. Sharay stood quietly behind Myra, looking as if she were waiting for the moment to act. I shook my head, hoping she would think twice. Sharay reached behind the door, reached for my father's autographed bat, and hit Myra over the head. Myra squeezed the trigger sending a bullet into my shoulder as my sisters scrambled away. Both Myra and I fell to the floor, facing each other.

"My baby!" My mother shouted before running down the stairs and kneeling by my side.

"Call the ambulance!" My father ordered.

Little feet scurried about as I began to lose focus. I wasn't sure if it was the pain from my shoulder or the loss of blood that caused me to feel faint and dizzy. I could hear Christian crying as tears poured from my eyes.

"Get him out of here." Lauren said to one of her children.

Taniqua gathered the young ones and ushered them into the kitchen. Sharay sat by my side crying.

"I'll be alright." I managed a whisper. "Watch over your brothers and sister for me."

"I'm going to call Daddy, Reese." Sharay said before brushing my hair out of my face.

When I woke up, I was laying on a hospital bed, arm bandaged and full of pain. My mother was in a chair beside my bed, head full of rollers and snoring. A nurse entered with a small white paper cup and a pitcher of water.

"Ms. Nettles, I have some pain medication for you. Do you need me to adjust the bed?" She asked as she set the pitcher of water and cup on the table by my bed.

"I'm fine." I replied.

My mother woke as I took the cup from the nurse.

"Oh, Reese. How are you feeling, Sweetie?" My mother asked as she stood from her seat.

"I'm okay. In a little pain but I'll be fine."

I sipped some water and tried to adjust myself into a more comfortable position but was too weak to move.

"How are my kids? How is Christian?" I asked.

"They're fine. Pop-pop is watching them."

"How's Sharay? Is she okay? I can't believe this is happening."

"Reese, she is fine. She and Lauren went down to the police station to make a statement. Everything will be fine. You trust your momma, right? Your family will not let you down." She tried to convince me but I wasn't sold.

"You already have." I stated.

"Excuse me? How have I let you down?" She asked.

"What possessed you to invite Myra over? You knew we were having problems. Last I remember she wasn't on your favorite people list. When did things change?"

My mother stood silent. My intentions were not to hurt her. It was time to let her know that she could not continue trying to run my life. I was tired of running away from her.

"Myra isn't my favorite person but you two were so happy together. I wanted you to be happy again. It broke your father's heart to hear you cry. Rodney has only brought you heartache, Honey. I thought that if I could get you away from Rodney long enough, you and Myra could rediscover whatever it was that y'all had. Whatever it was that made you happy."

"Ma, things have changed. Rodney is not only the father of my kids but the man that I am deeply in love with. Regardless of all the madness I went through with him, in the end, I will always want him. Myra and I did have something special but that was more than seven years ago. After I was raped, Myra helped me feel safe and whole again. She taught me how to have fun and find my strength. Yes, we had a bond. She showed me so much. I loved her for that however; I lost that feeling long before I met Rodney. Myra was not my soul mate, Ma. Rodney is."

"Charisse, you sound confused. How can you flip back and forth like that yet expect me to believe you know what you want? One man hurts you and you develop a relationship with a woman until you feel the thirst for a man again. That doesn't make sense and sounds like a pile of shit to me."

"Ma, even if the incident didn't occur I would have had a relationship with a woman. I am attracted to both women and men. However, I am only attracted to one person right now and I will be with that one for the rest of my life. Rodney is my twin spirit. Like Daddy to you. You don't have to like it but you are going to have to get use to it."

It was a huge relief to be able to express myself. For years, I avoided conversation with my mother. She was not a fan of my lifestyle, condemning it with harsh words and awkward glances whereas my father did not openly approve of it but would never treat me any different.

My mother wiped away tears as she sat on the hospital bed beside me.

"Charisse, I love you. I'm sorry I was so hard on you. Whom you chose to live your life with is your decision, but as your mother, I can't help but want the best for you. If you say Rodney is the man you want to spend the rest of your life with, then I wish you both the best, with all my heart."

Two doctors walked in as my mother kissed my cheek. One doctor, a young Asian female, brightened the room with her smile, while the other an older African-American gentlemen face remained emotionless.

"Ms. Nettles. I am Dr. Pierce and this is Dr. Chan. How are you feeling this morning?"

"I'm blessed." I replied.

"That's wonderful. We have been looking over your chart and everything looks very good. We were able to remove the bullet, there are no fragments in the x-rays and outside of the wound itself there was no major damage. We are going to keep you for today, to keep an eye on the wound. Hopefully you'll be out of here in the morning." Dr. Pierce said.

He closed the chart and put it under his arm.

"Do you have any questions or concerns?" Dr. Chan asked.

"Yeah. What are the Thanksgiving breakfasts like in here?" I asked.

Everyone laughed, even bold-faced Dr. Pierce.

"Your father and I are going to bring you breakfast. We will bring your babies, too." My mother stated before turning to the doctors. "How about Myra? Is she going to be okay?"

"Yes, she will be fine. We had to sedate her though. She gave us a hard time but we were able to close the wound with minimal stitches. However, after the medication wears off she may be in a lot of pain." Dr. Chan replied.

I giggled as I thought to myself, '*Damn, Sharay busted her head open.*'

"I'm sorry she was difficult." My mother apologized then looked at me with a chastising stare.

"It's fine. We have patients like her every now and again. Well, we have some other patients to see but we will see you before you leave." Dr. Pierce stated then turned and headed out of the room.

"So, what are you going to do with Myra?" My mother asked.

"Honestly, I don't know. I mean she's really not my responsibility. Maybe, you can call her sister and they can get her. Personally, I don't care what happens with her."

The room phone rang and my mother answered.

"Okay. Really, that's great! What? Oh no. Are they sure? Oh God. Okay, go on and help your father with dinner. I'll be home shortly."

The fear in my mother's eyes made my stomach quiver.

"What happened?" I asked.

"They let Sharay go. The police said that she acted on self-defense. Lauren retold the story to the police stating that Myra threatened everyone with the gun and as she turned away from Sharay, she saw it as the opportunity to attack Myra. They may have to arrest Myra though."

"Okay, now give me the bad news. I know that's not it." I said as I prepared myself for the worst.

"The police found Rodney's car in a ditch." My mother immediately covered her mouth and closed her eyes. It was her usual reaction to fear.

"Oh no! Is he okay?" I shouted.

"He wasn't inside. They're still searching for him." She replied.

CHAPTER 17

IMANI

Have you ever had that wicked feeling that something was about to go really wrong? Knowing the reasons that sent us to Atlanta were not positive, I still had this hope that everything would turn out fine. No violence involved, our family unharmed and our holiday would be a quiet yet joyous one. However, after that last phone call, my gut had a reality check. Not everything was going to turn out as good as I hoped. While Quinton and Bryan stood outside, I felt the urge to call Charisse. She was the one who kept me sane when my world was full of drama; however, this time was different. Both of our lives focused on the same drama. Since she did not call me, I figured no news was good news so I decided not to call with my troubles and let her have a peaceful visit with her family.

Kai-Aja sat beside me and laid her head on my shoulder.

"What's up, Sweetie?" I asked as I placed a hand on her lap.

"I wanna go home, now." She replied somberly.

"I know, Baby. I can definitely understand how you feel."

Quinton walked back to the table while Bryan stayed outside on his cell phone.

"Hey Baby Girl, are you okay?" He asked Kai-Aja as he stood behind us.

"I'm fine, Daddy." She replied.

"Come here, Baby. Talk to me." Quinton took Kai's hand and led her away from the table.

Bryan entered the restaurant with a worried look on his face.

"Mom, I think you need to call Aunt Reese. I was talking to Sharay and she said Aunt Reese is in the hospital. I tried to find out what happened but she said she couldn't really talk because she was at the police station." Bryan stated as he returned to his seat at the table.

"Are you serious? Did she tell you if Reese was okay?" I asked as I searched for my cell phone.

"No. She said it got crazy over there last night and Reese is in the hospital." Bryan replied.

"Where the hell is my phone?" I shouted as I stood from my seat.

Everyone fell silent as they looked in my direction.

"Quinton had it." Mama J said as she took dishes to the kitchen.

"Bryan let me use your phone, please."

"Here." He replied as he passed the phone across the table.

Immediately, I dialed Charisse's cell but it went straight to voicemail. I wanted to call her parent's house but the number slipped my mind. I played with the buttons until I remembered the number and dialed. Charisse's father answered. The tone in his voice didn't implicate that anything was wrong.

"Hello, Mr. Nettles. This is Imani. Is Charisse around?"

"Hey there Imani, how are you?" He asked.

"I'm fine, and yourself?"

"I'm doing well. Can't complain. Reese is not here."

"Do you know when she will be back?" I asked, hoping he would tell me what was going on.

"She will be home tomorrow. I will tell her you called."

"Please, Mr. Nettles forgive me if I am being inquisitive but my son received a phone call from Sharay. He said that Charisse was in the hospital. Is she alright?"

"Oh." He replied. "Yes, Charisse is in the hospital. Don't worry. She's fine."

Mr. Nettles went into details of what transpired the night before. Although it was a serious situation, I wanted to laugh. I held it back. I could not believe Myra shot Charisse. I was relieved to here that Charisse was in good health; I still wanted to speak to her though.

"Does she have a number I could reach her at?" I asked.

"When my wife comes in, I'll get the number and tell Charisse to call you. I don't have the number yet."

"Thank you so much, Mr. Nettles. Happy Thanksgiving."

"The same for you and your family." He replied.

Dinner was over, restaurant was clean, and everyone except Wil and Takiyah, was ready to get back to the house and relax. Mama J and Aunt Katherine decided to start preparing the dishes for the following night. If they did not agree on anything else, they shared a passion for cooking. James took the boys out to the backyard to play football while Quinton and I stole a couple of minutes in privacy. When we reached the basement, I gave him an once-over. Although the unkempt look was not his thing, it was somewhat sexy. I walked over to him and began to help him out of his sweater. Quinton stood before me with sculpted muscles under a gray t-shirt or what the kids called a 'wife beater', black jeans and a pair of Timberlands. He did not have to do much else; I wanted him badly, just like that. Quinton allowed me to have my time. He did not speak, just continued looking into my eyes, occasionally brushing my cheek with the back of his fingers.

"Do you want me to shave you?" I asked as I ran my hand over his facial hair.

"Yes, I would like that."

I led Quinton into the bathroom, motioning him to sit on the edge of the bathtub. I retrieved his travel case, removed his razor and shaving cream, and placed it in the sink. Quinton placed his hands on my bottom and pulled me close. He laid his head on my stomach and exhaled deeply.

"You okay?" I asked as I turned off the running water.

"I wish I could take you and the kids away from all this." He replied.

"Kai got to you?" I asked.

"Kai didn't have to tell me what I already knew. We do not deserve to be here. We traveled down our rocky road. The kids have been through enough for one lifetime."

"Remember when I thought I took all I could and was about to lose my mind. You were the one that told me that to ensure our family's safety and my own happiness sometimes the things we had to do and go through was never *too* much. Quinton, I know that you may think things are piling on your shoulders and you are not sure how much more you can carry, but it is never too much to see our kids happy, for us to be happy. Yeah, Baby it's a lot right now but years from now it will be another bump in the road."

Quinton looked up; his eyes filled with worry and hints of regret. I kissed the top of his head and whispered, "I love you. I got your back, Baby."

"Mrs. Banks, do you know what you mean to me?" Quinton asked.

He slowly rose from his seat then pulled me into his embrace. "You're my everything, Girl." He whispered.

Quinton began to undress. I followed. Both of us were standing naked staring at each other. His chocolate body yearned for affection, inviting me in. I stepped closer to him, looking up into his face. His face displayed all his hurt, confusion, and love. I wanted to make him happy again, take the pain away but I knew Quinton could not be satisfied until we were home and our family was back to normal. He turned on the shower, stepped inside and reached for me to join him. Once the curtain shielded us, he wasted no time finding passion. My back against the tile, Quinton leaned on me, his arms above my head and kissing my sensitive spots. My body moaned from deep down wanting him to touch me and he complied. As his lips trailed from my lips down my neck, his hands found their place on my breasts and my bottom. Lost in his touch, I closed my eyes and imagined being far away, him and me, under a waterfall, somewhere tropical and serene.

"Quinton, I don't want to fight with you anymore. The last couple of months have been so tense between us. I want us to be a team again." I said, eyes still closed, enjoying the moment.

"We never stopped being a team. It's been tough lately but no one said having kids, jobs and maintaining a home was going to be easy. I love you Imani. You're my Boo, remember? That's forever."

I laughed then grabbed the back of his head and pulled him in for a kiss that was full of fervor. Quinton parted my legs with his and wedged himself between. My body cried as he found my core. For the first time in months, we were making love. It wasn't just sex; it was loving and mind-blowing, intimate and emotional. I missed Quinton and our special moments. Moments like these, when we were able to find ourselves where we started—in love and in sync— are what made our relationship tight and unshakeable. After spending almost an hour in the shower, we decided to take it to the bed, where we continued to feed each other's desires until sleep claimed our drained bodies.

Quinton's cell phone began to ring, waking us both. He didn't bother to check his Caller ID, nor did he take the call. He turned the cell phone off and returned to the bed. With his strong arms wrapped around me, I felt safe and warm. As I began to find comfort, there was a small knock on the basement door. The knocking continued this time followed by a voice.

"Daddy. Mommy. Are you down there?" Naadira asked from the other side of the wood door.

"Quinton, you're angel is looking for you." I said as I turned to face him.

"Give me a couple of seconds." He shouted, replying to Naadira's relentless knocking.

"I'll take care of her. Get some rest." I offered but Quinton continued to hold me tight.

"You are staying here with me woman." He said as he pulled me closer. His eyes still closed.

There was another knock at the door. This one a little stronger.

"Yes." I called out.

"Mom, tell Dad his friend Mike called my phone and said it's important that he calls him back." Bryan stated.

"Alright." I replied.

Quinton finally opened his eyes. "He must have heard about his boy."

"What happened?"

"Last night we saw some of Trey's crew hanging out Downtown. One of Trey's men happened to be an officer from Mike's precinct. He was shot last night."

"Is he dead?" I asked.

Quinton never answered. He turned on his cell phone and returned Mike's call.

"Hey Mike, what's going on?" Quinton paused. "Seriously. Damn."

Mike dominated the conversation; Quinton never lifted his head from his hands. Then like a bolt of electricity shot through his body, Quinton jumped from the bed, manhood dangling and all, with a huge smile on his face.

"In the Stone Mountain area. Yeah. You got an address....Hold on let me get a pen."

Quinton jotted down the address, thanked him, and then ended the call.

"Mike said as they were running a check on the officer they found he had rental property in Stone Mountain that he was running an operation out of and thought Trey might be there." Quinton said as he reached for his boxers.

"Is that far from here?" I asked.

"Not really. I hope Mike is right because if he is, all this will be over real soon." Quinton stated while putting on a pair of tan sweatpants and matching t-shirt.

"So, where are you going now?" I asked as I reached for my robe.

"To check on the kids and grab us something to eat. Don't move I'm coming back for some more loving." Quinton said before leaning in for a kiss.

"Alright." I replied then returned to the bed. "Oh Quinton, pass my phone please."

He reached into his jacket pocket, retrieved the phone, and then handed it to me.

"If he calls, come get me." Quinton said referring to Trey.

"Okay. Go on. I'm starving." I replied.

When I turned on the phone, it displayed that I had three messages. The first two messages were hang-ups. The third was Charisse. She left her hospital number and I called her immediately.

"Hello." She answered, sleepily.

"Hey, Mama. How are you?" I asked.

"Imani. Girl, you don't know how happy I am to hear from you."

"What's going on? I spoke to your father. Did ole' girl actually turn psycho on you?"

"Hell yeah! Bitch shot me!" Charisse replied with hate in her tone.

"Tell me what happened. I got to hear this one."

Charisse ran through the whole story, from Rodney's phone calls and messages, her whipping Myra's ass, getting shot and Sharay busting Myra upside the head with a bat. Then Charisse began to cry.

"Its okay, Reese. Calm down. Everyone is going to be fine. Concentrate on getting better and getting back to your beautiful babies."

"Everyone is not going to be fine. The police said they found Rodney's car in a ditch this morning and they are still searching for him. The roads were really bad last night plus with all the traffic, I…"

"Don't think the worst. Did they check the hospitals? Are they still searching?"

"Yes. They have been checking everywhere. It's almost nine o'clock, Imani. His last message was about this time yesterday. He's been missing for a whole day. I'm sick to my stomach."

"Ask the doctor's to give you something to help you calm down. Hold on, did you say they found Rodney's car in a ditch?"

"Yes, off of I-95. Why?"

"Rodney had Quinton's car. Quinton and Rodney separated at the airport and Rodney took Quinton's car. Rodney would not have been on I-95 coming from Pennsylvania. Somebody is trying to throw the police off. Call them and have them check Rodney's car because his car must have been stolen and who ever stole his car probably knows where he is. Meanwhile, I am going to call in Quinton's car as stolen. Give the police Quinton plates and have them start a search. Don't worry, Reese. We'll find Rodney."

"Imani, do you think this has to do with that money?"

"What else could it be?"

"Myra mentioned that he was with another woman and the way she said it kind of had me thinking." Charisse stated.

"Mama, Rodney ain't thinking about no one else but you and his kids. She said that out of despair. Have faith, Charisse. Everything is going to be okay."

"Thank you. I love you, Sis."

"Love you too. Now start making those calls."

As soon as we ended our conversation, I threw on a pair of shorts, Quinton's t-shirt, and ran upstairs. Quinton was on the couch playing with the kids. Instead of disturbing him, I went into another room called our town's police station, asked for Mike and told him the situation. He assured me he would get right on it. Then I joined my family.

ജ്ഞ്ഞ്ഞ്ഞ്

<u>RODNEY</u>

I wasn't sure if it was because of the bright light or the blow to my head that made my head throb. I struggled to focus, my eyes fluttered open and close. As I attempted to rise from the bed, I realized that my hand and feet were bound together. There was a female voice coming from the bathroom, singing while the shower ran. I tried to drown out the song with thoughts of Charisse and our kids but it seemed as if she was getting louder like the cry of a Banshee. The unfamiliar voice made my stomach churn from anxiety. Then there was a buzzing sound coming from the single seat in the corner of the room. Once the buzzing ended, there was a faint series of beeps. I realized then that the mystery woman had missed a call. The thought of struggling against the restraints briefly crossed my mind but I knew it would be useless. Instead, I laid there anxiously awaiting my kidnapper to emerge from the bathroom.

With all that was going on, I could not get my mind off the fact that Charisse and Myra were together. If I was that type of man, I could have strangled Charisse and Myra. I felt deceived and overall disgusted. Then to top it all off, I must have left Charisse over twenty messages and she had not even tried to contact me. I left my cell phone on with the ringer volume set on high in case she called. I heard my phone ring several times but Charisse had a specific ring tone, and that one never played.

A young woman exited the bathroom with only a towel wrapped around her torso barely covering her ass. Her wet hair dangled down her back as water dripped onto the carpeted floor. I continued to lie still awaiting her acknowledgement, threats, or whatever it was she had in

230

store. She continued around the room as if I wasn't even there, which was fine with me. As I was becoming comfortable with the silence, the room phone began to ring. My heart skipped a thousand beats a minute. That was when I realized this madness was driving me to a breaking point. What I had first mistaken as comfort was quiet anticipation.

The young woman opened the nightstand drawer, pulled out a 9mm and said, "Don't say anything that will get you shot." Before picking up the headset and putting it to my ear.

I answered. The conversation was short.

She returned the phone to its cradle then asked, "Who was it?"

"It was the front-desk clerk. Check-out is at eleven." I replied.

"Why didn't you tell him that you're staying?"

"I wasn't planning on staying."

"Well you're not in the position to leave, are you?"

"I guess not. Well, since your hands are free, call back."

"You want to be a wise ass, huh! You won't be so smart after I shoot your ass."

I stood quiet as I watched beads of water run off her shoulders from her wet hair as she walked over to the single seat to collect her clothing. Her saunter was enticing and as awkward as the situation was I felt myself becoming aroused as if this was some kind of freaky fantasy fulfilled. The kind of kinky stuff you think about asking your woman to do from time to time. As she sat down in the chair and rested the gun on the table, I tried to force myself to stop watching but my eyes stood fixed to the dark patch between her legs. She turned her back towards me and I continued to watch as she slid her sweat pants over her bare behind. Then she dropped the towel to the floor but kept her back turned as she pulled on a t-shirt. She picked up the towel and roughly dried her curly hair. By the time she turned to face me, she was picking up her coat and placing the gun inside her large brown leather bag.

"I'll be right back. Don't move." She laughed as she walked out the door.

Of course, the first thing I did was move. I tried pulling my hands from the ropes but they were tight and seemed to get tighter. After a couple of minutes of tugging, jerking, and cursing, trying to loosen the ropes, I gave up.

She returned and my anger had reached its max. All sorts of devious plans had crossed my mind. I was ready to play her game.

"Are you hungry?" She asked as she placed a plastic bag on the table.

"Nah, Why don't you call Trey and tell him to handle his business like a man instead having his bitch play a thug."

"Trey is handling his business and I ain't his chick."

"I should have figured that." I whispered but I know she heard me.

"What?"

"You are too pretty for that nigga'." I complimented her in an attempt to challenge her mental, looking for that weak spot or that moment where she would become vulnerable to my bullshit.

This woman looked desperate and even nervous at times. She didn't have the heart to hurt anyone. I figured I could play on that until the opportunity to reverse the roles presented itself.

She never responded to my last comment. Instead, she sat at the table and started eating her breakfast. Everything was quiet until the buzzing sound started again.

"Yeah." She answered.

There was a long pause before she spoke again.

"I didn't hear my phone ring. Everything is fine. Did you get it yet? Well, what are waiting for? Look, Trey it's going to look suspect...but...yeah, I heard you."

She threw her phone across the room and rested her head in her hands. A small part of me felt sorry for her.

I realized she didn't want to be here as much as I did.

"Look, I know this ain't your kind of situation so why get involved. Trey ain't nothing but trouble. Is it worth it?"

"Mind your business!" She shouted as tears poured from her eyes.

"Alright." I turned my head away and asked, "Are you getting something from this? Or, does he have something on you?"

"Trey is my brother. We both have too much invested in this. For Trey, it is about money, for me its revenge. Imani took something from me and now I have the opportunity to take something from her."

A small smile crossed my face and obviously annoyed the woman as she questioned, "Something funny?"

"Imani don't even give a shit about the money. Hell, she didn't find out about it until all this. So, this ain't got shit to do with Imani."

"That bitch killed my man! It's her fault Omar is dead. When he died, it left a void in my life. Now it's my time to leave a void in hers."

"Your life is filled with greedy low-life niggas. Omar was a crack-head whose issues stemmed from his greed for money. Imani already lost enough. She lost her mother. Now your molester brother wants money that doesn't belong to him. Are you ready to loose someone else over money?"

"Are you? If Quinton doesn't stop playing thug, you might loose someone close to you." She calmly said before heading for the bathroom.

Her comment caused my body to ignite with anger. At this point, it was better I was tied up. I might have strangled her for her loose tongue.

After she exited the bathroom, she sat beside me on the bed, reached for the remote and began watching T.V as if all were normal. She had even become comfortable enough to lie upon my chest. I knew this woman wasn't playing with a full deck. An hour into the movie my phone began to ring again and this time I almost jumped out of bondage. This time Charisse's ring tone played. I must have startled the deranged woman. She jumped up from the bed and sprinted towards the bag where she hid her gun. When she realized my phone was ringing, she searched the drawer until she found it.

"I'm going to let you answer this call. Don't say anything stupid." She said before putting the phone to my ear.

"Hello." I answered.

"Hi Daddy." Christian replied.

"Hey. How are you doing? How are your brother and sister?"

"I'm fine. Damien is playing with Alaire." My heart began to swell as I listened to my little boy. "Mommy is in the hospital. Papa said she is okay and she is coming home tomorrow. Where are you Daddy? I want you to be here with us." Christian began to cry.

Tears streaked down my cheeks and I knew it was time to get out of here.

"Listen, you have to be Daddy's little man until I get there. What happened to Mommy? Why is she in the hospital?"

"She and Auntie Myra had a fight. They are both in the hospital. Sharay hit Auntie Myra with a bat and made her head bleed. Daddy, what time are you coming?"

"I'm coming soon. Christian, listen to me. When Mommy calls, can you remember to tell her something for me. Tell her that Daddy loves her very much. Tell her to call me okay."

"Okay. I love you Daddy."

"I love you too, Christian. Give your brother and sister a big hug and kiss for me. Bye."

The mystery woman then placed my cell phone back in the drawer and stood there staring at me.

"What?" I barked.

"Nothing." She replied.

She put the gun back in her bag and returned to her resting position on the bed. The room was quiet. Only the loud sounds of my empty stomach filled the room.

"Do you want something to eat now?" She asked.

She reached over me and picked up the plastic bag from the nightstand. She pulled out a wrapped sandwich and a bottle of water. She unwrapped the sandwich, ripped off a small piece, and brought it to my mouth. I barely chewed it; I was so hungry I could have swallowed the whole thing. She continued feeding me small pieces of the sandwich until she reached the final piece. As she placed the last piece in my mouth, I purposely sucked on her fingers. She inhaled deeply, signaling that she enjoyed it.

"I'm thirsty." I stated.

"Hunh? Oh, I'm sorry."

She then opened the water, placed the straw inside and held it as I drank the warm water. I finished the bottled in a few gulps. She placed the garbage in the pail beside the bed then returned to her resting place.

My mind continued to think of ways of escape but it still seemed impossible. Then the inevitable came.

"Yo, I got to use the bathroom." I announced.

Again, she went to her bag and retrieved the gun.

"I'm going to unloose your hands but I'm going to put on these handcuffs. You can hop to the bathroom."

Then she did exactly what she said and followed me into the bathroom. She helped unbuckle my belt and unbutton my jeans before turning around and allowing me to handle my business.

When I was done, I called to her. "I'm done. Can you help me out?"

She looked down at my penis then into my eyes and smiled. She must have thought I had an erection but it was just naturally like that. As she helped pull my jeans up and place my manhood back inside my boxers, she began to fondle it. I figured she must have found the whole bondage thing as kinky as I had earlier and was turned on. She never got around to buckling my pants. Instead, she brought her lips to meet mine. I wanted to spit in her mouth but thought of this as an out and played along. She backed onto the sink, parted her legs, and pulled me closer.

"You want some of this." I whispered.

"Yes." She panted.

"Take off your pants and turn around."

She did as I said and leaned over the sink. I grabbed the back of her head and banged it repeatedly against the ceramic sink until she passed out. Then without a second thought, I hopped out of the bathroom. There was a thunderous banging at the door and before I could reply, police kicked in the door and their flashlights searched the room to find me in the middle of the floor half-naked, dick hanging, and all.

"Are you Rodney Bennett?"

"Yes."

"Imani Banks called in her husband's car stolen. Coincidentally, when the highway patrol got the call, one of their guys was passing by and spotted the car right away. I contacted my partner Mike in Allentown, he explained the situation, and we got over here as soon as we can. Is everything okay?"

"Hell no! That crazy bitch has had me locked in this room since yesterday. Threatening to kill me and shit. *Do I look like everything is okay?*"

"Calm down, Mr. Bennett." The officer said as he removed the cuff.

Another officer was checking the woman lying on the floor, and calling for an ambulance.

Again, my cell phone began to ring; I checked the Caller ID but did not recognize the number.

"Hello." I answered.

"Rodney, oh baby. Are you okay?" Charisse cried on the other end.

"I'm fine, Boo. What hospital are you in? I'm on my way." I replied.

"I am on my way back to my parent's house. I miss you. I have something to tell you. Myra and I..."

I interrupted before she could finish, "I miss you, too. I am on my way."

I knew Charisse and I needed to handle that topic face to face

"Sir, we are going to need you to come down to the precinct. Promise not to take too long." An officer stated as I disconnected from Charisse.

"Look, *Sir*. No disrespect but I have been away from my wife and kids far too long already. I really need to go."

The officer waved his hand and with that, I was gone.

CHAPTER 18

BRYAN

While my father and mother were busy with family activities, I took the opportunity to sneak away. I slipped my grandmother's car keys off her key ring and snuck out the back door, around the front of the house and into her car. I did not intend to cause any more trouble but I was at the point where I was damned if I did or if I didn't.

Shortly after Detective Liggins called, I received another phone call. The caller said he had Rodney and threatened to kill him if I did not get them the money. The caller also gave me a set of rules: my parent's should not know about the call and keep my phone on. There was no specific destination. He told me to drive away from the house. So, I did. As I backed out the driveway, I checked my waistband to make sure I still had my father's gun. Without a plan, I knew I was like a fish out of water but I had no time to think, just act. As I drove I thought, *'Even if I gave him the information to get the money, he couldn't get it without the locket on Sharay's bracelet. What was I thinking?'*

As I got to the stop sign, my cell phone began to ring. I answered.

"Do you know how to get to the Georgia Dome?" The male caller asked.

"Not really." I replied.

He briefly gave me directions then ended our call.

My hands began to shake as I started for the highway.

The ride was long and gave me time to think about the trouble that I was getting myself in. As if I needed any further confirmation, my phone began to ring with the name *Dad* flashing across the screen.

Hesitantly I answered, praying that it was anyone else but him.

"Where are you?" Kai-Aja whispered over the line.

My prayers were answered.

"I'm on my way Downtown. Are they looking for me?"

"No, but it won't be long. We are about to have dinner. You took Grandma's car?" She asked.

"Why?"

"She thinks that Granddaddy took it but I know he went out with Wil earlier. Takiyah said they're on their way back home. Takiyah noticed that you were gone and asked me to call...huh...yes...Bryan hold on." Kai-Aja said before another voice came onto the line.

"Bryan, where are you?" Takiyah asked.

"I'm on my way to the Georgia Dome. Going to meet up with somebody and will be right back. Please do not tell my father. I need to handle this myself."

"You can get yourself seriously hurt out there. Are you alone?"

"Yes." I replied.

"Turn around and come back to the house. Let your father handle this."

"I can't, Kiyah. I think they got somebody following me. I'm not even supposed to be on the phone. But I got you on speaker so they can't tell."

"Bryan, please come home." Kai-Aja begged in the background.

"Sis, listen I can't do that but there is something you can do for me."

Kai-Aja listened intently as I explained my plan, which was simple, "Tell Dad to call the detective and tell him where I am going."

Then I hung up and prayed I did the right thing. The closer I got to the designated meeting place; my nerves calmed, no more jitters, no more fear. Trey did not know whom he was about to encounter. If he did, he must be desperate to put himself in the line of death. Quinton only knew violence when his family was in danger and this qualified as one of those meetings.

I knew there would be consequences for my actions but I did not fear that either. My dad and I had a subliminal understanding and he would lecture me but nothing more.

My eyes were beginning to get heavy as I waited for Trey. It had been a half hour and no one showed or called. Again, my nerves started to jump around, my stomach weak and head throbbing.   When I was about to lose my last bit of sanity, there were bright lights coming through my rear window. I struggled to regain my composure; Trey would not see my fear. After the car lights went out, the driver's side door opened, and Trey exited, alone. But not with empty hands, his gun was his back up.

"Open up the door slow." He demanded outside my window.

I complied but not before hitting the call on my phone, with my Bluetooth headset in my pocket I was sure that my father would hear if we were planning to change location. It was a corny idea but I was desperate and scared.

Upon exiting the car, he snatched me by my jacket and threw me against the car with his gun to my neck. I thought I was going to wet my pants when I felt the cold steel pressed on my skin but I manage to fight the urge. He searched my jacket pockets, found my Blue tooth, threw it to the ground and stepped on it. *There goes my last hope for safety.* I thought as he continued his search. He ran his hand up and down my back, around my waist and up and down my thighs then turned me around to face his gun. I was surprised he hadn't checked my calves but glad at the same time. Before he pulled up, I moved the gun from my waist to my sock.

"Where's the key?" He asked.

"On my chain." I replied.

Trey reached inside my t-shirt and I swallowed hard as the gun drew closer to my face. He snatched the chain off my neck and admired the key for a few before he began to talk.

"So, how's my daughter?" He said with a slight smirk that made me want to slap the freckles off his face.

"Your daughters are fine." I replied through tightly clenched teeth.

"And my son?" He asked this time with a full grin.

My stomach turned as I thought of how sick this dude was.

How can you be proud that your son, your grandson was bore by your daughter?

"You got what you want. Let me go. Sorry ass negro."

"You talk tough like your father except that punk couldn't use his tough talk to keep him alive or your mother, the whore. So sorry you had to go through that." He said before letting out the most evil laugh I ever heard.

Finally breaking my core, I felt tears trickling down my cheeks as the memories flooded my mind.

"Tell me something, Bryan. Did you know that the same man you call Uncle had something to do with what happened to your family?"

"LIAR!" I roared so loud I could swear the parking lot shook.

"Calm down young blood before you get yourself shot. Or do you want that family reunion?" Trey threatened. "I am trying to school you on those people you call family but if you don't want to listen that's on you. Your Uncle Rodney had your father killed over Sandra, Sharay's mother. Tell me you knew your Uncle Rodney is Sharay's father, at least? There is so much history on the streets, so much history between your family and mine. Did you know I've been playing daddy to your sisters? Them some fine young girls, nice ass..."

Before he could finish, I kneed him in the balls. Then used my elbow to knock his gun out of his hands and kicked it under the car. He quickly recovered and laid a blinding blow to my right eye. I felt it swelling rapidly but it did not stop me from charging the dude, both of us landing on the tar parking lot floor. I used ever ounce of strength to lay blow after blow to his bruising face. I felt victorious as blood began to run from his mouth and nose. However, my multiple hits were not enough to keep him down as he laid another blow this time to my nose. With swiftness, he pushed me to the ground and staggered to regain his balance as I lay there holding my possibly broken nose.

"You think you bad huh motherfucker..." He said as he started for the car.

I knew he was going for his gun. Fear filled me and the pain disappeared. Adrenaline pumped my blood. As Trey bent down to pick up his gun, I found strength to reach to my sock and stand to my feet. By the time, Trey reached his gun I was standing over him cocking mine. Trey immediately stopped his search when the cocking sound echoed through the parking lot.

"Stand up slow, Trey"

Trey didn't move fast enough so I used all my might and kicked him in his ribs causing him to land on his side.

"I tried to be calm. I gave you what you wanted. Why did we have to come to this?" I asked scared that I actually might pull the trigger.

"So, you're going to shoot me? Or, are you a bitch like your play daddy, Quinton? I know you got killer in your blood. Go ahead shoot me. SHOOT ME!" He demanded as if he was in control.

At that point, I aimed the trigger for his head. I was about to pull the trigger when I heard a woman's voice calling from a far.

"Bryan, NO!" My mother yelled as she ran towards me.

"Mom! Go back!" I shouted never once losing eye contact with Trey.

It puzzled me that my mother would show up before my father but I didn't lose focus. I knew that if Trey so much as flinched, he was dead.

"Son, put the gun down!" Quinton ordered as he ran from the opposite direction.

As I started to put the gun to my side, Trey kicked my feet from beneath me causing me to land on my back and the gun to go flying. But my father was close enough to grab Trey and toss him against the car. They began to rumble as my mother came to my aide.

"Baby, are you alright? What were you thinking?" She asked as she pulled me to her and kissed my forehead.

She pulled napkins from her bag and begin to dab at my nose as I lay there watching my father and Trey going blow for blow.

"Mom, did you call the police?"

"They're on the way." She replied, her eyes never leaving my face.

I knew it was because she couldn't stand to see Quinton fight. But I watched as my father laid blow after blow disfiguring his face and Trey trying to recover with his hits growing weaker and weaker. It was then; within that next second that Quinton laid Trey out with a hit that rang like thunder. There was Trey laying face down beside my grandmother's car, lifeless as my father tried to regain his breath then rushed over to check on me.

"I'm sorry," was all I could offer.

"It's alright. It's alright." Quinton repeated as he held my chin in his strong grip turning my face side to side, checking the damage.

Police sirens blared in the background as we sat and waited.

"Dad, can I ask you a question?" My mind was fixed on something Trey said. "Did Uncle Rodney kill my father and mother?"

Quinton was quiet at first, which caused my heart to sink further, but then he looked at my mother, back to me, and said, "No, your Uncle Rodney did not kill your father. This life killed your father—the guns, drugs, money. Did Rodney have something to do with it?" Quinton went quiet again before whispering, "I hope not."

It wasn't the answer I wanted, wasn't the answer I needed but for some reasons it gave me a sense of peace.

The police cars arrived and finally it was over. My mother stood first as my father reached down to help me stand. Something caught my eye, the good one, and then there was a shot. I dropped to the floor and crawled towards Quinton's gun as he fell to the floor grabbing onto his chest. My mind went blank as I pulled the trigger and let off two shots. One to Trey's chest and the next to his head. My mother screamed as Trey's body slumped against the car. This time I was sure he was dead.

When I became conscious of my surroundings, my mother was crying over my father's body as the officers gather around. An officer hollered into his radio for emergency medical units. The gun was still in my hands as the officers rushed the scene. First, fear shook me as I realized what had transpired. I shot a man. Then a huge surge of power ran through me as I placed the gun down beside me. What was supposed to make me feel scared actually made me feel stronger. I tried to fight it but it took over as a smile etched my face until I heard my mother cry out in pain.

"Quinton! Quinton!" My mother cried.

One of the officers ripped away my father's sweater and I saw the wound below his right shoulder, bleeding profusely. As I got closer, my father began to speak.

"Bryan, take your mother to the house." He said before grimacing from the pain of the officer applying pressure to the wound.

"But Dad, who is going to go with you to the hospital?"

"I'm fine." He said before pointing to circular scar not too far from his bleeding wound. "Trust me, I'll be fine."

I assumed that was from when my biological mother, Trina shot him.

How did she explain that? 'They say too much love can drive a person to do bad things. There's never too much love. Never too much.'

I believe that now. Like Trey said the street has history, I hope for our family sake that history does not repeat itself.

ಬಿಬಿಬಿ೪೪೪

CHARISSE

When we thought all was lost, our family wound up back together and as RUN DMC said 'tougher than leather'. Maybe Rodney was scared to leave the house or maybe he really wanted to be a family but he started keeping his black ass home, it worked for me either way. Home by the way was that house down the block from Quinton and Imani in Pennsylvania. New York was like voodoo for us so we agreed we needed to getaway to start over. Rodney was still trying to come to terms with the damage he's done to so many people. Above all, Bryan. They never spoke about it but Bryan knew and understood that what happened in the past should stay in the past.

Rodney protested daily about working a nine to five but part of making a marriage work was compromise, I will continue to be Charisse Bennett as long as he stays off the streets. That's the deal. Sounds fair enough, right?

Imani and Quinton were doing well and eagerly awaiting the arrival of their newest addition. Seems all their arguments were due to the baby messing with her emotions. We knew Imani was temperamental but this baby brought out the worst. Bryan, Kai-Aja, Jahlek, and Naadira were excited to learn they were getting an addition to the family. Sometime around fall, Imani and Quinton will be welcoming in their fifth child and from what the doctor's say their third girl. Still Imani prayed it was her boy. Quinton was happy either way.

Rodney and I have agreed that our trio was more than enough to keep up with while managing a business. Rodney and I have started our modeling agency for children. Of course, our boy's were our first clients but our business has picked up over that last six months. We have been doing well and were happy at last or something like that.

Imani got a call from an old friend stating that he was having a big celebration for a new fashion magazine he started and invited her to Maryland to mingle with some people he thought she should know since she had been trying to push her book. Naturally, Imani asked me to tag along. I convinced Rodney that we could get some good plug for our business but he could not stand the thought of me going out anywhere without him, which was really beginning to get on my last nerve. The fact that Imani and I made reservations to stay at a hotel after the affair really pissed him off.

Imani arrived to my house dressed in a sharp burgundy pants suit that complemented her beautiful glowing skin and hid her growing belly well. She came to borrow my black open-toe BCBG pumps. In addition, she brought over her gold shell necklace and matching earrings. I needed something to accessorize with my black knee length sleeveless DKNY dress besides my beaded shawl and black and gold stilettos. Imani's make-up was simple, eyeliner, mascara and a peach lip-gloss. I went without. Before we stepped out, I ran a hand over my freshly pressed mane, making sure all the little strands were flat.

It was a short drive, which Imani and I laughed the whole way. Still I was unhappy. The one thing I have yet to share with my best friend. Truth was I was afraid to say it aloud. Hoping all would get better if I kept it to myself. I was no longer happy with Rodney. At first, I thought I could not forgive him for the past but we got over that. But his jealousy and insecurities were making it hard to live with him and our house was not a home anymore. It's like my jail. This is the first time I've been without him in months and I feel free. I even left my cell phone home, hidden in the hamper. It felt wrong; what if there was an emergency? Still, I could not hide the fact that I was relieved.

"Reese, are you okay?" Imani asked.

"Huh, oh yeah. Yeah, I'm okay. Why?" I was so lost in thought I hadn't heard anything she said for the last ten minutes.

"We're here." Imani said as she pointed to the hall.

I reached for my clutch, which sat between us, and she grabbed my hand.

"Honestly, Reese. Is everything okay?"

It was hard to hide things from her. She knew me so well. It was as if she could read my mind at times.

"I'm fine, Sis. Let's go and mingle." I said putting on a fake smile.

A tall light-skinned brother greeted us at the door, sweet smelling and dressed like he stepped fresh off the page of GQ. I had to catch myself from staring so I tried to look around him but it seemed as if we kept making eye contact.

"Imani, how are you?" He asked.

It caught me off guard that he knew her on a first name basis.

"I'm blessed, Rahsaun and you?"

Rahsaun, why did that name ring a bell?

"I made it, Baby." He smiled and my heart melted he was gorgeous. Divine.

He pointed to a large poster of the cover of the magazine with his picture on the front. On the cover, he was wearing a tan suit with a rich brown shirt and posing with his arms crossed across his chest. All else that was going on I could not tell you because I was so fixed on his handsome face and green eyes that shined like gems.

"Charisse, you remember Rahsaun? You met in the mall once. It was years ago. Rahsaun Tyler, this is Charisse Nettles."

"Charisse, I believe we met more than once."

"Excuse me?" I was sure he had me mistaken with someone else.

"You have three beautiful children correct? From New York, Harlem to be exact. Two boys, one girl. It had to be like eight months ago. At the supermarket." He stated and the vision came back.

The man with the business card. That handsome man I dreamt of once a month since we met. After a while, he was a silhouette, faceless but there nonetheless.

Imani looked at me and her look told me she felt what I felt. My feelings for him were wrong. I was infatuated with this man and he had no idea.

"You never called." He said before grabbing my hands so gently and holding them as he peered into my eyes.

"So, how's your wife?" Imani asked trying to break our connection.

To no avail, he answered with out his eyes leaving mine. "She's gone."

"Well what do you know? You got divorced, Charisse got married. My, so many things happened in such a short time." Imani said while motioning for me to join her.

Rahsaun finally looked from me to Imani still holding my hands.

"She passed away, Imani. I thought I told you."

"Oh no. I'm sorry. You never told me. I'm so sorry." Imani offered.

At that moment, some men walked up and began talking to Rahsaun. He excused him self and everyone preceded into the hall.

"Charisse, I can't believe you. I can't believe any of this." Imani whispered as we walked from poster to poster admiring some of the fashions and topics he was presenting in his magazine.

"What Imani? What can't you believe? That I might actually be attracted to someone else? I'm human. Attractions happen. And yes I know I'm married but please don't remind me." I said, my tone revealed my aggravation.

Imani stood with a look of shock and confusion as I walked off. A tall, slim sister approached her recognizing her from her book photo, keeping Imani from following me.

As I managed to find a quiet spot outside on the terrace, I felt the urge to cry, scream something to release some of the emotions that were tearing at my heart and mind. I could not deal with it all. My heart was aching and I did not know whom to turn to for comfort or understanding since my best friend was in the dark and probably would not understand if I explained. She was so head sprung for love she was blind at times.

Behind me were some masculine voices but I did not want to turn to leave and risk anyone seeing my tears. I waited for a while longer and prayed they would rejoin the party so I could be at peace, alone.

I heard the music from inside get louder then fade again and the male voices were gone. I assumed I was alone again so I looked inside my clutch for my cigarettes—a bad habit caused by stress. I held one of the slim Capri cigarettes between my fingers as I searched for my lighter or matches. There was a tap on my shoulder followed by the voice of angel.

"You're too pretty to smoke, Charisse."

I turned to look into Rahsaun's face, which now looked to be filled with hurt.

"I waited for you to call."

"I wanted to call."

"Why didn't you?" He asked.

"So much was going on." I stated.

"So you're happily married now?"

"I wouldn't say happily. We're together." I replied looking away from him, fighting back the tears stinging my eyes.

"Charisse, I thought about you for years. Then when we met again, I knew it was fate. All I needed was for you to call."

"Like I said, so much was going on. My mind was all over the place. You would never believe all the stuff I've been through."

"You're still beautiful." He said as he brushed a strand of hair from my cheek.

"Thank you." I replied.

"I guess it's too late now. Too much time has passed, so much has happened."

"Yeah, I guess." I replied suddenly saddened by his comment and its truth.

We continued to gaze into each other's eyes. He ran his hand down the length of my arm and I think my heart skipped several times before he reached my fingers.

"Rahsaun, I'm sorry. This is wrong. I should…"

Before I could finish, he kissed me. It was not a kiss, it was passion, it was lust, and it was what I needed. Rahsaun pulled me closer with his hands resting in the small of my back as I placed my hands on his chest, not sure if to push him away or pull him closer.

Rahsaun backed away and I looked at him, puzzled by his actions.

"Charisse maybe this is wrong. This is too much for you to deal with right now I'm sure. I want you and I know I can't have you."

"Please don't think for me. I've been through it all. So trust me, there is never too much for me. Never too much." I said then leaned in for more.

As we ended our moment of desire, Imani walked onto the terrace. Rahsaun and I both turned to see who entered, I, with a smile plastered across my face for the first time in months, maybe years.

Can't remember the last time I felt this good.

"I hope you two know what you're getting yourselves into." She stated with a disapproving look and a hand resting on her belly.

We turned to look at each other, I passed him a mental message that everything was going be alright—they'll be some drama—but it will be alright. He replied with a smile.

Then as if his timing could not have been more accurate, Imani's cell phone rang and Rodney's name showed on the screen.

Imani passed me her phone.

"What's up?" I answered as I detached myself from Rahsaun trying to find a private place to talk.

"Nothing, wanted to make sure y'all made it there okay. I tried calling your phone but you weren't answering. What time y'all planning on heading back this way?" Rodney asked.

It was that, the interrogation, the jealousy, the insecurity—that was pushing me away.

"Rodney we haven't been here a good hour. Stop riding me. Please." I begged, weakened by the second.

He must have sensed my frustration and opted to end our call.

"Hey, I love you, Reese." He said.

"Yeah, I know." I replied.

TO MY READERS

I hope you enjoyed going through this journey with me again. In this, I hope I have filled your every desire and expectation. I listened to what you wanted then waited for the voices in my head to come up with what I hope is the perfect story, with the perfect ending for you. You know, these character take me over when I start writing so if you were one of the few that asked, "What's going to happened?" the truth is I never know until it is over. Therefore, I experience the shock, excitement, and happiness of every twist and turn with you. Thanks for reading!

Keep informed on what's going on in Envisage Publishing by vsiting our website: http://envisagepublishing.yolasite.com. There you'll be able to stay informed on all the latest as far as new releases, book signings and so forth.

Books and Blessings,

Danette Maroney

MORE FROM
ENVISAGE PUBLISHING

COMPLETELY SATISFIED
A NOVEL
RE-RELEASED MAY 2008
BY DANETTE MARONEY

THE MORE THINGS CHANGE...
A NOVEL
RELEASED JUNE 2008
BY DANETTE MARONEY
& MONIQUE MARONEY

NEVER SATISFIED
SEPTEMBER 2011
BY: DANETTE MARONEY

FOR MORE INFORMATION, OR TO ORDER OTHER COPIES,
PLEASE CONTACT US AT:
ENVISAGEPUB1@YAHOO.COM
OR (404) 955-4764

www.ingramcontent.com/pod-product-compliance
Lightning Source LLC
Chambersburg PA
CBHW071500170626
46811CB00007B/2652